"What are you drinking?" Letty asked. "Brandy?"

"A little destruction." He gave a mock salute and laughed bitterly, then made the mistake of looking at her.

Her expression turned serious. "Why do you do that?"

He brought his face intimidatingly close to hers. "Because it makes me feel good."

She drew in a breath and her eyes widened, but to her credit she didn't move. He felt as if he held her heart in his hands. He didn't want to be handed any hearts.

"I like things that make me feel good—strong drink, hard rides across the moors"—he lightly touched her cheek—"debauching innocent girls."

"And shocking people," she added, her face scant inches from his, her expression showing no signs of intimidation.

He could smell the scent of lavender lingering about her, clean and sweet ... and pure. It triggered something inside him. His mouth closed over hers hard and demanding. He intended to do exactly what she accused him of: shock the bloody hell out of her. . . .

For information call toll free: customer Can here orders above write to: Mall Order Department, Pocket Books, Inc., 100 Old Tappan Road, Old Tappan, N.J. 07675.

Books by Jill Barnett

Wonderful
Carried Away
Imagine
Bewitching
Dreaming
The Heart's Haven
Just a Kiss Away
Surrender a Dream

Published by POCKET BOOKS

JILL BARNETT

DREAMING

POCKET BOOKS

New York   London   Toronto   Sydney   Tokyo   Singapore

This book is a work of historical fiction. Names, characters, places, and incidents relating to nonhistorical figures are products of the author's imagination or are used fictitiously. Any resemblance of such nonhistorical incidents, places, or figures to actual events or locales or persons living or dead is entirely coincidental.

An *Original* Publication of POCKET BOOKS

POCKET BOOKS, a division of Simon & Schuster Inc.
1230 Avenue of the Americas, New York, NY 10020

Copyright © 1994 by Jill Barnett Stadler

ISBN: 0-671-77868-4

First Pocket Books printing June 1994

10 9 8 7

POCKET and colophon are registered trademarks of Simon & Schuster Inc.

Cover art by Lisa Falkenstern

Printed in the U.S.A.

Prologue

~

London, England, 1813

She believed in dreams, but this evening was fast becoming a nightmare. Alone in a small alcove of the crowded ballroom, Letty Hornsby watched the crush of English society swarm onto the dance floor for another set. Dripping in feathers and finery, they laughed and danced, flirted and fanned, all to the accompaniment of an orchestra of strings and woodwinds.

Anxious dandies fluttered around this season's bouquet of fresh females like butterflies in search of the richest nectar. They moved through the crowd, bowing and filling in dance cards, arguing in gentlemanly style over who would pluck a treasured waltz from this season's Incomparable.

Her first ball of her first season. Yet she had never felt so alone and far from home. She had wanted her father to be with her, but on that morning so many months past when they'd first spoken of her come-out, he had raised his head from behind the latest issue of

1

Roman Antiquities and said he was long past balls and the season's pleasures. She'd do much better with her mother's aunt providing her introduction.

However, Aunt Rosalynde hadn't introduced her to anyone except the hostess, then she'd shuffled Letty over to this side of the room whilst she scurried off to hear the latest *on dit,* leaving Letty to fend for herself in a ballroom filled with strangers.

She might be standing in a lonesome corner, but in her mind she twirled and spun and schottisched to the music. Beneath the long skirt of her gauze gown, hidden under a satin underslip and petticoat, she tapped a silk-slippered toe to the tune of a country dance. She closed her eyes and imagined that she was dancing and laughing and smiling, the belle of the ball, the princess she'd always dreamed she'd be, with long flowing titian hair and an even longer line of admirers waiting to dance with her.

The music ceased, the dance ended, and so did her dreaming. She sighed for what she wished would happen and opened her eyes to face sad reality. She wasn't a titian-haired princess and the belle of the ball. She was Letitia Hornsby, with nut-brown hair, long and curly as a pug's tail, and she was standing in a corner at her first ball, alone and forgotten.

From nearby a girl's gay laughter rippled into the air. Intrigued, Letty took a couple of steps out from the shadows, leaving a tall marble statue of Cupid alone in his alcove. Standing next to this icon of romance had done little to improve her situation.

The laughter sounded again. She watched a lovely blond girl snap open her fan, wave it playfully, and then, skirts in hand, sink into a deep curtsy before a group of doting young men. She fluttered her eyelashes slightly, then smiled up at her swains, who fought over themselves to offer her a hand up.

The girl denied them all, then rose so smoothly even Letty felt the urge to applaud. The men did applaud and argued over who would lead the divine and graceful miss in the next set.

Letty wished she knew the girl; then perhaps she could ask her to share. One dance was all she wished for. Just one.

As if in answer to her wish, a young dark-haired man stepped from the crowd and scanned the room, searching until his gaze stopped on her. His look changed to one of decided interest.

Every muscle in her body tensed in anticipation.

He slowly, purposefully, strode toward her.

Oh, this was it! Her breath caught in her chest and she prayed she wouldn't do something shameful, like burst into tears or swoon, especially before he reached her.

Beneath her gown she could feel her skin sweating nervous tears of its own. She supposed she should have fanned herself—she had made an attempt to learn the art of fanning—but at that moment her fan hung uselessly from Cupid's drawn arrow.

With each step the dandy took, Letty's heart pounded louder in her ears. In a flash of fancy she imagined it was a drum roll signaling the joyous moment she'd been awaiting. To dance. Oh, to finally dance!

The violins sang out an introduction to the next set. He was almost there. Not realizing she had even done so, she took a step toward him and stumbled, then felt his glove on her arm as he steadied her. She gazed up into his face and smiled her gratitude.

"Beg pardon, miss." His voice was so welcome a sound after no conversation for two hours. But not half as welcome as he himself was.

Still smiling a thank you, she raised her left hand, her dance card dangling from it by a pink silk ribbon.

"Pardon me," he repeated.

" 'Twas my fault," she said in a nervous rush. "I stepped on my hem. It's a bit long, you know. I told Aunt Rosalynde—she's a Hollingsworth, of the Exeter Hollingsworths? I told her it was too long, but she wouldn't listen, just told me to hush because I chatter too much and to let her handle everything since she knew what she was about."

Letty took a badly needed breath and raised her hand with the dance card a little higher. Now, standing inches from him, she waited for the question she'd been waiting for all evening.

"Beg pardon, Miss Hollingsworth—"

Her smile shined with pure joy. "Oh, I'm not Miss Hollingsworth. I'm Miss Hornsby."

Standing more stiffly, he said, "Miss Hornsby." He gave a sharp nod. "I need to pass by." His voice was curt.

Pass by? Letty looked into his eyes and frowned. He was looking over her shoulder.

With a sinking feeling of dread, she followed his avid stare. He wasn't looking at her, but instead at a raven-haired girl who stood behind her.

Letty turned back to him and blurted out, "You want her?"

His look turned hard as stone.

He hadn't wanted Letty.

She recovered herself quickly and stepped out of his path. "Excuse me." Her voice was so quiet she could barely hear it herself. To hide her humiliation, she averted her eyes. She could feel them well with moisture, and in a matter of seconds the small rosettes that decorated her hemline looked like nothing more than a pink blur.

The orchestra began anew with Letty still standing there, staring down, taking deep quivering tight breaths, and searching desperately for the strength to endure this long night completely alone.

There would be many more balls and routs, a thought that did nothing to improve the knot in her stomach. If anything, the thought of more nights like this made her even queasier.

Perhaps it was best she was alone. She didn't think she could speak to anyone at that moment and not make a utter fool of herself by sobbing uncontrollably on their shoulder.

She took one more fortifying breath, then another, and looked up again, her gaze drawn to the dancers on the ballroom floor, watching them with the same rapt hunger of an orphan watching a family celebrate Christmas.

Within seconds, she found herself looking at the young dandy and the girl of his choosing. Their dark hair caught the golden gleam of light from the hundreds of candles burning high above them. There was a magical quality to the way they glided and twirled through the intricate steps of the dance.

After a turn Letty met the girl's gaze, and she fervently wished the floor would just open up and swallow her. There was pity in the girl's eyes. Pity.

Biting her lips, she turned quickly, needing somewhere to go. She glanced at the terrace doors, but it was still pouring rain outside. Chin up and shoulders back, she snatched her fan from Cupid and strolled toward the refreshment table with what she hoped was the correct amount of *panache*.

Once near the table she just stood there, not wanting to be gauche and fetch her own cup. Her aunt had drilled the rules of etiquette into her head until she could repeat them in her sleep: A young lady *always* waits for a gentleman to help her down from a carriage. A young lady *always* waits for a gentleman to open the door. A young lady *always* waits for a gentleman to serve her. It seemed to Letty that a young lady's sole purpose in life was to wait for a gentleman to read her mind.

A young man walked up to the table. A moment later he turned back around, a cup of lemonade in each hand.

Letty glanced at the cups, then met his look with a smile.

He smiled back. And left.

Apparently he was no mind reader.

She tapped her fingers impatiently on her ivory fan and turned back to the table. Cups of lemonade were lined up like palace guards in neat regimented rows. She wondered what dire thing would happen if she just leaned over and picked up her own drink.

She cast a casual glance toward the wall where the turbaned chaperones sat gossiping and speculating. Referred to by many as the old crows' nest, it was from that illustrious corner that sight of one wrong move, one faux pas, could ruin a girl.

Letting her fan drag casually atop the tablecloth, Letty sauntered around the table until she was sure her person blocked their view. With the tip of the fan, she covertly pushed a cup toward the edge of the table, where, with just the right speed of movement, she could snatch up the cup without them seeing her.

One deep breath, and very slowly she slid her hand toward the table.

Closer.

And closer.

And closer.

"Thirsty, hellion?"

She gasped and snatched back her hand. There was

only one person who called her "hellion." There was only one person with that voice. The sound of it always made her feel as if she had drunk an entire pot of hot chocolate. Warm. Sweet, and a little sinful.

She spun around with a whispered "Richard ..." And looked up into the face of the earl of Downe, the man she had loved as long as she could remember.

He stood under the candlelight, his dark blond hair damp with raindrops that shimmered and sparkled and made it seem as if he had been delivered to her in a cloud of stars. He picked up a cup of lemonade and held it out to her. She stood there frozen, unaware that her heart was in her eyes.

"Are you going to take this or make me stand here all night?" He raised the cup until it was eye level and looked down at her, amused.

"Oh ... thank you, my lord," she said in a half croak, then took the cup and raised it to her lips and drank the whole thing in two giant gulps. She stared into the empty cup, searching for something brilliant and witty to say.

But before she could open her mouth he had reached out and tilted up her dance card. It was all she could do not to jerk her hand away before he saw the humiliating fact that her card was empty.

His face was unreadable, but he seemed to watch her for the longest time. Then, just as he had done in a thousand of her dreams, he wrote his name in a large masculine scrawl across the card. He dropped the card and held out his hand.

She just stared at it.

"I believe this dance is mine."

She met his look. It was all she could do not to throw herself into his arms and sob her gratitude. For once in her life, for once in the company of Richard Lennox, she did the proper thing. She placed her hand

7

in his, and felt a small flutter deep inside her. After a half curtsy, she let him lead her to the dance floor, praying to God that she wouldn't fall flat on her face and ruin everything.

The music filled her ears with notes more lovely than Mozart ever wrote. She moved slowly, feeling as if she were in one of her most enchanting dreams.

He touched her other hand and she almost cried out, so sharp was her reaction to him. Like one whose heart had just taken wing, every sensation in her young body came instantly alive. The air became tactile, the candlelight as warm as an embrace. Each breath she drew was honey, each note of music the sweetest of sounds.

In less time than it took a tear to fall, she was dancing. With Richard. She couldn't will her eyes to look up at him, and she was so nervous she had to concentrate on her steps.

"You miscounted, hellion."

She stumbled, but he pulled her into a turn, one strong arm keeping her steady. She looked up at him, then, half embarrassed, half thankful, completely besotted, and she whispered, "How did you know?"

He leaned down slightly and whispered into her ear, "Your lips are moving."

She flushed, red and hot, so flustered that she went in the wrong direction, throwing the entire line of dancers off. By the time she'd found her way back to him, he was making a serious effort to hide his amusement.

No one else was. She dipped her head to keep from seeing their smirking faces, and on the next turn her fan caught on the hem of his velvet coat. Shackled to his coattail, she was forced to follow him down the gentlemen's line of the dance as she tried to loosen her fan.

She stepped on his foot three times during the remainder of the dance. But at least she didn't fall. Next time she prayed for something, she'd have to remember to be more specific.

Ten minutes after they had started, the music, sadly, stopped. Eyes closed, heart pounding, she finished in a deep curtsy. Too soon, way too soon. She didn't even realize she had been holding her breath until she released it.

In utter silence, he led her from the floor over to Cupid's alcove. She turned, thanked him, then added quietly, "I'm sorry about your foot, my lord."

He said nothing. His face carried that same look of casual indifference it always wore of late, and she wondered what he was thinking when he wore it. Vaguely she heard him voice his pleasure before he made a quick bow and walked away.

Her gaze locked on his broad back, clad in a dark green velvet coat that matched the deep color of his eyes. Even when he had joined a group of men on the opposite side of the room, she could not will herself to look away. His friends clapped him on the back and stood there talking and laughing. Never once did he give her another glance, but she didn't care because he had danced with her.

Her mind in cloud castles, she sagged back against the wall and stared at nothing. If, for the remainder of the season, she never danced again, it wouldn't matter, because Richard Lennox, recently the earl of Downe, the center of her dreams and the object of her affections for six long years, had actually danced with her. At a ball. In front of everyone!

She looked up at Cupid, balanced on a pedestal, his arrow drawn. Then she stared down at her dance card for the longest time, watching Richard's signature as if she expected it to just disappear, to fade as so many of her dreams had in the cruel light of morning. She ran her fingers over the handwriting. But it didn't fade.

His name, bold and dark, stared back at her. She knew then that it hadn't been a dream. It had been real.

She took a deep breath. His scent lingered around her. She could still feel the warmth of his hand touching her, still see his face looking into hers, still hear that chocolate voice.

She could still feel the tingle of his grip on her waist as if he had marked her. She looked at her hand, the one his had touched, and wondered if she could ever bear to wash it. Her mind flashed with the impulsive youthful thought that nothing but lemonade would ever touch her lips again.

Ever so slowly, she untied the pink ribbon around her wrist. With a huge sigh, she clasped the dance card to her heart. And out of the corner of her eye, she could have sworn she saw Cupid wink.

10

Chapter 1

Devon, England, 1815

*T*he earl of Downe was known for his horsemanship—which was fortunate because it was harder than hell to stay on a horse when one was drunk. It was even harder at night, and this night was darker than a rake's past.

But Richard Lennox and his mount knew these dank moors. Over the years, they had ridden hell and hounds to the cliffs and on to the small cove below, where he'd found solace away from a house that had never been a home.

He rode across those moors now, away from his estate, until he couldn't taste the stale air of the past, only the briny scent of the sea. He could breathe again.

Horse and rider slowed as they neared the cliffs, and Richard relaxed. Two years before things had been different along this coast. England had been at war with France. Yet now all appeared quiet on the Channel. No storm-swept seas, no dark clouds, no

11

French navy lurking off the opposite shore, nor the frequent sight of British blockade ships zigzagging through the water.

Until a month before he, like everyone else, had thought the war was over. Then Napoleon had escaped Elba. Most recent rumors had the Emperor marching through the French countryside on a campaign to gather support.

Richard stared out at the Channel until it dawned on him that he was behaving like some idiotic dreamer who fancied for one instant that he could see what was happening on the opposite shore.

He saw only black—an expanse of dark water and the night sky. It was that one time of the month when the moon turned coward and its back was all one could see. A smuggler's moon.

He shook his head in derision and guided his mount along the cliff. Smugglers' moons and French armies. He must be bloody drunk, prattling on like one of those superstitious old fishermen from the village. He gave a humorless laugh. Dreamers and fools, the whole lot of them.

He stared off at the southern cliffs, where lights glimmered dimly from the neighboring Hornsby estate. An instant later his mind flashed with the image of a young woman's face framed in a wild mane of curly brown hair.

Letitia Hornsby.

God ... there was a thought. He blanched slightly and rolled his shoulder, the same one she'd accidentally dislocated. Instinctively his hand rose to his right eye, the one she'd once blackened with a cricket ball. His foot twitched as if it suddenly remembered the pain she'd inflicted dancing on it, and more recently when she'd driven over it with his curricle. After that incident he'd been forced to use a cane for two months.

Leaning on his saddle pommel, he watched the manor lights flicker and wondered if she was rusticating in one of those lit rooms. No sooner had the notion crossed his mind than he felt a powerful, instinctive, and self-preserving urge to put a vast number of miles between them.

No, he thought. Not miles . . . continents.

The Hornsby hellion—his recompense for every black sin he'd ever committed. Her London season had been one of the most disastrous in recent history, and her unflagging infatuation with him had been partly to blame.

As vividly as if it were yesterday, he could see her standing in a corner during the first ball of the season, trying to look comfortable and failing miserably.

Gallantry was one of those moral attributes Richard usually eschewed. With good reason. Being gallant, civil, or moral hadn't lit a fire under his father. Through years of rebellion, he had acquired a certain expertise at patrimonial arson.

But the night of that ball, he'd asked the hellion to dance. The motive for his doing so still escaped him. Logic had naturally dictated that, by the age of seventeen, the chit would have outgrown her childhood affection for him. But she hadn't. If anything, that one dance had only made matters worse. Every time they met, at every social event they both attended, some catastrophe happened.

It didn't take long for malicious word to come of her banishment with only half her season done. Society thought her a joke and had laughed cruelly. He remembered the brief twinge of guilt he'd experienced when, on a fluke, it had been he, the object of her unwelcome affections, who had won two thousand pounds in a tasteless wager on the exact date of her season's failure.

He looked away from the lights of the manor house just as a man's shout, startlingly loud in the silence, echoed up from the cliffs behind him. Turning suddenly, he faced the sound and paused for an instant, then rode toward it, stopping at the edge of the north cliffs, where he used a thicket of gorse bushes and a huge granite rock as a shield.

An outcropping on the cliff beneath him blocked his view of the cove, so he eased his mount toward a narrow dirt path that cut along the cliffside and led to the shore below. About halfway down, just past the outcropping, he stopped.

In the cove, dim lanterns moved like fireflies in the darkness. Again he glanced out toward the sea, searching for some sign of a ship, but still seeing little. He scanned the shore and spotted two skiffs beached below.

A small group of men was unloading crates of contraband, more than likely brandy, Belgium lace, and salt. More dark-clad men moved out from the cave beneath the cliff, lugging long wooden boxes to the boats.

Odd that they would be loading—

A twig cracked above him. He stilled.

A sudden commotion thrashed in the bushes overhead. He tensed, and his mount shifted slightly. Slowly he slid a hand inside his cloak and drew a pistol, then tightened his thighs and nudged the horse forward. Looking upward, he leaned back and took deadly aim.

Another loud rustle . . . and the bushes parted.

The Hornsby hellion peered down at him. Their gazes met.

He looked at her in horror. She looked at him as if he were the sugar for her tea.

Groaning, he closed his eyes and lowered the pistol.

"Richard . . ." She whispered his name like a prayer.

With her anywhere near him, he needed a prayer—a long prayer.

There was another rustle and a vicious growl. Richard stifled another groan as a huge and droopy canine head poked out of those same bushes.

Her dog.

Forget the prayer. He needed a benediction.

The animal took one look at him and snarled. His horse shied. He struggled to control his mount on the narrow path. Dirt and rocks tumbled down to the beach below.

The beastly dog barked.

Quickly he turned in the saddle, scanning the cove. The smugglers must have heard it. Hell, Napoleon could have heard it.

A lantern had stopped directly below him, then another, and another. Richard froze. The men below stared up at the cliffside.

He was caught between two evils—the smugglers and the twosome from hell.

Her blasted dog barked again.

His horse sidestepped, nearly sending them both over the crumbling edge of the path.

"Oh no!" Letty called out and reached toward him, her face stunned, then horrified. "Richard!"

Naturally, the dog growled.

His horse reared. With an odd kind of resigned horror, he felt the reins sliding through his hands. And Richard slipped off the saddle, his graphic swearing the only sound as he fell.

Down . . .

Down . . .

His last conscious thought?

He'd be better off with the smugglers.

* * *

Letitia Olive Hornsby believed in fate, in hearts destined, in love at first sight. And she had loved him forever.

Well, perhaps not quite forever, but at nineteen, eight years was nearly half of her life. She could barely remember a time when her heart had not belonged to Richard Lennox, her neighbor and, of late, the earl of Downe.

His enviable title had nothing to do with her devotion. The earldom should not have been his. In fact she'd heard that he held nothing but scorn for his father and the title. Richard was a second son and grossly out of favor if rumor had been true.

But two years before all that had changed with two shots from a highwayman's pistols. His father and older brother had been killed. Richard was suddenly an earl.

No, to her the earldom meant nothing. The man meant everything.

No one tried harder, or with less success, than Letty to make her dreams come true.

But she had hope, and the solid belief that God never closed one door without opening another. The strength of those beliefs and her tenaciousness were what carried her through the times when God slammed that proverbial door in her face.

Her mother had died when Letty was seven. Although her father loved her, he was no substitute for the gentle hand and guidance only a mother could give a daughter.

Not a day of her awkward girlhood had passed that she didn't miss her mother terribly and wonder if perhaps she might have turned out differently—better, more refined, less inept, and perhaps less lonely—had her mother lived.

Her father spent most of his time with antiquities—anything ancient, buried, and Roman, which accounted for her horrid name. *Letitia* was Latin for "delight," and her parents thought it most appropriate at the time. Her papa christened her with the ghastly middle name of Olive, which was the Roman symbol of peace—something he'd also claimed he'd had little of since the day she was born.

The first disaster she could remember happened when she was eight. It had been a difficult and lonely year for a suddenly motherless girl. Her father's attention had become so terribly important to her.

She had practiced talking for hours, until she could cover numerous subjects and thoughts in one breath. Intending to dazzle him with what she considered her oratory skills, she'd plotted a reenactment of a discourse by the famous Roman orator Cicero.

She had donned a toga—one of the crisp white bedsheets from the linen closet—then painstakingly cut Roman sandals from one of her papa's saddle flaps and ingeniously fashioned the sandal straps from his finely tooled Spanish bridle.

With a pair of dressmaking sheers, she had cut her long hair into a short cap of curls just like that on her papa's bust of Julius Caesar. And she topped those curls with an olive leaf crown that was in truth a wreath of elm leaves.

Confident she accurately looked her part, she gave her newly cropped hair a swift pat, took one last look at her Roman costume, and proudly marched into the great room where her papa was playing host to England's major antiquity society and their honored guest, a renowned archaeologist.

When she was not more than ten steps into the room, her sweeping toga caught on the leg of a candle stanchion, knocking it over into the next one, and it into the next, which tilted toward a line of surprisingly flammable potted palms. The palms rapidly set flame to a wall of velvet draperies.

There was so very much smoke, and when it finally cleared, the only reenactment given her father and his esteemed guests was that of Rome burning.

Then at nine years old she had attempted to build a miniature model of the Roman aqueduct. As it turned out, she was quite the engineer. She drained the entire lake.

Unfortunately, she drained it into the stables.

Next came the incident of Hadrian's Wall, too long and disastrous a story to tell, but one should imagine the worst. All those fieldstones rumbling down the marble staircase. To this day if she closed her eyes she could still hear the clamor.

Thus was her quest for her papa's attention, which continued until the object of her attentions shifted from her papa to their neighbor's son, Richard Lennox.

Most young Englishwomen meet their heart's desire across a crowded ballroom, on a casual drive in the park, or through an arranged marriage. Not Letty. But she had ever been one to march to a different drummer.

She was eleven when she first clapped eyes on Richard Lennox. It was one of those bright English days when the sky above Devon was as blue as a hedge sparrow's egg, and the clouds seemed as white and fluffy as goose down.

Her papa's hounds barked gaily at the chattering birds, and the stable cats chased fluttering butterfly shadows. She and her cousins fled the stuffy confines of the schoolroom to the fresh freedom of the west pasture, where the only eyes upon them belonged to the dairy cattle.

It had all started on a dare. Her obnoxious cousins,

Isabel and James, had challenged her to ride a cow. The delighted gleam in their eyes should have warned her that something was afoot. But pride can make one blind.

Confident that she could easily accomplish so simple a feat, Letty marched into the midst of the grazing herd, rope in hand, and proceeded to examine each cow, looking for the one with the kindest eyes.

A plump Jersey with eyes like Father Christmas appeared just perfect. She even had a small indentation in her brown back that Letty judged to be the size of her very own bottom.

Now, one would think by looking at them that cows were placid, calm, most biddable animals, content to graze in the fields and chew their cud, their tails whipping up occasionally to swat a few pesky flies.

They are, usually.

Her cousins sauntered over near her as she spoke softly to the cow and slid the noose around its thick neck, not realizing that it was her own neck she'd noosed.

A quick prayer, a deep breath, and she leapt swiftly onto the cow's bone-hard back. Dear Cousin James slapped its rump with a hand that had a nail hidden in it.

She hadn't known cows could scream. The animal bawled and pitched and twisted, landing so hard that Letty's teeth rang together. At the sound of her cousins' cruel laughter she gripped the rope even tighter in her small hands and managed to stay on, her pride being at stake along with her life. The former, however, was most important to her at the time.

One blurred glance at her cousins' surprised faces and Letty knew she would ride that bovine beast as long as physically possible. So with her teeth ringing and her bottom battering the cow's spine, they trotted down the hill at a fast clip, splattered through a small brook, and cantered up a dirt road that led to a split-rail bridge spanning the river.

It was there, on that hollow wooden bridge, atop a bawling, runaway Jersey cow, that Letty Hornsby first met Richard Lennox, who, as divine fate would have it, was returning home from the university.

Even fate must sometimes succumb to cliché, for he was astride a white horse. Richard Lennox, a blond god whose looks could put the angel Gabriel to shame. A knight to slay dragons. An unsuspecting young man whose blasphemous profanity echoed upward as he was thrown over the side of the bridge and into the mossy waters of the River Heddon.

Meanwhile Letty clung tightly to a beam of the bridge and watched the cow trot along after his spooked horse. Two rather vivid curses caught her attention, so she turned back and peered over the side to the river below.

Until the day she died she'd always be able to remember his face as he surfaced to scowl up at her. Oh, it was chiseled classically: high cheekbones, a firm square jaw that carried just a shadow of a dark beard, and a straight, somewhat hawkish nose.

His skin was tanned a deep golden brown and his hair—now wet, slicked back, and peppered with green moss—was the color of her papa's fine French brandy, only streaked with blond. He had a dark slash of thick male brows over eyes the color of which were impossible to determine from such a height, but they glittered up at her from a face that said he'd love to get his clenching hands on her.

The incident set the pattern for their future encounters. Some were more disastrous than others, but, through the years, through the heartache and the embarrassment, never wavering was Letty's devotion.

With a faith as strong as a disciple, she'd clung to the heartfelt idea that someday Richard would be hers. He was the center of her lonely world.

She'd dreamed her hair would suddenly turn into long red tresses guaranteed to catch his eye—which was, by the way, green. She'd discovered the color during an unfortunate incident with a cricket ball.

Actually he didn't have one green eye, for if he'd had only one eye he'd have worn a patch—like a dashing pirate. As romantic a thought as that was, Richard Lennox had two green eyes, and they were not the rich green of spring grass nor the bright green of a leprechaun's suit, but the same dark green of the sprawling Devon moors, of the Channel sea just before the sun sets, of a dangerous forest in which an innocent fairy-tale princess could become hopelessly lost.

A green for a lonely girl to weave fanciful dreams about. And dreaming was one of the few things she did well, because in dreams there were always happy endings. In dreams she could imagine anything, no matter how preposterous, no matter how unlikely, without the world outside knowing. In dreams she had a glimpse of perfection that never existed in the real world.

So she dreamed that someday Richard Lennox would awaken with the sudden realization that he couldn't live without her. She fancied their first kiss—which she practiced by pressing her lips to her bedchamber door—and she remembered every rare smile, every chance meeting, and the one time he'd actually danced with her.

Oh yes, she remembered that time. Every girl remembered the first ball of her season, and Letty remembered hers as much much more than merely a ball. She had been the damsel in distress and Richard, her knight in shining armor.

Such a moment! If she closed her eyes she could still remember his scent. He'd smelled of sandalwood and raindrops . . . and heroes.

She still had that dance card, hidden in special box along with her mother's pearls, the nail James had used to slap that cow, and a small sampler with which her mama had taught her to stitch. It said: "Speak from your heart."

After the debacle of her London season and the humiliation of her banishment, she had tried to make her papa understand. He, like everyone else, had known how she felt about Richard. It was no secret. But with that came the fact that her papa was also well aware of her disastrous history with the young man, aware of every plan gone awry, of every foolish thing she had done to win the attention of a young man bent on destroying himself without her help.

Love had been her downfall, she had argued when her papa tried to talk to her. Couldn't he even begin to understand? She'd been in love with Richard for half of a lifetime.

Her papa had said that if things continued on as they had, half a lifetime was all Richard Lennox would get.

And here it was a year or so later that Letty was looking down at her love, lying so still, his blond head in her lap, his dark brows flecked with sand, those dark green eyes closed. She hoped her papa's jest had not been prophetic. He had taken quite a nasty fall from his mount.

"Richard?" she whispered.

Her English bloodhound, Caesar Augustus, drew back his lips in a canine snarl and growled.

"Hush, Gus," she scolded. He blinked once, whimpered, then sank his large brown head with its floppy black-tipped ears onto his outstretched paws and watched her through bloodshot hazel eyes.

She turned back and searched Richard's face for signs of consciousness. She saw none. But there was little light—only one guttering candle nearby. As she had a hundred times since his fall, she stared intently at his chest.

It rose and fell slightly. She gave a sigh of relief and moved her face just inches from his. "Please wake up, my lord. Please. You've been unconscious so terribly long."

He stirred, then mumbled something unintelligible.

She watched him ever so closely, looking at the strong angles of his face, his square jaw stubbled with a bit of beard growth that was so much darker than the golden streaks in his hair. She slowly drew a tentative finger along his rough jaw, then touched her own jaw.

She sat completely still for a moment, thinking. Deep in her chest, she felt a strange little thrill when confronted with the simple contrasts between a man and a woman.

Unable to stop herself, she slid her hand into his large one, holding it. For the sweetest moment she just stared at their joined hands, looking at the difference in size, the dark hardness of his hand, the pale softness of hers. Then she sighed. "I'm here, my lord . . . my love."

He slowly peeled open one green eye, then the other. Both appeared slightly glazed, then they cleared and filled recognition. Richard moaned like a man dying.

"Are you in pain, my lord?" She frowned and

reached out to gently stroke the bits of sand from his forehead.

"What the hell did you do to me this time?"

"You fell."

"You're flicking sand in my eyes."

She drew her hand back. "I'm sorry."

He blinked for a moment. "I fell," he repeated, as if he had to do so to comprehend. "Off my horse?"

She nodded.

"From the cliff path?"

She nodded again.

He tried to lift his head and winced. "What did I land on? The rocks?"

"Your head."

He raised a hand to his head and appeared to feel around for wounds. "Good God . . ." He paused on a spot and gave a small groan. "What a knot!" He lay there for a second, his eyes closed, then asked, "Is anything missing?"

"No."

He opened his eyes and pinned her with a stare. "Broken?"

She shook her head. "I don't think so, my lord, but I can help you see if anything's broken. You did moan a bit when you first awoke."

"That wasn't from pain." He sat up very slowly and looked straight at her. "Only the anticipation of all the pain to come." He grimaced, rolling his shoulders as if they were stiff. He shook his head slightly, blinked, then took in the dark room. His express filled with dread. Facing her, he gripped her arm tightly. "Where the devil are we?"

Gus shot up in a stiff protective stance, nose to nose with Richard, who quickly released her arm and said, "Never mind. Now I know where I am." He scowled directly at Gus. "I'm in hell."

"I think you're confused my lord."

"That usually happens when you and I are together, Miss Hornsby."

He was calling her "Miss Hornsby" and her heart dropped just a bit, because it always did something wonderful to her when he called her "hellion." But he hadn't called her that in so terribly long.

"I've been told I have a habit of creating confusion. I don't try." She gave a small sigh. "I never thought you were confused, probably because you seem quite clear eyed when you shout."

He pinned her with a hard stare for a moment, then flinched slightly.

"Does your head still hurt?"

"Yes."

"I thought so. You look queasy."

With an even sicker look, he studied the dank surroundings of the ship's hold. "I think I might be ill."

"Oh," she said knowingly. *"Mal de mer."*

"No. *Mal de la femme,"* he said under his breath, then added in a flat tone, "We're on a ship."

She nodded, leaning closer as she lowered her voice to a hushed whisper. "I believe it's a smugglers ship, my lord."

He closed his eyes and took some deep breaths. The silence ate at her nerves and she clasped her hands in her lap and nervously tapped her fingers together.

Finally he looked at her. "What were you doing on those cliffs?"

She flushed and stared at her hands. "Following you."

"I haven't been back to Lockett Manor in over two years. How in God's name did you know I was back?"

"I heard the servants talking. One of the kitchen maids saw you leave the tavern and she told Cook, and ... I, uh, overheard."

"Hiding in the back staircase?"

Surprised, she looked up. "How did you know?"

He gave a sharp laugh that held no humor. "Lucky guess."

Again there was no sound except the slosh of the waves hitting the side of the ship. She waited for him to say something, anything. But he didn't. There was nothing but *slap! whoosh,* and an occasional creak. Unable to stand the silence a moment longer, she said, "I think, considering the situation, you and I are rather stuck together, my lord."

He gave a wry laugh. "That, Miss Hornsby, is the ultimate in understatement."

"Yes, I suppose it is," she said with a sigh. "But since we are going to be together, I think we shouldn't worry about formalities. You should call me 'Letty' or 'Letitia,' although I prefer 'Letty,' but not 'Olive.' I cannot abide that name. But 'Letty' is just fine." What she really wanted was to tell him to call her "hellion," but she didn't have the courage to let him know how much that name meant to her. She waited for him to say something.

He didn't say anything, just looked at her the way Cook looked at a fallen soufflé.

She cocked her head and said, "Please ... my lord?"

He turned away and rubbed his head "Fine," he said shortly.

She smiled, then waited for him to speak. He said nothing. After her season, short as it was, she had decided that men were not mind readers at all. And ladies were expected to be patient. She was certain that it was a man who coined the phrase patience is a virtue—a way of keeping it a man's world by fooling women into waiting patiently for love until they, the men, deigned to succumb.

But patience was not part of her. The times she'd been patient, waiting for something to happen, the world went round and round, but without her. For Letty, patience was the same as allowing herself and her dreams to fade into nothing.

She watched him a moment longer, then gave up and said, "Considering the rules of etiquette, I suppose I should continue to defer to your title and say 'my lord.' But you've hardly been a lord very long, barely two years, and besides which, I heard that you didn't want to be a lord at all." She took another breath.

He shook his head, then gave her look of astonishment.

The perfect chance for her to make her point. "But since you didn't want to be one—an earl, that is—I shall call you 'Richard.'"

Gus snarled.

She turned and shook a finger at him. "You be a sweet dog!"

A loud choking snort came from Richard's direction.

She turned back around.

He scowled at Gus, who grumbled and scowled back.

"Gus . . . it's not polite to growl every time you hear his name."

Gus looked at Richard, barked once, then flopped his head on his paws and just watched them.

Letty turned back to Richard and gave him a tentative smile, hoping he'd return it. She had no idea that her eyes gave away her heart.

His expression was that of a man suffering. He had taken quite a nasty fall. "I'm sorry your head pains you."

He gave her an undefinable look, then turned his

gaze on the locked door for long minutes, during which her smile slowly died. Finally, when he turned, his gaze swept over her, then shifted to Gus.

Richard shuddered slightly, which she attributed to the dampness of the ship, then sat there for a long time, looking at the dark walls of the cargo hold, eyeing the wooden barrels and crates stacked nearby, then staring at the bolted door.

A full minute passed before he glared up at the ship beams overhead and said, "To think they say You are a kind God."

She was unsure how he meant his words. And after a moment, very quietly, she said, "God is kind."

Richard gave her a look of male bewilderment.

She smiled warmly, then added with bright and simple honesty, "Very kind. You see ... He gave me you."

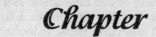

Chapter 2

$\mathcal{A}$ gift from God. She actually believed that balderdash. He pinned her with a hard stare. She smiled as if it was endearing.

He closed his eyes and was instantly aware that his head pounded. Which wasn't surprising. He'd fallen on it.

While his friends might have suggested that his body was rebelling against all the brandy he'd dumped into it, he knew differently. With the stubbornness of an English ox, he looked at the hellion's face and rationalized that she could give anyone a headache.

Here they were, locked in the hold of a smugglers' ship, probably on their way to France, where Napoleon was on the loose and once again advocating war. Meanwhile the hellion sat only a few feet away with her hands properly folded in her lap, babbling about gifts from God and chattering niceties as if they were about to have tea.

Quite the image. He watched her shake the sand

from the soiled hem of her blue dress. Her cloak hung off one shoulder and her nut-brown hair had fallen down into a wild and curly mass. It looked as tangled as her thinking.

And he was more than familiar with how her mind worked. Her infatuation with him had been blatant, and nothing but trouble: spying on him from trees, rescuing him from duels, concocting situations that her furtive mind had thought would impress him. She was a tenacious thing.

He glanced back at her and saw what he didn't want to see: her heart laid open. And it made him more uncomfortable than crossing paths with the most blatant of London flirts. Yet unlike those experienced flirts, there was no guile to her look, no all-too-familiar come-hither expression that most Englishwomen practiced for long hours in front of a mirror, and most Englishmen played to their best advantage.

She was ignorant of those games, and he didn't know how to play her. Her face held no secrets, and he didn't care for what he read in it. Adoration. Innocence and honesty. She was too honest, too sincere, traits that were foreign to English society.

Honesty had been at the root of one of the first ripples of gossip she'd created by walking innocently up to her aunt during a card party and announcing to the whole table that she thought Almack's was dull as dry toast and that Sally Jersey, while certainly a bit of a tragedy queen, wasn't half as ill bred and despotic as her aunt had implied. Lady Jersey had been playing at the card table behind her.

The hellion had only voiced aloud what everyone else thought but never dared say. They chose not to welcome her, because she didn't fit into society's accepted mold.

Now there was an interesting image, he thought

wryly. The Hornsby hellion in a mold. She'd probably break the blasted thing, and if it was heavy—enormously heavy—he had no doubt it would somehow land on him.

He turned his gaze to her and was struck by the contrast between what he saw and what he knew. Sitting there as she was, with her feelings bared for all the world to see, no one would ever believe that she could wreak such havoc.

But she could. Had. And probably would, perhaps before the day was out.

He looked around the hold again, then said, "Miss Hornsby . . ."

She glanced up and smiled. "Letty."

"Letty. How long have we been locked in here?"

"I'm not certain. Perhaps an hour. Why?"

He rubbed his chin thoughtfully, looking for some way to escape. "I'm trying to figure how far out into the Channel we are."

"I don't know. I've never been on a ship." Her voice lowered to a furtive whisper. "Especially a smugglers' ship."

"I think they know we're down here, so you needn't whisper." Shaking his head, he turned his attention to the rafters, looking for a trap. All he saw was an expanse of wood darkened by dampness and time.

"Don't you think this is exciting?"

"No."

"Oh." Her voice trailed off. "Well, I certainly think it's exciting."

He stopped his search and looked at her. "I fail to see how you can find this exciting."

"Oh, well, to me it is. Rather like a novel come to life. A true adventure. Why, we could be Tristan and Isolde, Robinson Crusoe and Friday, almost any romantic characters. Now do you see what I mean?"

"No."

She tilted her head as if she were trying to understand him. Hell, he didn't understand himself. After a pause she added, "I suppose that's because you're a man."

"And what's wrong with being a man?"

"There is nothing wrong with being a man," she said bluntly. "However, it's been my experience that sometimes men are not too perceptive."

"Your experience?" There was a sardonic bite to his voice.

"Oh, now I've offended you, haven't I? I never meant to imply there was anything *wrong* with men. They can be perfectly wonderful. Our monarch is a man. Well, I suppose that's not the best example of 'wonderful,' is it? And the Regent ..." She clapped her mouth closed and flushed. The look he knew so well. There was a commonly used saying for guilt: a hangman's hands. The hellion had hangman's face.

"Vauxhall," he said.

She looked as if she wanted to fade into the wood. "Were you there?"

"No, but half of society was."

"It was just horrid."

"Yes. I suppose it was."

She looked up at him with a question in her eyes. "I have never quite understood how, with such a bevy of valets to help one dress, His Majesty's stay strings could have possibly trailed behind him like they did. I do believe almost anyone could have happened along and stepped on them. To this day I don't which was louder, the Regent's shouts or the cry of springing stays and rending velvet."

The incident had been the brunt of more jests than Richard could count, the two most memorable of which were published in the *Times:* "Ode to a Bun-

32

gling Miss" and a parody on Milton titled "Clad in Naked Majesty."

She turned silent, her discourse on men and heroes and royalty thrust away by the unpleasant memories of her failure. He wondered what went through her mind when she thought about London or her season.

Looking at her left him with a sense of awkwardness that was unknown to him. He had thought his cynicism and his long association with every side of society had equipped him to handle most any situation.

Yet he could still remember the gleam of anticipation and excitement he'd seen in her eyes at that first ball, and he knew that all of the social functions that had grown so tiresome to him were of supreme importance to her.

He knew enough of females to understand that they saw balls and parties and teas in a different light than did males.

In retrospect, he supposed that was why he'd danced with her. She had looked as if she desperately needed a dance. And now she still looked as if she were in desperate need of something.

But he was no knight to slay dragons, no guardian angel there to make her dreams come true. He turned away, choosing to go on with his search of the hold. But a few quiet minutes of searching gave him no means of escape, so he started to walk across the room. The rustle of her skirts stopped him, and he turned.

She was looking at him as if she were a soap bubble ready to burst. He leaned one shoulder against a wall and crossed his arms, instinct telling him this would take a while. "I take it from that expression that you have something to say."

She gave him a tentative look, then nodded.

He waved one hand. "Go ahead."

Her demeanor said this was very important to her.

She chewed on her lip an extra second, then took one long breath and raised her worried face toward his. "I was wondering why you haven't come home for so long."

That was not the question he had expected, and he wasn't sure he wanted to answer it. Truth was, he hadn't been able to bring himself to come back since he buried his brother and father.

"Home" she had called it, but Lockett Manor was not home. It was his father's house. His brother's house. But it wasn't home, which is why he'd not come back until last night.

And then he'd come back because the only two men of any importance to his wretched excuse of a life—his friends Belmore and Seymour—had both challenged him to do so with the comment that he'd better bury old ghosts before he bloody well buried himself.

He stared at her bowed head and thought of how to answer her. He came up with nothing polite enough for her innocent ears. She still hadn't looked at him but fiddled instead with some flowers on the hem of her dress.

Finally she must have sensed his look, because she raised her head, then promptly averted her eyes again as if she knew her face showed her thoughts, and those thoughts were too wounded to show the world. When she spoke, it was so quietly he had to move closer to hear her.

"Did you stay away because of me?"

"You?" he said, then repeated, "You?" And because he couldn't help himself, he began to laugh.

Her mouth fell open, then she frowned when he laughed harder. Her expression said she didn't know whether to be offended or to laugh with him. After a moment her chin went up and she just sat a little straighter, watching him through eyes that were both puzzled and hurt.

He stopped laughing so hard. "Considering our past, I suppose I'd have good reason to stay away."

She nodded seriously while plucking at her skirts.

"But I don't think I can lay the blame at your door, hellion."

Her head shot up and she stared at him as if he had given her an unexpected gift. She smiled so brightly his breath caught for an instant, and he stood there feeling as if he'd swallowed a torch.

"Why did you stay away?"

Why? According to his friends, he been doing little else but drinking and gambling, drinking and dueling, and drinking and trying to bed every willing woman in England. Hellbent on destroying himself. He wondered how she'd react if he told her the bald truth. That her hero hadn't the courage to come home. "I'd have come back if I could," he finally said with a shrug of indifference.

He could see by her expression that he'd not satisfied her question.

"You don't want to tell me where you've been, do you?"

"No, I don't."

"Then the Reverend Mrs. Poppit was right."

"Just what did the Reverend Mrs. Poppit say?"

"Quite a bit, actually. You are her favorite topic during tea at the weekly meeting of the Ladies League for Moral Stewardship. She said you'd come to no good drinking and gambling and carousing about with rakes and such." She gave him a direct look.

"Of course you know she claims to be an authority on rakehells, one of which she claims you are. And no one dares question her." She paused for a thoughtful second, tapping a finger against her lower lip while she chewed on it. "I must say, however, that I've often wondered at the propriety of the wife of a reverend being so knowledgeable about sin. But I don't think anyone has the starch to question her authority."

She gave him a soft look of blind faith. "You needn't worry, though. I have never believed that of you."

He waited, then asked, "What would you say if I told you she was right?"

She searched his face, looking for God only knew what. Then her expression became mulish and she shook her head. "I don't believe you are wicked."

He laughed. "Well, I suppose to Mrs. Poppit and that Ladies League, I am the very epitome of wickedness."

Her eyes widened just enough to make the devil in him reach out and slowly run a finger along her jawline.

"I've tasted my share of sin."

Her lips parted and her breath caught.

Through a lazy gaze he stared at her mouth for the longest time, feeling the inexplicable urge to run his thumb across her full lips, especially the full lower one that she so often chewed, perhaps even dip a finger into the damp pink of her open mouth.

In a natural response, he slid his hand behind her neck and stroked her ear with his thumb. Once. Twice. "And you should remember that, hellion." Three times. "I am wicked." He paused for effect. "Very . . . very wicked."

She stared up at him, her mouth still open, her eyes uncertain. Slowly, he pulled his hand away, then chucked her under the chin. "Now be a good girl and go sit down by that beast you call a pet while I try to find some way for us to escape."

She blinked once and he laughed again. She flushed

bright red at his laughter and looked away, her eyes disillusioned.

He found suddenly that he felt more cruel than cocky, rather like he'd just drowned some kittens. So foreign a feeling it was that he paused for a moment, then instinctively looked back at her. She had retreated and was sitting by the beast, her face pensive.

Perhaps he had succeeded in frightening her off. That was his intention. However, he felt no sense of relief.

After a small lapse of silence she shifted, and again he heard the rustle of her skirts. He ignored it and began pounding on an inside wall, looking for a door. He could feel her stare for long minutes, accompanied by a silence that should have worried him.

"I think that is some of your appeal."

"What?"

"Your wickedness." She sighed.

He froze.

"I had thought this adventure might be even more romantic than a dream."

He turned. "You think this is romantic?"

She nodded. "When you were unconscious, I wondered if perhaps this might be the most romantic thing that ever to happen to me." There was a frankness in her face. "You and I—us, together—being kidnapped by smugglers."

"This isn't a silly romantic novel." With that he turned back around and away from that face, choosing to continue down the wall, randomly tapping on the boards. "And the fact that you find smuggling romantic does not surprise me. However, I think it would be better if you viewed the situation more realistically. We are locked in the hold of a smugglers' ship." Having no luck with this wall either, he turned and scanned the hold.

"They were quite nice when they locked us in here," she said in a chipper tone.

He straightened to his full height. "How fortunate for us. Nice smugglers. Do you suppose they'll throw a little soiree for us when we get wherever the hell it is we're going? And if they were so bloody nice, then why did they lock us in here?"

She gave him a curious look and casually scratched the hellhound's ear. "Of course they would lock us in here. I mean to say, they were smuggling ... and smuggling is illegal ... and we saw them smuggling, illegally. It seems quite natural that they would lock us up."

"You don't seem very concerned."

"I was more concerned about you. You were unconscious quite a long while. Although I suppose I should admit that I was frightfully upset for a few moments. It would take nerves of steel not to concern oneself when one was in the midst of being nabbed. But then I remembered."

"Remembered what?"

"I'm with you, and you'll protect me."

She was making him out to be some hero. He found humor in the irony of that, he who had wanted so badly to be a soldier and been denied the chance, first by his father and then by fate. He hadn't thought his first taste of battle would be with a love-swooned hellion hunting for a hero.

"Truth be told, if I was concerned about anything, it was whether or not you had been seriously injured. I'm perfectly fine. However, I must say the smugglers looked rather shocked when I ran toward you instead of down the beach and away from them. You were my only thought—so much so, I ran past the two men they'd sent to chase me. They were quite confused.

Ran into each other before they came after me. I quite believe they expected me to become hysterical."

"Most ladies would be hysterical. But if there's one thing I should be aware of, it's the fact that you are not 'most ladies.' "

Her bright look died suddenly. She wore the expression of someone who had failed miserably. "I've never acted as I should." She sighed, staring at her lap where she had just clasped her hands. "It's been the bane of my existence." She glanced up. "However, I'm certain I would have been hysterical had something happened to you. I need only to think of you lying there on that beach, ever so still, while I wondered and worried if my papa's jest had come true."

"What jest is that?"

"He told me that if I didn't leave you be, half a lifetime was all you would get."

He gave a bark of mocking laughter.

"Papa laughed too," she said quietly. "He doesn't take me seriously. I think perhaps you don't either. But that won't change how I feel."

Her faith in him was so strong he tensed, as if deep down inside he was rebelling against the responsibility of caring for another, as if he didn't deserve such blind faith and wouldn't accept it from her. Everything about her screamed vulnerability, a vulnerability that was somehow linked to him.

She looked back up at him, her eyes wide with honesty and little hope. "Would it help if I acted concerned now? If it would help I could, you know."

She might as well have just said I'll do anything for you. Be anything for you.

"I'll decline your offer of feigned hysteria," he said more sharply than he intended. He found himself staring at her bowed head. "Hysterical females have no appeal," he added gruffly. "Just be yourself."

She looked startled, then turned to stare at the locked door. After a few minutes she asked, "What do you suppose will happen to us?"

"I have no idea."

"I'm certain they won't harm us."

He snorted with disbelief. "Blind faith needs some element of logic, hellion."

"While we were in the boat, rowing out to this ship, they let me hold your head in my lap." There was an illogically hopeful tone to her voice.

"Enlighten me. Please." He crossed his arms. "What does that have to do with anything?"

"Well, it makes perfect sense to me."

No wonder I'm confused.

"They wouldn't have let me hold your head if they had meant to harm us. They wouldn't have given a fig about your head. If you really think about it, doesn't that make sense?"

"I'm beginning to wonder if anything will ever make sense again," he muttered, turning to look at the crates behind him. They were long and coffin-sized, he thought, giving fate credit for a sublime sense of humor.

Besides bodies, crates that size could contain almost anything. Curious, he tried to pry the top of one open with his hands, but it was nailed shut, so he stepped around and searched for some identifiable markings.

"Perhaps it was the fall on your head."

"What?" he asked offhandedly, rubbing at some kind of lettering on the crate.

"Why, surely you've heard of the expression 'knocked senseless'? It seems to me that term wouldn't exist if it didn't happen, so perhaps that's why nothing makes sense to you."

"My sense is just fine."

"Oh." There was a small snatch of silence. "That's good, isn't it?"

"Hmmm." Barely listening to her chatter, he examined the crate closely, then squinted to try to read the writing on it.

"Are you aware that a moment ago you claimed nothing made sense?"

He straightened. "What I said was . . ." He looked at her and words left him. She stared at him as if awaiting the most important answer of her life. Her expressions always seemed to ask him for things he could never give.

Her face was somehow different than he remembered. Not as young or as full, yet still innocently inquisitive. He ran his hand through his hair in frustration and stood there, silent. Time seemed to tick by in aeons, then he finally admitted, "I seem to have forgotten what I said."

"I remember!"

He held up his hand. "Whatever I said doesn't matter, because there is still no logical reason for them to lock us in here."

"I don't understand."

"Then let me explain it to you. There are plenty of locals involved in an innocent degree of smuggling. For some families, handling contraband is the only way they can survive."

"I know that. I was raised in Devon too. That's why I wasn't concerned."

"You didn't let me finish."

"Go ahead. Finish." She gave a wave of her hand, yet he had the distinct feeling that her mind was already set.

"They don't, however, kidnap peers and innocent women and lock them in a ship's hold." He leaned against the crate, crossing one boot over the other while he awaited her next argument.

Her eyes lit with secret admiration and her voice lowered with a tad of drama. "Have you known many smugglers?"

Yes, he'd known his share. Half of Devon smuggled some type of contraband. The village wheelwright and some of the fishermen smuggled lace, silks, and glass. Even the stable master at Lockett Manor had dabbled in brandy. Richard suspected most of what he drank the night before hadn't had a ha'penny of duty paid against it.

He leaned down closer to her inquisitive face. "Didn't the all-knowing Reverend Mrs. Poppit fill your ears with lurid tales. Perhaps I smuggle brandy, spit fire, and devour inquisitive young ladies who ask too many questions."

She watched him as if she wasn't certain if he was teasing her. He tried for a fierce look.

Contrary as ever, she laughed and smiled up at him, her hand gently touching his arm. "You can be so witty, Richard."

The next instant her dog leapt onto the nearest crate, stuck his loose lips and damp black nose directly in Richard's face, then growled.

Chapter

3

*F*ifteen minutes later the beast finally moved. For the first five minutes Richard and the obnoxious dog stood in challenge, at eye level; the second five minutes the beast followed his every movement with a pair of bloodshot and leery canine eyes. Now Gus lay in a dark corner, making noises not unlike that of a sleeping bull with some lung affliction.

In that same fifteen minutes, the hellion had scolded Gus, offered to help Richard, then chattered in circles while he'd examined every crate in the hold for legible markings.

There was one candle, and it gave barely a breath of weak thin light. The hold was dark as dusk, so he gave up squinting at the last crate and straightened. Good fortune was on his side, for he spotted two rusty oil lanterns lying in one dark corner. Each was about half filled with oil, and he brought them over to the wooden crates, where he set one on each end.

He lit lanterns with the nub of candle, and soon

they were casting a dim yellow glow over the corner. He slid a lantern closer to the edge and bent to try to read the smudged words on the crate.

A curly brown head suddenly popped up next to his line of vision. "What are you doing?" She looked intently at the crate.

"Trying to read this." He stared at the back of her head.

"What does it say?"

"I don't know. I can't read it with your head in the way."

"Well then, I'll do it for you." Before he could respond, she'd shifted in between the crate and him, blocking his entire view. Her head cocked at a curious angle. "It says ... *F-o-r*," she spelled out, then paused. "I can't see ..." She pulled the lantern closer to the edge. "There's a darker smudge, then it looks like *P* something *d* something *y* And *l-o-n-d-o-n* ... oh, *London!*" She turned to him and grinned proudly. "Whatever it is, it's from London."

She whipped her head back so quickly he had to step back to keep from getting snapped in the face with her hair. She continued, "Then beneath that it says *p* again, *e-r-c-u-s-s-i-o-n*—"

"Locks," he finished.

She faced him again, surprised. "How did you know?"

Richard swiped her hair from his face. "Forsyth and Purdey are gunsmiths. They market new percussion locks for rifles."

She stared at him blankly.

He added quickly, "The locks make the rifles fire balls in rapid sequence."

"Oh." She straightened. "Is that good?"

"Probably to Napoleon's supporters it is."

"Napoleon!" she gasped.

He nodded, eyeing the hold. "Now I think I understand why we're locked in here."

"Why?"

"Because they're smuggling arms, and that's a treasonable offense."

She was uncommonly quiet. One look at her face and he saw that she had finally realized this was not some romantic little fairy tale.

Very quietly, with a slight quiver in her voice that made him take pause, she asked, "What do you think they're going to do with us?"

"Probably nothing," he lied.

She gave an enormous sigh of relief.

"They'll deliver the crates to the French, then more than likely return to Devon. Just a little adventure for you to tell your grandchildren." He knew that wasn't even probable, but he wasn't sure what the truth was. They could be sailing toward their deaths, but he didn't intend to tell her that.

He did, however, intend to find some means of escape. In which case she'd never have to know the danger they might be in. He glanced back at her, aware she was keeping incredibly quiet.

She watched him for another peaceful moment, then took a deep breath and said with utter openness, "There's no one I'd rather be kidnapped with."

He gave a small mocking laugh. "Of that I have no doubt."

She smiled at him again.

He looked away. His sarcasm had gone right over her head. When he looked back at her, spurred to do so by another lapse into female silence, she was leaning against one of the gun crates with her eyes closed. She wasn't asleep, because one hand was again twisting one of those flowers on her hem.

"What *are* you doing?"

45

"Dreaming," she answered, without opening her eyes.

"I'm certain that you will find this extraordinary, but most people dream when they're asleep."

She laughed and opened her eyes. "Not that kind of dreaming. *Day*-dreaming, silly."

He flinched. He didn't consider himself as pompous as his friend Belmore used to be, but he still preferred "my lord" to "silly"—a word that brought to mind geese and girls, not that he thought there was much difference between the two, and the last hour had done little to change his view.

She sat very still, almost relaxed, but what gave him pause was the peaceful expression on her face. "You do this often?"

"Umm-hmmm." She had closed her eyes again.

He shook his head and turned away but for some reason stopped midturn. "Why?"

"Because I can see things no one else ever sees. Close your eyes." She began to hum Mozart.

"Wait!" He held up a hand.

She stopped humming and looked at him.

"Why do you want me to close my eyes?"

"Because that's how one dreams, silly."

"I prefer 'my lord' to 'silly,' " he said sharply.

Her face flushed red with embarrassment, and she averted her eyes. "I'm sorry."

He looked at her bowed head and wondered why it was that she was able to spark guilt in him more often than anyone else. He felt a sudden need to find a way of escape. Quickly. He turned away and searched for some kind of hatch behind the stack of wooden crates.

There was none. Let her dream her little dreams. He would look for a way out.

"I didn't mean any disrespect . . . my lord. I forgot

you weren't Richard Lennox anymore." She made it sound as if he had died.

He slowly counted to ten, then leaned against the crates, crossed his arms, and closed his eyes. He was about to rescue a kitten. "There. I've closed my bloody eyes. Are you happy?"

He heard her skirts rustle with movement and could feel her face move just inches from his. He caught a whiff of lavender just before he felt her wave her hand in front of his face, apparently to make certain he wasn't peeking.

"Thank you, my lord."

"You're welcome." He paused. "And you can stop 'my lording' me."

"But my lord, you said—"

He opened his eyes. "I know what I said." He took a long breath, then admitted, "I was wrong."

She smiled up at him so brightly he couldn't look away, so he closed his eyes again.

"Just let your imagination go . . ." she said in the low and dreamy voice of a mesmerist.

He stood there leaning against the crate with his eyes closed when he should have been looking for a way to escape. "Why am I doing this?"

"To put wickedness from your troubled mind," she said very slowly.

"And here I was, plotting my latest debauchery."

"I don't think debauchery is allowed."

"Ah, yes, well, I do believe I'm as familiar with gambling. Suppose I dream that I've wagered a small fortune."

"Gambling's not allowed either."

He opened his eyes. "Fine wine—"

"No."

"French brandy?"

"No." She shook her head, her eyes still closed.

47

He wondered how long she'd keep her eyes closed if he mentioned seduction and used the most base and elemental English word for it. Not long. And no doubt it was not allowed either. However, the thought brought to mind some interesting and decidedly sinful images, and he closed his eyes willingly this time.

"Are you imagining something?"

He gave a wicked grin. "Yes."

"In your mind's eye, do you see something personal, something that I can't see?"

"I'm certain this would never be among your dreams, hellion."

"Is it wonderful?" she asked, the rustle of skirts telling him that she was stepping away.

"Umm ... I'd say so."

"So is what I'm imagining." There was a moment of utter silence. "Do you want to know what it is?"

"What is this? You show me yours and I'll show you mine?"

"I don't know what you mean."

"No, I suppose you don't."

"Dreams aren't like wishes. You can tell what they are and they can still come true."

He laughed.

"Do you want to hear mine?"

"No, but I'm sure that won't stop you."

"I'm dreaming that—"

"Ha!" He opened his eyes and looked in the direction of her voice. "I was right."

She stood barely three feet away, her head swaying to some imaginary tune, her eyes closed and her expression still dreamy. As if she stood in front of a star, she was limned in the dim light of the lanterns. Every curve, every line that was in essence her, had sharpened in clarity before him. For the first time ever, he saw her as a woman.

48

Wild and untamed, her hair spilled down her back almost to her waist, and instead of being charmingly ramshackle, it was suddenly sensual in its disarray. It brought to mind the deep hot images of the morning after—after a night in which every minute was filled with sensual pleasure. Her figure was not that of the young girl he'd known as a pest. She had a woman's fullness, and he asked himself when she had grown up.

The faceless woman in his imagined seduction suddenly had a face, a young face, with full lips and a dreamy expression that was the result of the most intimate fulfillment. He could almost taste her on his lips. He stood frozen, unable to catch air, to move for an instant. He'd had this feeling only once before, when Gentleman Jackson had given him a hard right cross.

"Oh, truly? What were you right about?" Her curious voice broke the spell.

He blinked a few times, stupefied, and stared at nothing, the only thing on his mind the carnal images of soft naked thighs wrapped tightly about his hips, his waist, his head. "I don't remember."

"That's a shame. Now we'll never know."

"This seems to happen often."

"My being right?"

"No. These memory lapses. Perhaps the fall did knock you senseless."

Senseless. Yes, he was senseless. He looked at her face and focused on her mouth. He shook his head to clear it, but it didn't help. Too much brandy the night before. His hands shook slightly, a sign that he had lost his control.

"This conversation is going nowhere," he said in the cold tone he used with someone he wanted to dismiss.

"That's because you won't answer me," she said with an innocent frankness that couldn't be dismissed.

She sat down suddenly, leaning against the crate

and arranging her skirts. When she had them just so, she looked up at him. She frowned, then searched his face. "You don't look very well. Does your head still hurt?"

"Yes!" he barked.

Gus barked too.

Richard slowly turned to glare at the dog. The beast glared back at him.

"He barks like that whenever you shout." She cocked her head and frowned thoughtfully. "You look as if you're in pain again. Perhaps your head hurts from the fall, although I hate to bring up the subject because it seems to agitate you. A rest would probably do you good, so why don't you sit down right here." She patted the floor next to her. "And rest your eyes. All that glowering must make them tired."

He didn't move.

"Richard?"

Gus crept forward in a crouch, growling, his eyes darting toward Richard, his teeth showing white against his black lips.

"Come over here, Gus." She patted the floor on the other side of her.

The beast eased past him, grumbling, then slunk near her other side, where he walked in a leery circle a few times, then plopped down with a loud thud and rested his damp snout on her lap. His narrowed eyes never left Richard's.

She smiled up at him expectantly, then patted the floor on the other side of her again. "Sit here. You'll feel better, I'm certain."

Richard gave up and slid down the crates he'd been leaning against. He sat next to her on the plank floor, stretched his legs out, and crossed his boots.

His arm touched her and he heard her slight intake of breath. He could feel her stare and returned it, only to find her gaze on the point where their arms had touched.

He shook his head, aware that he had completely surrendered to her silliness. But perhaps if he did as she asked she would be quiet for a blessed minute.

With a sigh as big as her imagination, she leaned her head back against the wooden crates. There was a sweet silence, then she began to fidget.

He could feel it coming. About one blessed minute of quiet was all he was going to get.

"Are your eyes closed?"

Not again. He took one long breath, then leaned his own head back and snapped, "Yes." Closing his eyes was easier than talking to her. He amended that thought: Listening to her.

"My eyes are closed too. Do you feel better?"

"No."

"Give it a few minutes. I'm dreaming that we're on a smugglers' ship."

"How inventive."

She laughed. "As I said before, you can be such a wit."

I must be a halfwit to be doing this. He gave a derisive laugh.

"Keep your eyes closed," she warned.

To avoid another round of senseless argument, he kept his eyes closed. He heard her getting up and he could sense her standing before him. "Try to imagine this," she said. "In my dream, I'm the damsel in distress."

Good God ... a bloody fairy tale.

"And you are ... my lord hero."

His eyes shot open.

She sank to a deep curtsy, until her gaze was even with his. She batted her eyelashes.

Staring, he wondered how long she could flutter

those eyelashes at him and not appear cross-eyed. Settling back against the crate, he rested one arm atop a raised knee and let himself be entertained. So this was how the hellion flirted. Interesting.

She started to rise, but her knees cracked like Christmas walnuts. "Ouch!" She grabbed onto the crate, frowning down at her knees as she rubbed one. muttering, "How did she do that?"

He was struck with an overpowering urge to laugh.

After a space of time she stopped rubbing her knees and straightened. She looked at him and frowned. "You're just sitting there."

"You told me to relax."

"This is exactly what I meant about men not being very perceptive."

"Then tell me, hellion, what do you want?"

"You're not living up to your reputation."

"Which reputation is that? Drinking, gambling, or debauching?"

She planted her hands on her hips. "You are supposed to be a rake."

"Ah, the Reverend Mrs. Poppit. Didn't she warn you about flirtations with rakehells?"

"Yes, but you're different."

"I see." He nodded. "Known a lot of rakes, have you?"

"Oh no. Only you."

"Yet you seem to have a vast amount of knowledge on how I am supposed to act."

"I've been told I have a vivid imagination."

He laughed then, because he could do little else. and because she probably had more imagination than the Grimm brothers and Charles Perrault put together. "I'm certain you do. Now, do you want to tell me what that little display was all about?"

She sighed, then plucked at her skirts for so long

he actually became used to the rarity of silence. He stood. Then he felt her look, felt the tentativeness of it, and he watched her even more closely.

She was searching for courage. After some interminable minutes she took a deep breath and she blurted out, "I've never been kissed before. But there's a good reason. I wanted you to be the first. Winston Easterly tried once—to kiss me, that is. He cornered me behind the rectory after the services on Sunday, but I couldn't imagine anyone else's lips ever touching mine, so I shoved him in the Reverend Mrs. Poppit's roses ... the ones with the witches' thorns that are so long?" She held up her hand to show him how long "so long" was.

He shifted closer.

"He was rather surprised—Winston Easterly, not the Reverend, nothing seems to surprise the Reverend—and he, Winston, shouted words that should never have been said on a Sunday, let alone behind the rectory."

She took a quick breath. "I was saving myself for you. I told him so. And he never came near me again. His sister Emmaline said that the physician spent two hours plucking the sharp—"

Richard grabbed her waist and pulled her against him.

"—thorns ... oh my—"

His mouth covered hers. The silence was a second taste of heaven. He'd found the perfect way to keep her quiet and teach her not to go around asking gentlemen to kiss her.

She stiffened, and the proof of her inexperience showed when she puckered her lips tight as the Regent's stays. He touched her jawline, stroking softly. With a sigh of submission, she slowly curled one tentative hand around his neck.

He opened his eyes and watched her face, then dev-ilishly swept his tongue across her pursed mouth. Her eyes flew open, wide and questioning. He pulled her tighter against him until he was aware of every soft woman's curve he'd missed before.

Her eyes grew misty and drifted closed. Her lips softened, and he explored her mouth with an intimacy that was foreign to first kisses. Her first lesson.

An apt pupil, she kissed him back, and to his sur-prise the lesson was lost, for the kiss became real. Too real.

His sanity returned—fast—and he pulled back, star-ing down and running a hand through his hair in frus-tration. One arm was still about her back, the only thing supporting her. He heard her mumble something about this being so much better than kissing a door.

He awaited her reaction and ignored his. Her foggy gaze cleared, and she smiled as if she'd just been given the world.

Before he could tell her what she'd really been given, she touched her lips reverently. Her look held the joy of a miracle, and she backed away.

Her elbow hit the closest lantern.

It crashed to the floor.

The lamp oil burst into brilliant orange and blue flames.

So did Richard's cloak.

Unfortunately, he was still wearing it.

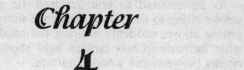

Chapter

4

"**H**ell's teeth!" He shot up and ripped the cloak off, stomping out the flames. He bent and picked it up, using it to whip out and finally smother the oil fire that spilled blue-orange across the floor.

"I'm so sorry . . ." she whispered, her hands to her mouth as a cloud of smoke drifted ghostlike between them.

Richard waved it away and glared at her for as long as his patience and the sting of smoke in his eyes would allow.

The silence was so tense the smoke almost vibrated. He stared down at the floor where the cloak still smoldered, then stomped on it with a vengeance. It was a foolish action for a grown man, even more foolish for him, but it kept him from killing her.

He watched his cloak smolder. It was a recent Bond Street purchase with five capes. He bent down and picked it up. It now had one and a half capes, and the half it had was burning.

55

As he counted to one hundred, he glared at the smoke rising to the rafters. His gaze sharpened on the ceiling above, suddenly noticing the small snatches of what he realized was lantern light showing from the cracks between the wooden rafters.

The smoke was slowly rising toward those cracks. He wondered if perhaps there might be some sort of trap door, but he couldn't see clearly enough because thick smoke hovered among the rafters.

He could feel her stare, and after a pensive minute she asked, "Are you terribly angry?"

A grunt was the only sound he could make with his jaw so tight.

"I thought so." She paused, then said, "It was an accident."

"I'm quite familiar with your accidents."

Her face was so defeated. She pulled her arms tightly to her. He had the uncomfortable feeling that she hugged herself because of a desperate need for comfort. He was not one for giving comfort to anyone. He chose to look away.

In a too quiet voice, she said, "I'll pay for it. Although it might take me a while. I'm sure it was very costly. I have a few pounds saved, but probably not nearly enough. I could sell my mother's pearls. They are very valuable. Perhaps you would take them as a sign of my good faith; then when I have all the money I need, I could buy them back and you could have a new cloak and I wouldn't lose one of the only things I have left of my mother's."

He shut his eyes, but he couldn't shut his mind to the most impassioned and sincere speech he'd ever heard. And he felt about as petty as he'd ever felt in all of his twenty-nine years. "It was an old cloak," he said gruffly.

"It was?" There was a touch of hope in her voice.

"Yes. Very old. I needed a new one."

"Well then ... if you're certain ..."

"Keep your money. I can buy a thousand cloaks should I choose to."

"Oh ... I forgot. Now that you're an earl, you must be very wealthy."

He didn't respond. He was too busy trying to figure out how she had manipulated him into sounding like such a pompous ass.

"I wonder how I shall repay you, then."

"I told you to forget about it. Keep your pearls and your money."

She managed, despite the cloud of smoke, to heave a sigh. "Oh, I couldn't do that. You just saved me. I need to thank you. Why, if you hadn't acted so bravely and quickly, we would have been burned into sheer nothingness."

Life isn't that kind. He looked at her. "If there's one thing I've learned it's to be prepared to move quickly whenever I'm around you."

"And you certainly did," she said seriously.

He shook his head, half expecting to hear a loud *whoosh* as his sarcasm flew over her head. When he glanced at her, she had that about-to-burst look again. "Why do I have the feeling you have something monumental to say?"

"You're becoming very perceptive ... for a man."

"I'm not certain how I should take that comment."

"It was a compliment. Surely you don't think I would insult you after you saved my life, do you?"

"I'm not some hero, hellion."

There was a gleam in her eyes. Trouble was coming. He'd seen it often enough.

"Did you know there are cultures that believe that if someone saves a person's life, then the person saved must devote their entire life to the one who saved them?"

He stood rooted to the floor. Trouble was here.

"It's a matter of honor." She gave him a devoted smile. "Have you heard of this before?" She paused for a thoughtful second, then her face brightened with understanding. "Oh, perhaps you don't remember. You are having those memory problems. Do you suppose one fall on your head could cause such trouble? Now don't glare at me. I'll be more than pleased to help you remember things. After all, Richard, you saved my life."

Gus growled.

She reached out to scratch the hellhound's ears. "And Gus's life too."

He stared at the dog and had the absurd thought that perhaps he should have just let them burn.

The beast's growl had faded into a gurgle, and the dog closed his eyes in ecstasy, tilting his head so Letty could scratch the other floppy ear. After a second, the dog opened his bloodshot eyes and gave Richard a smug stare that held nothing akin to devotion. It said *This is wonderful and I am smarter than you.*

Richard wondered briefly if the dog was right.

He didn't move. He didn't breathe. He couldn't. He stared at the smoking cloak in hand, his head already in a state of utter confusion. He tried to fathom his situation, only to find himself taking long, slow breaths, smoky breaths.

Until a moment before he was only stuck with her and that beast of a dog, in a twenty-by-twenty-foot space—with no escape. In the smoke. On a smugglers' ship.

The wicked and wild earl of Downe and his recompense.

Now the hellion had some bacon-brained idea that

she and that obnoxious hound of hers were honor bound to him. No one, he thought—not fate, destiny, even God—could possibly be that cruel.

"I realize that our past encounters have been ... rather, uh, awkward," she admitted honestly.

"Rather awkward?" He was on the verge of shouting. He didn't care. He shook the cloak at her, ignoring the new cloud of smoke that swirled around him in favor of anticipating the pure pleasure of bellowing at her.

She winced, then looked down. "Sometimes ... things just seem to go wrong."

Now there was an understatement. The woman was bound to be the death of him. Black eyes, broken bones, hot fires. God only knew what other delights awaited him. And yes ... she was a woman, which irritated him even more.

Ready to bellow the bloody ship down, he opened his mouth, but a shout in the distance silenced him. There was the sound of running, as the wooden rafters above them suddenly rattled and thundered.

These were the first sounds of life he'd heard above deck. Before he could move, the door flew open and slammed hard against its jamb.

"Fire! Fire in the hold!"

A wall of icy salt water hit him. He staggered backward, coughing.

"Oh, dear," she said.

With the smoking cloak still in his hand, he turned. "Stop!" she shouted.

Another ocean of water hit him. The cloak sizzled. He slowly swiped the water from his face, trying to see through a burning blur of sea water.

Two scruffy-looking smugglers with empty buckets stepped away from the doorway, and another older man in a bright yellow shirt stepped inside. He pointed an ominous-looking pistol directly at Richard's chest.

The hellhound barked a greeting, then jumped up and trotted cheerfully over to the smugglers, where he sniffed their shoes and legs, his tail wagging, his canine face filled with the joyful, panting welcome of man's best friend.

Water dripped from Richard's cloak, from his head, from his clothing, to plop loudly onto his sandy boots. He turned slowly, intending to tell the hellion what he thought about the honor and loyalty of her pet.

He froze.

She and her dog wore the same expression.

"For God's sake woman, what the devil are you smiling at?"

She gave a huge sigh. "You look just as you did on the first day we met."

"Stand where ye be!"

Letty reluctantly tore her gaze away from Richard and looked toward the smuggler who had shouted. He raised the gun slightly before he glanced down at Gus.

"There, there, ye hearty fellow. Took a liking to old Phelim, did ye?"

Gus, who had taken an instant dislike to Richard, was licking the smuggler's free hand as if they'd been friends for life.

Letty cast a quick glance at Richard and blanched. Never taking his eyes off Gus, he gripped his dripping cloak in a white-knuckled hand, then raised his other hand and began to slowly, methodically, wring and twist the garment. Water pattered onto the wooden floor.

"Psssst! Gus! Come over here!" Letty patted her skirt.

Gus ignored both her and Richard, preferring the flavor of old Phelim's hand.

"Gus!" she whispered more loudly, then heard Richard make a comment about the effectiveness of whispering when a roomful of people were looking at you.

She glanced up.

His expression said he thought her wits had walked to Wiltshire. Then she scanned the room. All the smugglers were staring at her in the same foreign way.

"Oh, I suppose you're right." She covered her mouth to stifle a giggle and patted her skirt again. "Heel, Gus!"

Gus finally looked at her through drooping hazel eyes, then he gave Phelim's hand a last long swipe of his tongue before trotting happily back over to her side.

He sat, haunches pronounced, tail battering the wet floor with a sloshy *thump, thump, thump,* while he eyed everyone. A second later he showed what he thought of them by yawning loudly, then shifted his head to the side and began to vigorously scratch his ear with a damp back paw.

Out of the corner of her eye Letty saw Richard take a step.

"Don't move!" Phelim aimed the pistol directly at Richard's head.

Richard froze, his eyes locked on Phelim for a moment so tense Letty didn't dare breathe, let alone speak. Then Richard's expression became curiously hooded, his body stance relaxed, and he leaned back, resting an elbow on the crate behind him. "I take it that you're in charge?"

"Seeing as how I have the gun and ye don't, I'd say so." Phelim grinned and preened when the men chuckled.

"Ah, a man with a sense of humor," Richard said, smiling companionably. "I take it we're prisoners aboard a smuggling lugger. Such a foolish move."

The men stopped laughing.

"I suppose you'll also find it increasing humorous that you have kidnapped two innocents. What do we care if you indulge in a bit of contraband?" Richard looked at her. "Do you care, my dear?"

"No."

"There, see?" He gave them all a rather bored look. "Why, I purchase French brandy myself."

"Everyone knows of Richard and his brandy," Letty added, trying to be helpful.

His gaze flashed to hers. He looked as if he wanted very badly to say something, but he turned back to the men and continued. "But of course, all can be rectified easily. You need to but weigh into the nearest port and release us. We'll go on our merry way and so shall you."

She imagined that perhaps his quick look to her had been instinctive. He most likely wanted to thank her for helping. She smiled, rather proud that she'd thought so quickly and jumped right in to help him.

"We are no threat to you," Richard went on. "An innocent lady and a country earl. Isn't that correct, my dear? We could care less about smuggling."

"Yes." She nodded, seeing her opening, then improvising, "Richard is a rake. Rakes have better things to do."

Something flickered in Richard's eyes, but he continued coolly. "Kidnapping a peer of the realm is punishable by a much stiffer sentence than smuggling."

Phelim glanced at the other men.

"I wonder if it is worth it." Richard slowly eyed each of the men. "All those years in prison for, say . . . a few kegs of brandy?"

He paused for so long she decided to help. "And some bolts of silk," she volunteered.

Richard frowned at her, shaking his head ever so slightly, then said, "We'll say nothing—"

"About the gun locks," she finished for him.

He stiffened to his full and intimidating height. His face quickly turned a deep red. His jaw clamped tight. His eyes glittered, disarmingly so.

And her stomach sank. With a sudden and sick feeling of dread, she realized that if those eyes had been arrows, she'd be the bull's eye.

The smugglers were all smiling, and the smiles weren't friendly. Letty turned back to Richard. One look at his face and she felt like running. "You're upset with me again, aren't you?"

His eyes gave her the answer she needed.

"But you said the smugglers knew—" She clamped her mouth shut at the sight of Richard's livid look.

Phelim grinned, a smile that held not a whit of humor.

Before she could say another thing, Richard had spun in a flash and snapped out the wet cloak.

It covered Phelim's head.

Letty gasped.

Phelim dropped the gun.

Caught as off guard as the smugglers, Letty took a step backward, her eyes locked on Richard, who stood with his arm clamped around the smuggler's neck. The man struggled beneath the cloak that held him prisoner, his curses muffled.

"Now it's your turn not to move." Richard looked at the others and warned, "Any of you." He tightened his arm around Phelim's neck, making him cough. "Or I'll break his neck."

He turned his harsh features toward her and gritted slowly, "Pick up the pistol."

She glanced down. The gun was at her feet. She bent and picked it up. She'd never held a pistol before. It was much heavier than she would have thought, and cold, very cold.

"Bring it here."

She glanced up.

Richard gave a quick nod of his head. "Quickly!"

She took a step.

Gus shifted and stretched.

She tripped.

And the gun went off.

Chapter 5

Someone was calling his name.

"Richard?"

"Grrrrrrrrr."

"Hush, Gus."

Richard felt a soft hand stroke his cheek.

"Please wake up."

He opened his eyes. The hellion stared down him. Out of instinct he shifted to move away. A jab of fire shot down his arm and across his shoulder. He groaned and let his head fall back onto her lap.

"Don't move!" she cried, gently patting his jaw. "Please. I've been so very worried."

The pain faded into a dull throb and he took slower and deeper breaths. He felt clammy, chilled, and realized his chest was bare except for his torn shirt, which lay tucked around him like a blanket. He looked at her and rasped, "What happened this time?"

Her face paled, looking suddenly white against the black soot that smudged her cheeks and chin. There were streaks in the soot on her cheeks. She'd been crying. She swallowed hard, sniffled, then took a deep quivering breath. "I—I shot you."

He looked at his shirt. A wide brown blotch of dried blood stained the left sleeve. He moved his gaze to his left arm. It was wrapped in a piece of lacy white petticoat linen, the ends of which were tied in a neat but puffy lace bow.

It all suddenly came back to him: the gun at her feet, the dog yawning and stretching his long body out in front of her, the shock on her face as the pistol fired.

He looked up at her now. Her eyes were misty and red from crying, and she chewed nervously on her lower lip. Her whole demeanor showed self-censure. She blinked back her tears, took one quivering breath, and just sat there, waiting, a strange mixture of courage and defeat. He closed his eyes so that he wouldn't have to stare into hers.

So the hellion had shot him. Nothing unusual there, just another day in the humdrum life of Richard Lennox.

For a brief instant he asked himself what else she could do to him, then realized that he was only asking for trouble. He opened his eyes. There before him was the face of trouble. She looked like a child waiting to be whipped. Her head hung down and her misty gaze was locked on her clasped hands, the knuckles of which were white from a tense grip.

His upper arm throbbed, a painful reminder that in truth, he was to blame. He'd told her to hand him the gun, which was rather like asking the Devil to pray for him.

Stupid fool. He might as well have just put the weapon in her hand and told her to pull the trigger. He stared at the rafters and asked himself what else could have happened. He supposed that if luck had been with him she could have shot one of the smugglers. But based on past experience, he was her usual target.

He looked at the wound again. It was no scratch, but he'd received worse in a duel. He waited a moment. She still wouldn't look at him. "Letty?"

"What?" she said in a rasp of a whisper, still staring at her hands.

"Next time . . . try to aim for the smuggler."

Her head shot up and she stared at him for a dumbfounded second. He knew the instant she realized she'd been forgiven. She glowed, and he thought for a moment she might begin to cry.

He gave a quick nod toward his arm. "Is the ball still inside?"

She shook her head. "It went out the other side." She paused and held a breath, her expression not unlike that of an executioner who'd just killed the wrong man.

He was fast becoming familiar with that look. "And?"

She glanced past him. He started to look that way but paused, the niggling voice of experience demanding he ask himself if he really wanted to look.

He did. One whole corner of the hold was charred black. Burned timbers lay at fallen angles as if some giant hand had tossed them like pickup sticks. Pieces of weathered canvas had been nailed to a huge hole in the ship's side, but sea water still leaked in streams through the sides. The lowermost part of the hole must have been at just about sea level, for he could hear the slosh of waves slapping the canvas.

"No single gunshot could have caused that," he said, staring in amazement at the size of the hole and its makeshift repair. He was surprised the ship wasn't listing.

"It wasn't the shot ... well, it was, in a way, but not truly."

"This ought to be interesting."

"It was the gunpowder."

"What gunpowder?"

She pointed at the hole, then said, "There was a tin of gunpowder over there. It was destroyed in the fire."

"The fire?"

She nodded. "From the oil."

He waited.

"Remember your cloak?"

"I assure you, the incident is seared into my memory."

She flinched slightly, then admitted in a quiet voice, "It happened again."

"You knocked over the other lantern," he stated flatly, finally understanding.

"I didn't. The pistol ball did."

Richard glanced down at his arm and tried to string her story into some logical sequence. "Let me see if I understand you. You tripped and shot me."

She nodded.

"The ball went into my arm and out."

She nodded again.

"Then it hit the lantern? And ..."

"Knocked it over and the oil caught fire and burned a path to a tin that held gunpowder and then ... *Bam!*" She threw her hands up in the air. "There was all this smoke and water and shouting. It was quite chaotic."

He just stared, suddenly understanding the smudges on her face.

"The men moved very quickly."

"I'll wager they did," he said, picturing the scene in his mind.

Neither said a word for long seconds that stretched into minutes. The ship creaked and waves slapped like clapping hands against the canvas.

Richard began to laugh. The hellion had struck again. Perhaps the foreign ministry should send her to France as Britain's own secret weapon, guaranteed to destroy the entire French army in a single gunshot. He laughed harder. Better yet, they could make her Napoleon's gaoler.

She stared at him through puzzled eyes, and that only made him laugh all the more.

"You're not angry that I shot you?"

He shook his head. "No, although I'd appreciate it if you'd avoid doing so in the future. I'm not certain how much torture my body can endure."

She gave him a tentative smile and relaxed. "I'm so relieved. I thought you'd be especially angry, considering you weren't too pleased with me before."

There was a long pause, which should have warned him that she was thinking again.

"Forget it."

"Thank you, Richard."

Gus growled.

Richard turned and looked at the beast. No luck there: Gus was unscathed. He lay stretched out on his side, his eyes closed; he looked to be asleep.

Richard examined him more closely. He wouldn't put it past the devious Gus to feign sleep. But the dog didn't move. No doubt he was bored because there were no pistols around.

He turned to Letty. "Your dog growls in his sleep?"

"Only when he hears your name."

He looked back at Gus, waited a minute, then snapped, "Richard!"

The dog curled his lips into a snarl and growled from deep within his chest. Yet the beast never opened his bloodshot eyes, never flinched. He lay on his side, sound asleep.

He waited, then repeated, "Richard!"

Again Gus growled but never awoke.

"He's done that since the first time he saw you," she explained.

"I remember. It was just before he bit me."

"You were dueling, and dueling is illegal and—" She stopped in midsentence and was too silent. "You really do have a rather shaded past. Drinking, dueling, befriending smugglers . . ."

"I wasn't befriending smugglers. I was trying to persuade them to release us unharmed. And I was doing a rather good show of it too, until you sealed our coffins by spilling the tea about the gun locks."

Her hands fell to her sides. Her face paled. She just stared at him, then slowly whispered, "Sealed our coffins?"

Damn his mouth.

"You mean they're going to kill us?"

He shifted, wincing from the pain that shot up his arm, then slowly sat up and put on his shirt. "I don't know what I mean anymore."

"You told me they wouldn't harm us." She looked betrayed.

He silently worked the buttons.

"You said it was just a tale to tell our grandchildren."

"*Your* grandchildren," he said, angrily jamming his shirttails into his breeches.

She stood silent, and to him the silence seemed even longer than it probably was. She looked directly into his eyes and whispered, "You lied to me."

"It was for your own good," he said curtly, not liking the fact that he was made to feel guilty.

"You don't lie to someone you care about."

"I don't—"

The door flew open and banged against the wall. Two smugglers filled the doorway, one anxiously waving a musket, the other a sword. Soot covered their clothing and blackened their wary faces.

One man's hair was singed and stuck out like that of a Punch puppet. He had a ratty bandage wrapped around his forehead. Scattered remnants of a black beard spotted the other man's chin and his face had a blank look, due to the fact that he no longer had any eyebrows.

Their excited gazes quickly scanned the hold and lit on Letty. Almost in unison, their weapons rotated toward her.

"Stay where ye be!" came a shout from behind them.

Gus shot upright, suddenly awake, and trotted toward the doorway, his tail wagging and his face alight with a slobbering canine grin.

Phelim stepped from behind the wall of singed smugglers, holding in each hand a bowl with a battered tin cup poised atop it. He cautiously walked toward them. Gus trailed along behind him, sniffing at the closest bowl.

"Oh, Mr. Phelim!" Letty said. "You're awake now!"

"I'm Philbert, Phelim's brother. He just came to a while ago. Ever since he's been running 'round the ship giving orders. His head is still looby. Thinks he's Admiral Nelson. Refuses to use one arm and he keeps askin' fer his eyepatch." He stopped in front of Letty—not too close—and held out the steaming bowls. "Here, Missy. Take 'em, real quicklike."

71

Chewing on her bottom lip, she took the food, and the man was out the door so fast that even Gus hadn't time to move. The other smugglers grumbled something about the fires of hell and women before they slammed the door and the lock. Richard could almost hear the sighs of relief through the locked door. He looked at her.

She just stood there, staring at the locked door.

He wondered what she was thinking, then decided that whatever it was, he'd probably be better off not knowing.

As an afterthought, he ran a hand through his hair, which was still there and didn't feel singed. He turned away from her and covertly rubbed a hand across his forehead, expelling a breath when he felt the thickness of both eyebrows.

He glanced down at his bandaged arm and decided that perhaps he'd been lucky. He relaxed, but his relief was short-lived. He could feel her look and slowly turned, expecting to see the timid, hangman expression she usually wore after a disaster.

To his surprise there was an odd sparkle in her eyes—a look that said she was simply delighted about something. Instinct told him he should be worried. Common sense told him he could never come close to imagining what she was delighted about. Past experience told him not to even try.

She grinned and handed him a bowl of food. "They aren't going to kill us."

"Ah, I see. I was wondering what you had to be so jubilant about. How did you come to that conclusion?"

"It's very simple. I'm surprised you didn't notice."

"I lost the ability to be surprised years ago."

She cocked her head and looked at him, as if she

were trying to understand him. Despite its innocence, the look was penetrating.

Don't look too close, hellion. There are no pretty little dreams inside here. He gave a hard stare meant to quell her a bit.

"You and I do seem to see things differently. Do you suppose that's just one of the differences between man and woman? It must be," she said, unfazed by his look and answering her own question before he had a chance to respond. "It couldn't possibly be us."

"God forbid."

She smiled at him. Once again his cynicism had gone sailing past her.

Odd thing: He felt like an ass.

"Do you still want to know how I know they're not going to kill us?" There was a tinge of gloating to her voice.

"By all means, do tell."

"You don't feed people you're going to kill."

His first instinct was to ask her if she'd ever heard of a last meal. But he realized that the less she knew the better—for both of them.

And perhaps it was the fact that the men had no eyebrows that had made them look so bewildered, or perhaps it was something else, but whatever, he felt no threat from them. As a matter of fact, the smugglers had looked downright fearful. His gaze drifted to the hellion. He laughed to himself. Perhaps they had good reason.

"Ouch!" She dropped her spoon and rubbed her lips. "Too hot."

He watched her blow lightly on her food, then shook his head and glanced down at his own bowl. He set it aside. His gaze swept the dank room and saw no means of escape. Whether the smugglers were dangerous or not, they still needed to escape.

His wound wouldn't hinder him. He glanced down at his arm. It was sore but not unbearable.

He glanced at the dog. He was unbearable.

At that moment Gus was lying quietly beside his mistress, his snout atop his paws and his whiskered lips sagging to the floor. A pair of bloodshot eyes looked directly at Richard. The beast lifted those lips in a snarl, but he made no sound.

Richard ignored him and looked at his mistress. She had relaxed and was leaning back against the crate behind her, her eyes closed, her face full of peace.

He found that ironic, considering that she brought little peace to those around her. "Dreaming again, are we?"

"Ummm-hmmm."

He doubted his own face had ever worn such a quiet look. "So tell me, hellion, what are these incredulous magical dreams of yours?"

She opened her eyes and smiled the you-are-so-wonderful smile that usually irritated the hell out of him. Instead of feeling irritated now, he felt the spread of some elusive unnamed emotion, but before he could counterbalance it with some sharp caustic comment, she spoke: "Dreams can be anything one wants that is special to them. Take, for example, the servants at home. I taught our gardener to dream. He chose to dream about roses, prize roses. The coachman dreamed he was playing cricket at Lord's. The stable-boy dreamed of jockey's colors and the Newmarket races. The cook chose soufflés, chocolate soufflés. Ummm." She gave him a little grin. "The dreams don't have to be incredulous. They are magical because of how one feels about that which they're dreaming.

"I can dream about blue skies and puffy white clouds and chattering birds in the middle of a winter storm. I can dream that I danced every dance. I can dream about . . ." She looked him in the eye as if she was going to admit she dreamed of him, but to his surprise she didn't. She looked away.

"Sometimes I think of romantic myths. Perhaps I'm a titian-haired princess riding a runaway horse. And fresh from his dragon slaying comes a knight atop his white charger. He rides across a bridge just in time to save me."

Ah, he thought, she didn't need to speak of him because she'd turned everything into her own romantic tale.

She looked back at him and gave him a misty smile. "Dreaming is magical because no matter what the tale, I can be whomever I want. Either the most romantic or the most tragic figure I can think of."

She gave him a direct look. "Did you ever notice that in those romantic tales, the women always have long and lovely titian hair? I imagine Helen of Troy and Juliet both had titian hair."

She paused and sighed. "I've always wanted titian hair." She grabbed a curly strand of her brown hair and held it in front of her, frowning at it as if it were curling earthworms.

"Don't you think I'd look more dramatic if I had titian hair? Oh, you needn't answer that." She dropped her hair. "Of course you do. Men always look fairly upon women with titian hair." She stared at her hands.

He had wanted to speak, his usual sharp biting words that would tell her this was the cruel world, not some bloody adventure; to tell her that she should give up believing in fairy tales and to tell her how foolish she was.

But for the first time in his life the caustic words wouldn't come. He'd used them on fools, on friends, and he'd spent years spitting them at his father, yet when he looked at her, he was suddenly at a loss for something to say.

She had managed to get him kidnapped by smugglers, had set fire to him, and had even shot him, yet he couldn't say what came naturally. He couldn't tell her to be quiet, to give up all her idiotic dreams of princesses with titian hair and knights on white horses.

And most of all, to tell her that caring for him was an absolute lost cause. He wasn't a hero, and probably would never be one.

"Letty," he said more sharply than he'd meant to.

She straightened and looked at him questioningly.

He looked away and tried to find the right words. The earl of Downe at a loss for words. No one who knew him would believe it.

He glanced up at her again. She sat there, waiting, an expectant look in her eyes. She placed too high a value on him and his words. It was a responsibility he could shirk easily, because he didn't want to mean anything to her. He couldn't, even if he wanted to, and he didn't want to. He didn't want to be here. He didn't want to look into her eyes and see her heart. He didn't want to be part of her world.

He caught the high color in her cheeks and found himself thinking of things that he'd never thought of before. He'd never noticed a woman's skin, whether it was dewy or soft or pale.

Yet he noticed hers. He came to a new understanding of why throughout time poets compared a woman's skin to a white rose. Of all the women he'd seen and flirted with, of all he'd even bedded, he'd never once been intrigued by something as simple as the look of their skin.

He stared down at his own hands and realized they were rough and hard, weathered. He wondered whether he could still feel softness with those hardened hands.

For one brief instant, he knew that he might have given her almost anything should she have asked. The air around him turned heavy and was strangely silent, as if the world had suddenly stopped. There was an odd tightening in his chest. If he hadn't known better, he'd have thought it was his heart. But he'd stopped caring long before, when he'd lost the ability to believe that the future held anything for him.

He knew with surety that he could never give her what her eyes begged him for. He willed with every ounce of his being for these strange feelings to pass. And the seconds turned to minutes.

"Your food's getting cold," he said finally, giving a curt nod at the bowl in her hand while he blamed his addled sense on the fall.

She blessed him with one of those smiles that seemed to irrationally irritate him, then set a cup of water aside and took a bit of stew. "This is quite good."

Self-preservation made him look from that smile to the food in her hand until he'd blocked her out with thoughts and smells of food. He'd had nothing in his stomach but the brandy he'd known he would need to be able to walk through the front door of his estate for the first time in two years.

One couldn't confront old ghosts sober. But all those glasses of false courage were now nothing but a sour memory in his empty stomach. He felt his stomach tighten. He was hungry after all.

A loud slurping sounded from behind him. He turned around.

The hellhound quickly sat back on his haunches, staring at him, his canine face set in a sly and truly satisfied grin.

With a sick feeling Richard looked down at his bowl—his empty bowl.

And Gus burped.

Chapter 6

The lock slid open with a rusty scrape that Letty could feel clear through to her teeth. She turned just as the door cracked and a musket barrel poked through the opening. The musket quivered, and after a slight pause, Philbert stuck his gray-haired head inside. He quickly tossed a large soup bone toward Gus. It landed with a loud thud and rattled across the wooden floor for a foot or two.

One would never have known that Gus had just eaten Richard's food from the way he pounced on that bone. Like an animal starved, he hugged it between his large paws, then clamped his teeth around it, his droopy eyes darting left, then right. He stood up and trotted around the hold, tail wagging and ears flopping, as he proudly displayed his prize.

He carried it as if it were a brace of pheasants. He pranced past a tight-jawed Richard three times, then settled into a corner and began to ravenously gnaw on the bone.

"Excuse me, Mr. Philbert?" Letty said, ignoring Richard's bullish snort.

The smuggler looked up and pointed the gun barrel at her, using the door as a shield. "I'm not Philbert."

She paused, a little apprehensive. It was Phelim, and the last time she'd seen him he was being carried out unconscious. She supposed he would not be too pleased with her. She gave a tentative nod and searched for the correct thing to say.

From his appearance, she figured he had come out fairly unscathed. After all, he did have his eyebrows. Just for good measure, she decided a compliment was the most politic. "Mr. Phelim. You look well."

"I'm not Phelim."

Her mouth fell open. "Another brother?"

He nodded. "Aye."

She held up three fingers.

The man nodded. "Triplets."

"Oh." She cast a quick glance at Richard, who sat in a corner near a brandy barrel. His knees were drawn up, his injured arm resting on one of them, while he watched Gus from narrowed eyes that made him look as if he were ready to snatch the bone away and eat it himself. "Have you ever met triplets before?"

Richard said nothing. He just watched Gus the way the Duke of Wellington might have eyed Napoleon across a battlefield.

She sighed and turned back to the other brother. "Gus ate Richard's food. I believe he's terribly hungry. Do you suppose someone could fetch him another dish of stew?"

The man remained in the doorway, the musket still aimed at her and his stance very cautious. After one of those long strings of male silence, he frowned and shook his head slightly, then appeared to think long and hard. He shrugged at the room in general and turned toward Richard. "Sorry, yer lordship. The crew ate everything and there be no meat left to stew."

Richard slowly faced them and, through a tight humorless smile, said, "We could always stew Gus."

Gus looked up from his soup bone and smacked loudly.

"He doesn't mean that," Letty told the man. "He wouldn't stew Gus." She looked back at them and wondered which one of them was going to outlast the other, Richard or Gus. At that moment it appeared that Gus was winning.

She crooked a finger at the newest brother. He shook his head vigorously and hugged the door a tad closer to his stocky chest.

She moved closer, not minding too much when he took two steps backward and raised the gun a notch, the knuckles on one hand turning white from gripping the door. She supposed he had his reasons. She glanced back at the repaired wall. The blast had shaken the entire ship.

"Perhaps you could bring him something to eat—bread, water, something." She leaned toward the smuggler and lowered her voice. "I believe that then Richard might stop sulking."

"I am not sulking."

"Oh." She spun around. "What do you call it?"

He glared at her, then at Gus. "I call it hell."

"You're quibbling over words because you're angry at Gus and at this situation. And probably hungry. I understand." She looked at the smuggler. "He is usually a perfectly wonderful man. He acts as if he doesn't care about anything, but he does. Why, he saved our lives ... Gus's and mine. Yours too. He did put out the fire. Isn't there some saying that there is nothing more feared by sailors than a fire at sea?"

"Aye, but since last night, some of the men might be arguing that a fire aboard ship can't be as bad as a woman."

"I'd suggest, then, that you throw us overboard," Richard said, still looking at Gus. "Him first."

Letty watched Richard tentatively. "I do believe he needs to find his sense of humor again." She swung back around to the older man. "He is very witty, you know." She paused, then asked, "What is your name?"

The man crinkled his eyes suspiciously, and his gaze darted back and forth between Richard and her. "Why do ye want t' know?"

"Because it would be easier to converse, and I can't very well call you 'Phelim' or 'Philbert.' Since you all look so alike, I daresay that people must call you by the wrong name constantly. And if I address you by your family name, then that would be the same as your brothers, Mr. So and So, and any one of you could answer, now couldn't you? Of course you would all answer to the same name, so you could all answer at once. I imagine that must be terribly confusing, mustn't it?"

"Probably no more confusing than this conversation," Richard said under his breath.

"Are you confused . . . Mr. . . . ." She stopped and turned toward the man.

The musket hung forgotten from his hand and his mouth gaped open. "Phineas," the man answered, trancelike.

"Oh, truly? I had a great uncle named Phineas." She glanced from Phineas to Richard. "He was the brother of an earl, just as you were. But now you're not, because you're earl, but before you were—his brother, that is. He was so terribly interesting."

Richard looked up and asked, "My brother?"

"No," she said. "You aren't listening very closely."

"It wouldn't help if I were."

She looked at him glowering and gave him a smile. He didn't smile back. She sighed. "Now where was I?"

Richard just gave her a telling look.

"Oh yes, I remember. We were speaking about my great uncle Phineas." She took a breath and looked at the smuggler. "He has the same name as you do."

Phineas was scratching his head.

"He had very large ears—which was strange, because he studied frogs." She looked from one to the other.

The men exchanged one of those male looks that said they didn't understand. Richard was silent for a moment—probably the count of ten, like her father.

She waited expectantly.

He cast a quick glance at Phineas, who was stunned into silence, then he looked back at her and waved a hand in capitulation. "Fine. I'll bite. Why was that strange?"

"Because, silly, everyone knows frogs don't have ears."

There was a huge, silent pause. And Richard finally laughed.

The silly earl of Downe drank his third cup of smuggled brandy and contemplated the auricular structure of amphibians.

He stared into his empty tin cup and asked himself who at Boodles would lay high stakes on the idea that frogs were deaf. Next he calculated how much blunt he could win on the odds of the actual existence of a band of smuggling triplets. It was just the type of rakehell foolishness that had always angered his father.

So Richard had partaken, making certain he was prominently involved in whatever foolishness his father despised. He had played the rake well, had even, on occasion, created enough of a spectacle to ensure that news would travel home swiftly and with lavish and vile detail.

No one had defied the old earl of Downe. Except his second son. If the earl said sit, Richard stood. If he said eat, Richard starved. If he said no, Richard did it anyway, and usually right in front of his father.

The earl wanted a bishop for a son.

Richard wanted to be a soldier.

Not that he had anything against God, he just didn't wish to spend his days returning stray lambs to the fold and writing sermons for mankind to sleep through.

He had told as much to his father, then with brutal honesty added that having a bishop for a son didn't necessarily ensure the father's place in heaven. Their subsequent shouting match had almost brought down the two-hundred-year-old walls of Lockett Manor, while leaving an even higher wall between father and son. One that couldn't be breached.

Richard had always created battles because he thrived on conflict. In retrospect, that must have had something to do with his determination to follow the drum.

As different as he and his father were, they were both stubborn bastards, and when in the same room both were primed for battle. This particular battle had gone on for years.

Time had changed nothing. The earl had staunchly refused to purchase a military commission.

Finally, seeing no other way to defeat his father, he set out on a four-year path of blazing sin—assurance that the Church of England would never recruit him but instead pray heartily for his black soul. He learned he could defeat his father by destroying himself.

He stared now into his empty tin cup, his mind caught in a past he wanted to forget. He reached over and tipped the brandy barrel, refilling the cup. He heard the rustle of skirts and looked at Letty.

When he'd last glanced her way she'd been asleep, curled into a ball, her face resting peacefully on her hands. She had looked . . . innocent.

He had asked himself how long it had been since he'd thought about anything chaste. The answer made him feel soiled. So he'd refilled his cup and tried to drown the feeling.

But now she stood a few feet away, her hands clasped in front of her, her expression a little tentative. "I'm sorry."

"About what?"

"About Gus eating your food."

He shrugged and took a drink. His stomach was full—of brandy.

She moved closer. "How is your arm?"

He glanced down at the wound, at the idiotic way it was wrapped in white petticoat lace and tied with a fluffy bow. His blood had long since stained the lace a dirty brown. The symbolism didn't escape him. "It's still there."

She sat down next to him and leaned against the crate, straightening her skirts again. She shifted and wriggled and fidgeted.

He did his best to ignore her by swilling back another cup.

"What are you drinking? Brandy?"

"A little destruction." He gave a mock salute and laughed bitterly, then made the mistake of looking at her.

Her expression turned serious "Why do you do that?"

He finished the brandy in angry silence and set

down the dented cup, then shifted slightly, bringing his face intimidatingly closer to hers. He pinned her with a hard look. "Because it makes me feel good."

She drew in a breath and her eyes widened, but to her credit she didn't move.

Foolish, naive chit. He felt as if he held her heart in his hands. He didn't want to be handed any hearts.

Some selfish part of him felt the intense need to tarnish her innocence. Because seeing all that shining virtue only reminded him that he had none.

"I like things that make me feel good: strong drink, hard rides across the moors." He lightly touched her cheek. "Debauching innocent girls."

"And shocking people," she added, her face scant inches from his, her expression showing no intimidation.

He could smell the scent of lavender lingering about her, clean and sweet ... and pure. It triggered something inside him. He reached out with sudden fierceness and gripped her hair tightly until her head tilted back.

She flinched.

His mouth closed over hers, hard and demanding. He intended to do exactly what she'd accused him of: shock the bloody hell out of her.

This was no gentle meeting of lips. He forced hers apart with his tongue and filled her mouth, catching her small gasp of surprise. He slid his hand inside her bodice and cupped one bare breast while he pressed her down and down, until he'd pinned her beneath the length of his body.

He kissed her harder, with anger and intensity and some elusive thing he couldn't name, some pure emotion that was both passion and violence.

She wriggled a hand free and he waited for her to

pound his back with her fist, to grip his hair, to instinctively fight him.

Instead she stroked his wrist with soft and gentle fingers, then slowly lifted his hand from her breast and placed it on her shoulder, where she held it in place with little more than a soft and stroking touch.

It was so quiet, so tender a reprimand, that he froze, overcome with a sudden sense of shame. He stared down at her face and knew with sudden clarity that he'd sunk to a new and vile low. He was so jaded and used to self-destruction that he'd tried to destroy her.

He moved off her so swiftly that his brandied brain saw nothing but a blur. He fell back against the crate, drawing up his knees and resting his arms on them.

He stared at his shaking hands, his breath coming hard and fast. He heard her sit up and felt her watching him for the longest time.

"Why?" she finally whispered.

He turned, feeling inexplicably bitter and still so very angry at himself, and at her for being who and what she was. "You're the one who seems to have all the answers. You tell me why I kissed you."

"You misunderstood. I didn't mean *why* did you kiss me. I meant why did you stop?"

Chapter
7

Letty waited for his answer and watched Richard try to control his emotions. He was livid. But aside from anger there was an aura of something he seemed to be fighting. She could read it in his face, and it was so powerful that it overshadowed his usual crust of anger.

She was used to his anger. Anyone who knew him was well aware of the fact that, of late, the earl of Downe was either angry, cynical, or drunk. But there was something else there, something uncontrolled.

His hands shook with it. She wondered what it was he worked so hard to hide, and she searched his face for the answer. She found nothing but a look so scornful she wasn't certain how to react.

His look didn't change when he said, "You should have hit me for doing what I just did."

She cocked her head. "Why would I ever want to hit you?"

"Good God. Didn't your mother teach you anything?"

It would have been kinder if he'd slapped her. She stiffened.

As surely as if his hand had left its mark, her face heated and flushed red with humiliation, forcing her to look away. Any joy born from the magic of his kiss faded into nothing but a deep quivering feeling of disgrace.

Her throat tightened, and deep within her chest, where her heart and happiness had been but a moment before, there grew a fresh shame so painful she clutched her belly.

For the hundredth time in the last twelve years, perhaps the thousandth or more, she wished her mother had lived. She stared at the floor, because she didn't think she could look him in the eye and not cry.

Whatever she was, she was because she had grown up mostly alone. She'd had the best education her father's money could buy, yet there had been no guidance, no life lessons taught other than the ones she had learned her way—through mistake after mistake, despite the fact that most of those mistakes had initially carried a wealth of good intentions.

There had really been no chance for her mother and her to be much of anything. For the first seven years of her life, her mother was not a friend and mentor, but instead a safe warm haven for a babe, a pair of comforting arms when she had fallen and was hurt, a quiet reassuring voice when dreams turned into nightmares.

At the age when she needed a mother's wisdom, there had been no one to teach her about men and women. The ways of romance were foreign to her.

She knew only how she felt inside her heart, tattered as it was at this moment. Richard was her hero. Her everything. Her dreams, her hopes, and every moment existed only because he did.

She took a quivering breath. "But I love you," she whispered, hoping the truth would, perhaps, win her forgiveness for not knowing how to behave.

"You're too young, too naive to know what love is. Bloody hell! I don't even know what it is!" He stood barely a foot away, towering high above her like the god she thought he was.

Gus leapt to his feet and wedged his way between them. He raised his head and looked up at Richard, snarling.

"Come here, Gus." Letty swallowed around the lump in her throat and patted the floor beside her.

Slowly, never taking his eyes off Richard, Gus moved to stand protectively beside her.

As she had done so often before, she put an arm around her pet and rested her head against his thick neck. There were times, not unlike now, when it felt as if the entire world was some foreign land where she didn't speak or understand the language, where nothing was familiar, where she was so completely alone that fear was an incomplete word for what she felt. So she held onto Gus and tried to think about the one thing in her life that was constant and true.

Her love for Richard.

Her hand softly scratched Gus's ear, and he cocked his head so she could scratch the right spot. He stopped glaring at Richard, who, Letty was certain, had not stopped glaring at her.

The tension he'd had so much trouble controlling was a live, animated thing that she could feel as surely as she felt his touch and as surely as his harsh words had bored painfully through her heart.

With her gaze locked on the sand and crusty dirt that marred his black boots, she quietly began, "I know what love is."

When he said nothing she looked up. "I knew the

first time I ever saw you. You can shout and you can bluster and you can try to shock me the way you try so hard to shock everyone else, but all the brandy, all the wild ways and anger in the world, won't change what's inside here." She pointed to her heart. "I love you."

The taut anger in his face slipped, and something akin to desperation flashed through his expression. Her Richard was there, somewhere, guarded, underneath everything he showed the world. He had for one instant lost that guard. But just as quickly it was back up, and once again he hid behind a mask of dark cynicism.

"You love me?" He laughed cruelly and squatted down in front of her, his look as intense as his being. With one knuckle he tilted her chin up until she could look nowhere but at him. "I'll give you this warning, hellion." His dark green eyes carried the cold hardness of marble, and he shook his head and said, "Don't."

Then he stood up swiftly and crossed the room, his shoulders straight, his long lithe strides taking him back across the hold to another barrel of destruction. He bent and refilled his cup, then stood there leaning against the crates, his gaze pensive, cold, and distant. And the minutes felt like hours, vacant, empty, because he never bothered to look at her again.

For the long hours of the blackest of nights there was no sound but the sea, nothing but the constant rocking of the lugger. There was also little wind, as if the gods of irony had decided to play little games with those who chanced to be aboard.

With a purple dawn came a breath of wind, enough to fill the sails, enough to send the gulls cawing and wheeling out over waters that rippled like the gods' laughter. And later, from deep within the still dark depths of the ship, a loud and constant thudding echoed above board.

"Open this bloody door!" Richard raised a fist and pounded again.

"Do you think they'll come soon?"

He cursed under his breath and turned toward the hellion.

"The water seems to be rising," she informed him from her perch atop the gun crates. He watched her peer thoughtfully down at the sea water that was now a good foot deep. Her skirts were damp and her slippers and stockings were piled in her lap, while her bare feet dangled impatiently. One arm was around the hellhound's neck.

Richard would have liked to get his arm around the beast's neck too. The damned dog had spent the better part of the last hour shaking water on him whenever it could.

He hammered the door again. "Open. Open, I say! Do you hear me? This is the earl of Downe! I order you to open this door! The earl of Downe, you hear! The earl of—" He froze, frowning. "Good God, I sound like Belmore."

The lock slid with a rusty clunk and Richard stepped back. The door slowly opened. Water from the flooded hold spilled into the passageway with a loud swoosh.

There was a gruff curse, and one of the triplets stuck his head inside. A second later he slogged into the hold, followed by the sailor with the singed beard and no eyebrows. Both men held pistols.

Sluggish Gus sat up, suddenly alert, and he barked a greeting.

Richard took a step and found himself staring into a gun barrel held by Phelim. Phergus? Phineas? Phelix? Philbert? Phleabrain? Whichever.

"We are not staying down here," Richard said, his tone unyielding, and his plan underway. He'd loosened the canvas in the small hours of the morning so the sea water leaked through in streams instead of trickles. He reasoned that this was the only way for them to have a chance of escape. They would have to get topside whichever way they could.

The smugglers stared at the water, frowning.

"It's been filling faster for the last hour. And I've been pounding on the bloody door for half that time. You'd think the entire ship was deaf."

"None of us be hearing too well after that blast," a sailor said in the overly loud voice of an old cannoneer. He kept his pistol aimed at the hellion. The gun quivered slightly.

"Ye're shouting again, Harry," the other smuggler told him. "Here." He handed him the other pistol. "Keep an eye on 'em since yer ears ain't no good." He crossed over to the canvas, inspecting the edges until he came to one of the five spots where Richard had removed the nails. He glanced down at the floor, bent down, and felt around the water, coming up with one of the nails. He crossed the hold and started out the door.

The damned fool was going to leave them in the flooded hold. "Where in the bloody hell are you going?"

"Topside. We need volunteers." He gave a covert look toward Letty. "Men willing to come down and renail the canvas."

"You cannot leave us in here." Richard moved toward the man, but Harry the eyebrowless stopped him with a pistol barrel in the chest. "Now see here, Ph—" Richard frowned. "Which one are you?"

"Why do ye want to know?"

"That's Phineas," the hellion volunteered.

Richard gave her a look that was meant to quiet her.

"I'm right, aren't I?" she asked the man, ignoring Richard's look like she did everything else he said, ordered, or asked, which was why she had no idea he had a plan. He'd made sure she was asleep when he'd loosened the canvas.

"Aye." Phineas turned to Richard and eyed his wound. "I don't suppose ye could cause any more problems with that arm, now can ye?"

"Oh, Richard won't be one bit of trouble."

"Letty . . ." he warned.

"Well, you won't. It's obvious we cannot stay down here. And Mr. Phineas isn't a cruel man, are you? Of course not. I can tell by his kind eyes. As brown as sorghum molasses. No one with eyes like molasses could possibly be cruel and mean, now could they? You do have very kind eyes, you know. Just like my very own Uncle Phineas." She blessed him with a smile so brilliant even Richard was caught off guard for an instant.

He recovered and glanced at Phineas, whose suspicious and gruff features were anything but kind. Until now. The man now looked as if he'd just been handed a fleet of duty-free goods. "I suppose there'd be no harm in ye coming topside."

"Her?" Harry shouted in a tone that said he considered Letty, who weighed scarcely near seven stone, more of a threat than a hundred of Richard. "Can't we lock her up somewhere else?"

"Give me the pistols," Phineas told him, taking the guns. "Tell the crew to stow all gunpowder in the mezzanine." He glanced at Letty. Ye'll keep away from the stern?"

She nodded.

Harry scurried from the room, his shouts to the crew echoing back down to the hold. Richard heard the words "female" and "topside." There was a sudden rash of cursing and the rafters above the hold thundered as if the men on deck were running for their lives. Rumbling downward was the sound of barrels rolling over the deck toward the stern.

Richard moved toward the crates to help the hellion down. Before he could offer his hand, she hopped down with a small splash, her skirts in one hand and her slippers and stockings in the other. She sloshed past him, her face glowing with that look of half excitement and half delight.

Richard shook his head and started to follow her from the hold. A loud howl stopped him cold.

"Come along, Gus!" Letty called out from the passageway.

Before Richard could think, let alone move, Gus had vaulted from the crate, his legs outstretched and his ears flapping. He plunged into the water, splashing and shaking and spraying sea water with more eagerness than a mad retriever.

Richard wiped the burning salt water from his eyes and face just in time to see the beast's wet tail disappear around the door.

Richard slowly slogged through the water toward the doorway. His plan was a success. Except that even he had trouble convincing himself he was any kind of Machiavellian strategist with a gun barrel in his damp back and water dripping from his long aristocratic nose.

Damned dog.

Letty stepped onto the deck and into a cold slap of welcome wind. She could taste the brisk flavor of briny sea instead of the musky ancient taste of damp wood and burned timbers. Gulls cried overhead and the sails flapped and shimmied and swelled a hello.

Hugging her slippers and stockings, she just stood there for a moment and reveled in the freedom—the wind whipping back her heavy tangle of hair and plastering her damp skirts against her bare legs, the frosty spray of salted sea that pricked her cheeks and made her feel more alive than she had since Richard had kissed her.

Even the sun peeked out from a billowy white cloud and winked down at her. There was silver green sea everywhere, and the sky, blue and clear with only a cloud or two drifting overhead, and no land on the horizon, just the mirrored glassy shine of the bright sun bouncing off the sea water.

She smiled and strolled over to a covered hatch, where she sat on the smooth wood and began to roll her stockings. Gus thudded up the stairs and then skidded to a stop once he was on the deck. He sat near the hatch waiting, a canine grin on his homely face.

Not more than a minute later Richard's wet head cleared the hatch beam. Gus shot up and shook every drop of water from his lanky body, shimmying and shuddering as if he were ridding himself of fleas instead of water.

Letty watched as Gus ignored Richard's muttered curses and trotted over to plop down next to her. Richard seemed to bring out the worst in Gus. Or was it the other way around?

She shrugged and rolled one white stocking up her leg, pausing to slowly tie the blue ribboned garter with a perfect bow. When it was just so, she gave it a quick pat and turned

Humming the romantic notes of a sonata, she grabbed the other stocking and bent down to slide it onto her bare foot, wiggling her toes in one last gesture of freedom before she confined them again. She pulled up the stocking and casually glanced at Richard.

She stilled.

He no longer glared at Gus. She followed his intense look right to her legs. Chewing her lip, she slowly, and with sure dread, scanned the deck. The crew was frozen in place, every man wearing an expression exactly like Richard's.

Unfortunately, the ship was not frozen in place.

She jerked down her skirt, but it was too late. The sails billowed, and billowed . . . and billowed . . . until the batten ropes slid from a mate's hand. They whipped wildly through the mast rings and curled out into the full wind like tendrils of a siren's hair.

The sails slapped together, loud and whipping, then blew loose and outward to hover over the deck. There was a shout. The mast creaked. Someone swore.

Letty turned toward a man who was calling out for his mother. She listened more closely: Yes, that was it. Harry, the sailor with no eyebrows, dangled by a foot from one of the mast lines, bellowing over and over.

The poor soul must have been frightened terribly, a grown man, a smuggler yet, calling as he did for his mother's comfort. Before she could find help for him the frozen crew came alive, shouting, running, leaping at the flying ropes.

A second later the ship slowly leaned toward the west. Just as slowly, just as certain, Letty began to slide. She gripped the edge of the hatch cover.

The ship listed more. The crew's shouts were loud as cannon. Barrels rolled by to crash into the sea. A mop tumbled after them while swab buckets teetered and skidded and slid past her. One banged against the hatch and tilted, spilling soapy water over her arms and hands.

She looked up, clinging to the hatch rim, and saw a mast bend under the pull of its wild sail. Her fingers began to slip.

There was a loud crack.

"Richard!" she screamed, barely hanging on.

A canine howl rent the air.

"Gus!" she cried and struggled desperately, trying to look over her shoulder.

She lost her grip and slid. She clawed helplessly at the slick wood, grabbing for anything.

There was nothing but wet, flat wood.

The ship tilted again. It almost touched the sea.

"Oh, please!" she called out and slithered across the slick deck on a last prayer.

Chapter

8

Richard's words were nothing even close to prayer. He took one look at the hellion sliding across the tilting deck and swore viciously.

He moved to grab her. Gus slid into him first, howling and whining, his paws frantically scrambling on the wet deck.

Richard wobbled slightly. "Hell's teeth!"

Gus bit on to Richard's ankle, hanging on for all he was worth—which was, in Richard's mind, about two ha'pennies.

Four gangly paws slapped the deck like clabber boards. Both dog and man began to slide, Gus sprawling on all fours and his weight dragging them both backward.

Richard reached for the ship's rail. And missed.

They slid again. He gripped the closest thing—the rim of a dinghy.

The ship lurched again and Letty slid past him, mumbling the Lord's Prayer.

He grabbed for her leg. He got a wad of her skirt.

The sound of tearing fabric ripped through the air, along with her divine plea that God forgive all of Richard's trespasses.

He wound her skirt fabric round and round his hand, pulling her close enough for her to grab hold of him.

"And lead him not into temptation . . ."

"Quit praying for me, dammit! And hold still!" He felt Gus growling around his ankle and snarled back, "You too! Bloody damn dog!"

The dinghy creaked, but he knew it was secured to the rail. Only moments before that same dinghy had been part of his escape plan, until he'd seen that there was no land in sight.

Now that same boat and a few yards of silk were the only things keeping all three of them from falling into the sea.

The ship shuddered. He felt it through his aching arm, which was damn well killing him. He gritted his teeth together, tapping strength from an innate wealth of English stubbornness.

He pulled her toward him in spite of the throbbing of his wound, the rocking and listing ship, or the chaos on deck; in spite of the damned dog that had managed to wedge himself between his splayed legs, of the animal's sharp teeth digging into his booted ankle, and, most of all, in spite of the fact that if he just let go, all his troubles would end.

He tightened his grip on the dinghy. *Coward.*

He glanced down at the hellion whose hands were folded in prayer, whose eyes were tightly squeezed shut and who still muttered something about delivering him from evil. "Letty!"

She opened her frightened eyes and looked up at him.

"Unfold your blasted hands and try to hang on to me!"

She reached out for him and slipped, jerking his arm. Pain like stabbing knives shot from his wound to his fingertips.

Her face was stark white with panic and he could feel her literally begin to shake with fear. Jaw tight, he pulled, ignoring the sweat that dripped into his vision. "Hellion!"

Her gaze locked with his.

"Try again."

She stretched toward him, reaching, never taking her eyes off his. Her fingers closed over his forearm. Sighing with relief, she said his name. He could feel Gus growling around his ankle. Ungrateful wretch.

Just then she reached up with her other hand.

"Not my arm!" he warned. "My—"

She gripped his wound.

He spat the most foul word in his vocabulary. His vision flared with stars, hundreds of stars, thousands of stars. Everything was white. Then black. For long seconds nothing existed except the burning agony in his arm.

To his credit, he didn't let go.

But neither did she.

It would have been less painful if she'd shot him again. In the same spot. At point-blank range. A hundred times or so.

"Waist!" he finally said through clenched teeth. "Grab my waist!" He sucked in a deep breath and shouted, "My *bloody* waist!"

His vision cleared and focused on her stunned face. Her eyes widened with realization. She slid her free arm around his waist and let go of his wound, clinging to him and mumbling something into his belly that sounded like "love" and "sorry."

The ship shifted again, and he steeled himself for another tug of war, but to his surprise it surged upward instead of slowly turning into the sea as he had expected.

Stunned, he looked around. The crew had somehow managed to secure the mainsail, and the wind was cupping the sail once again. However, the mast was no longer straight. In fact, it was bent at a strange angle. Arched.

His gaze followed it upward, where the sun, bright as hellfire, blinded him for an instant. A large shadow flew by once, then again. His eyes adjusted. A moment later he realized why the mast was bent.

Some poor sailor, snared by one foot, swung like a human pendulum from the mast lines, bellowing curses on womankind that were so vitriolic, so original in their venom, that even Richard flinched.

The hellion huddled closer. "He was desperately calling for his mother a few minutes ago."

"His mother?"

"His mother's kiss, actually."

He frowned.

She looked up at him and said seriously, "He kept screaming 'mother pucker.'"

"I see," Richard said with a ghost of a smile. He felt an odd sense of kinship with poor Harry, who still swung high above them, screaming dire threats.

"Did you hear what he just shouted?"

"Yes."

"You don't suppose he was referring to me, was he?"

"You're the only female aboard."

"Could he actually do . . ." she paused, frowning in horror. "That?"

Richard shook his head. "It's not physically impossible. Inventive." He rubbed a finger over his chin thoughtfully. "Interesting. But not possible. Of course, if I were in his ... position, I might relish the thought of tying your legs in a cinch knot around your throat."

She shivered suddenly, looking very vulnerable. Without thought, he did something completely idiotic. No doubt due to starvation, pain, and loss of blood.

He slid his arm around her.

Fool.

"You wouldn't let him harm me."

He gave a droll laugh. "I wouldn't?"

"No." There was certainty in her voice. "You wouldn't." Her hand drifted down his good arm and she seemed to try to get even closer to him, as if by doing so she'd be sheltered from danger.

He felt that chill of unexplained emotion, the strength of it, and he glanced down, seeing nothing but a familiar and tangled mane of curly brown hair. He frowned momentarily because he didn't recognize the emotion until suddenly it had a name, a long and forgotten name: something called *tenderness*.

She raised her head. There was utter worship in her blue eyes. She looked at him as if he had just cleansed the world of sin. He fought to ignore his reaction—the fistlike tightening inside his chest, the incomprehensible urge to keep her close to him.

She blinked back some emotion that scared the hell out of him, then tore her soft gaze away and slid her hand into his, touching it gently and turning it over to just stare at his palm for the longest time.

He watched her over her bent head, then asked, "Looking for nail holes?"

She sighed then, one of those dreadful and dreamy exhalations that meant she was in her own little world. One he couldn't fathom. One he didn't want to.

He knew too that she probably hadn't heard him,

and that even if she had, she wouldn't have understood. His cutting remarks and his bitter cynicism were lost on her, for to be bitter, one had to have hatred in their heart; to understand cynicism one had to see the world through a jaundiced eye.

In her heart, she knew no hatred, no bitterness or self-mockery. These things were as foreign to her as was the sordid and unproductive life he'd led. Surely she'd been the recipient of those cruel things. Her London season had subjected her to people who knew little else but to mock those they didn't understand, those who didn't think or do as they did. Yet she had acquired none of those cruel traits London worshiped as town polish.

'Twas hard to believe that someone benevolent had turned her loose in the world, this woman who could innocently change absolute calm into a disaster. Yet a woman who was so vulnerable that he felt an overpowering urge to protect her when he should have been running the bloody hell away from her.

Running away before he suffered another kind of wound—a crippling kind that threatened to render him helpless should he ever give in to it, for that might mean he needed someone.

Richard needed no one. He deserved no one. He wanted no one.

He had always felt his lot in life was already ordained by God or fate or whatever grim fortune guided mankind. But now he steeled himself against an urgent emotion he didn't understand, and in his ignorance of heart, he just stood there, watching her as warily as if she were the one in control of his destiny.

Reverently she turned his hand over and ran hers along his knuckles, then laid her palm flat against his.

He stared down at their hands positioned so and realized how very fragile and small her hand was. Despite the fine, feminine bones, the thin veins and soft skin, this was a hand that could, more often than not, turn a scene into utter chaos with one innocent motion.

But instead of looking destructive, it appeared pale and fragile. The thought crossed his mind that he could crush it in his own should he have wished to.

"This is the hand that saved my life," she whispered. "Again."

Those words, whispered with such awe, had the warning power of a cannon blast.

"No," he said gruffly and pulled his hand from hers, waving it in front of her dreamy face. "*This* is the hand that's going to do you great harm should you ever again lift your skirts higher than an ankle."

She was silent. Her arms had slipped back around his waist and her head was slowly drifting toward his chest.

"Do you understand?"

Silence. Dreamy silence.

"Letty!"

"Hmmmm?"

"Did you hear what I said?"

"I heard you bluster, but I almost always ignore that. You don't really mean those things."

He unwrapped her hands from about his waist and gripped her wrists, giving them a small shake. "Open your eyes!"

She stared up at him through misty eyes that asked him for the impossible. Then they drifted closed again.

"Letty!"

"Yes?" she said on a heavy sigh.

"*Open* your eyes." He gave her a small shake.

"Yes, Richard."

"Grrrrrrrr."

Richard released her and slowly his gaze shifted to the hellish dog, who still had a muzzle clamped around his boot. A pair of bloodshot eyes frowned up at him, challenging, and too intelligent for a mere animal.

"Let go!" He shook his foot.

Gus growled and kept his teeth clamped around Richard's boot.

"I said. Let. Go!"

Gus hung on tightly.

"Now, Gus," Letty scolded, shaking a finger at him, "be sweet."

Those sly canine eyes darted back toward him, narrowed in a message of power that was unmistakable, then the beast bit down just a little harder before he looked back to his mistress and grudgingly released the boot. He sat there, hanging his head, his eyes cast downward—the image of contrition.

"Good boy ..." she said, giving him a light pat on his big droopy head.

Richard would have liked to give him a pat on his head with the anchor.

Gus sat there, his canine face in a half grin, half pant, and his tail beating a gay tattoo on the planking of the deck.

"That animal bites too often."

He was acting instinctively."

"He should consider himself fortunate that I didn't act instinctively."

"You wouldn't harm Gus," she said in a tone that sounded as if she was going to call him "silly" again. She looked up at him. "You wouldn't. I know that. You two just like irritating each other. The Pringle sisters do the same thing."

"Who?"

"The Pringle sisters. Surely you—oh ..." She

106

paused thoughtfully. "I forgot. They moved to the parish after you left. Now wasn't that—"

"Silly," he finished.

She cocked her head. "How did you know I was going to say that?"

"Instinct."

"We're becoming kindred spirits," she said with a touch of excitement. "You are actually beginning to think as I do."

Only if God has a morbid sense of humor.

"You look as if you want to say something."

"Nothing vital."

"Well, where was I? Ah yes, they, the Pringle sisters, came to live at Crestmoor cottage, on the north end of the village green? I'm certain you know where that is because it's not too far from the Boarhouse Tavern, and you seem to have an affinity for taverns, gaming halls, and the like, being a rake, and since that's the closest tavern to Lockett Manor I'm certain you know of it. Not that it's the type of place one should go to, but the Reverend Mrs. Poppit says that men are fickle creatures, especially influenced by those with whom they associate themselves, and since you've been with rakes and smugglers I suppose it's more than understandable in your case."

She looked at him then, her face bright and smiling. "Besides, I did ask God to forgive you."

"I heard."

She laid a hand on his chest, near his heart, and she gave him a pat. "Now, you needn't worry about your past. I'll wager that God has forgiven you already. Perhaps as we speak. Which reminds me ... Weren't we talking about the Pringle sisters?"

"You were." He crossed his arms and leaned against the skiff. *Here we go again.*

"Well of course it was I. They moved to the village

after you had left. I was certain we had established that fact. That you didn't know them, that is. I must tell you that they are the most humorous ladies I've ever met. Well, almost the most humorous. I suppose one could argue that Matilda Kenner and Lady Emily Harding were similar to the Pringle sisters. But then they weren't sisters, were they?"

"Why are they called the Pringle sisters if they're not sisters?"

"Not them."

He frowned.

"Lady Emily Harding and Matilda Kenner. The Pringle sisters are sisters, of course. Otherwise they wouldn't be referred to as sisters. That doesn't make any sense."

"I'm beginning to wonder if anything will ever make sense again."

"Life can be so confusing, can't it? Take the Pringle sisters. They are sisters, so one can refer to them as the Pringle sisters. But sometimes things are not always called by what they are. Did you know that a cucumber isn't a vegetable at all? In actuality, it is a fruit. And squash also.

"Now one would think by looking at a summer squash that it was surely a vegetable. Why, even the flavor isn't particularly sweet, and most fruits are sweet, like cherries and peaches and apples. But it isn't a vegetable."

Sisters. Squash. Cucumbers. Cherries. Peaches and apples. A mental string of things unconnected, not unlike the thoughts of someone who had just arisen from being conked on the head, he thought.

"And, speaking of fruits, I'm sure you do know of them. One had a bright shade of hair, the color of ripe persimmons. That's a fruit too, which is why I spoke of fruits. And the other one had titian hair."

She sighed. "Surely if you think very hard you can remember. I don't believe any man would forget someone with titian hair. Don't you think so?"

"The fruits with titian hair," he repeated.

"No, silly. I was speaking of the women."

"The Pringle sisters."

"Lady Emily Harding and Matilda Kenner."

"I don't know what the devil you are talking about."

"Oh. Weren't you listening?"

He waited a long time before answering. The count of ten slowly, three times. "What do Lady Harding, Matilda Kenner, and these infamous Pringle sisters have to do with what I was talking about?"

"Oh, you're confused again. *I* was speaking of the Pringle sisters. You don't know them."

"I knew I was talking about something," he muttered.

"You were blustering."

"I was not blustering."

She gave him a maternal look of understanding that did nothing to lighten his mood. "You're just a bit out of humor because you're still hungry."

"I am not hungry."

"Well of course you are. Gus ate your food. I understand how the lack of sustenance can affect one."

"If you'll remember, I said nothing about being hungry."

"Certainly I remember. I'm not the party who has trouble remembering who said what."

"I am not hungry." His look must have shown he was ready to wring her neck. He moved toward her.

She took step backward. "Now Richard . . ."

The growl came loud and clear and expected.

They both looked at Gus.

"*Now* I remember what you were talking about.

109

You were talking about Gus. You shouted 'let go' and
I told him to be sweet."

"A keg of molasses . . ." he gritted, following her anxious steps backward. "A hundred loaves of sugar . . ."

He stalked her for a change, and he had the satisfaction of watching her eyes grow wide as she kept back-
ing up. He took another longer step. She scurried
back.

"And all the honey in Devonshire couldn't make
that bloody pet of yours *sweet!*"

She bumped into the rail. "He can be very sweet.
You just don't understand him. Come here, Gus!
Here, boy!"

Gus trotted over to his mistress's side, then sat, that
stupid grin on his face as he looked up at them.

She patted the top of a storage hatch. "Up, Gus!"
He leapt up and sat, waiting with eager expectation.

Letty gave Richard a look that had just enough I-
told-you-so to make his jaw tense.

"Roll over!"

Gus rolled over, his long gangly legs flailing in the
air and his ears flopping. Then he was sitting again,
his haunches bowed and his big paws flat on the
hatch.

"This is a wonderful trick. Watch: Play dead, Gus."

"Let's not play, shall we?"

"Just ignore him, Gus, and we'll show him how perfectly sweet you can be. Now play dead."

Gus rolled over onto his back, his paws held limply
in the air, then he flopped his big head to one side,
his lips loose and lazy. The beast lay still as stone.

"You were right, hellion, that is very good. Leave
him that way. Permanently."

A sudden shout broke the air. As quickly as the
ship had righted, it listed again.

DREAMING

Richard grabbed Letty before she could slide away. He pressed her to the bulwark and gripped tight. His body kept her pinned. There was a deafening howl.

"Gus!" Letty screamed.

The howl faded in the distance. And Gus hit the water.

Chapter 9

"**What** in the hell do you mean, *I* must save him? He's a hound. He can swim." Richard ignored the plea in Letty's eyes and scanned the deck. The men had righted the ship and were trying to secure the sail lines and lower Harry.

"I can't see him. Oh dear God, I can't see him!" She gripped the railing and stood on her tiptoes, straining over the rail.

Reluctantly, Richard shaded his eyes against the glaring sun and searched the water.

She gripped his arm. "Do you see him?"

Off in the distance, a brown head surfaced, gave a watery whine, and went under again. "He's out there." He pointed at Gus, who resurfaced and paddled in a small circle, howling.

"Oh, Gus . . ." She hiked up her skirts and started to climb over the rail, but Richard pulled her back against him and jerked her skirts down.

"You are not going to jump in the water after that dog."

"I knew you'd save him."

"I'm not going to save him."

"Of course you are."

"No."

"Then I am." She started to struggle.

"I will not let you jump into the Channel to save that dog."

"Then you must save him." Her voice quivered with panic.

He stood there silent, stony and immovable.

She looked at him, horrified and a little disillusioned. "Gus ..." Her whisper came out ragged and torn.

Then she did the only thing that could possibly make him rescue that dog. She cried. Gut-wrenching, pitiful sobs.

He ignored it when his belly tightened in reaction. Tears, he told himself, were only a form of manipulation. But she cried harder, and the sound was real, honest, and affected him more than he cared to admit.

"Oh, Gus ..." She stared out at the water and rasped, "He's the only thing I have." She quietly sniffled. "My only friend ..." Her breathing began to hitch and her sobs stuttered. "In—in the wh-whole world."

"Stop crying, dammit!" Richard hobbled on one foot, pulling off a boot.

She was unable to take a full breath, and when she inhaled it was in loud pathetic wheezes.

He tossed the boot aside and angrily ripped off the other. "I'm going over."

"Ple-he-ease hurry! Ple-hease!" she hiccuped.

He turned and pinned her with a hard stare. "You hang on to this rail. The ship could list again. Understand?"

She nodded, swiping at her tears.

"Now. Before I jump."

She gripped the rail.

"Both hands."

"Hurry. Ple-hease."

He fixed her with a hard look. "Do *not* let go of that rail."

"I'm holding on. Just save him."

He ducked under the ship's rail and braced himself on the ledge.

A second later he was sailing through the air on a rake's curse. He hit the water. It was like ice. But the cold water numbed the pain in his arm.

He surfaced and collected his bearings, turning toward the deafening canine wails, then swam with a kind of limping one-armed stroke toward the stupid dog that despised him as much as he despised it.

He took a long stroke and asked himself why he was in the icy Channel, wounded, and swimming to save a dog that bit, howled like a banshee, and made his life hell.

Pausing, he looked back at the ship, where Letty gripped the railing and watched him intently. Turning to swim on, he sighed. "That's why."

He was five feet away when Gus looked straight at him, stopped howling, and lifted his lips in a nasty snarl.

Richard began treading water. "Look, you son of a—"

"Aahoowoo! Aahoowooooooo!"

Richard winced and shook his head, his ears ringing from the noise. He glanced back and could see Letty still at the rail. Her shoulders were still shaking, and he could see her wipe her hand across her eyes.

Resigned to rescue the beast, he turned back. Gus was paddling away from him.

"You'd best come back here! Now!"

Gus stopped paddling away and began to paddle in a wide circle. Around Richard.

"You have about one minute to swim your ungrateful ass back here, or I'm going to turn around and swim back to that ship." He tightened his jaw and gritted, "Tears or no tears."

Gus continued to circle him.

Richard waited a minute, then another. He glanced back at the ship and could see Letty leaning way over the rail, waving her hands and holding on to nothing. Should the ship list again she'd go headfirst into the water.

He started swimming back.

"Aaahoowoo! Aaahoowoooooooo! *Aaahoowoooooo!*"

Richard kept swimming. He be damned if he was going to let that dog manipulate him.

Letty called his name and he listened for a familiar growl. Gus was strangely silent. Richard gave thanks for small favors and kept swimming, his stroke ungainly and awkward.

A moment later something thrashed through the water. He knew without looking that Gus was splashing along behind him. He didn't give the animal the satisfaction of looking at it. He just kept swimming.

So did the dog, swimming at an angle, until it was alongside him and just scant inches away. They both moved through the icy water. Neither looked at each other.

Then, with a sudden burst of speed, Gus outdistanced him by three bodylengths. It was as if the dog was suddenly swimming for its life.

Frowning, Richard glanced over his shoulder, half

expecting to see a mythical sea serpent or something equally dangerous swimming after them. There was nothing there. He slowly turned back, his gaze locked on the dog, then he glanced to the ship's rail, where Letty was still waving at him.

No. Behind him there was no sea serpent, no ferocious monster with its mouth open and ready to swallow him.

He wasn't that lucky.

The hellhound was, in Richard's estimation, incredibly fortunate, for it was even farther ahead.

Out of strangling distance.

Richard picked up his stroke again, something that was easier now because he was so blasted cold that he'd lost all feeling in his arm. When three strokes separated them, sly Gus looked over at him, then paddled like the very devil.

It was then that he knew. The damn dog—the same one he'd jumped into the water to save—was racing him back to the ship.

Letty peered over the side of the ship and watched Richard and Gus swim toward her. Both appeared unharmed, until Gus began to furiously slap his paws through the water. All she could see was his floppy brown head amid sprays of splashing water. He seemed so panicked she wondered if he was hurt after all.

Richard swam harder too and was almost to the ship when Gus, who had lagged behind, suddenly stopped.

"Aaaahooooooooow! Aaaaahoooooow!"

Gus sounded like he was dying, and Richard was still swimming away! She couldn't believe that Richard couldn't hear him.

Panicked, she grabbed the nearest thing: a coil of

knotted ropes tied to the ship. She quickly untied them and with a heave flung them over the rail.

They splashed into the water just inches ahead of Richard, who swam right into them. They tangled about his head and arms. He stopped swimming and began treading water. He scowled up at her, looking like a netted fish.

"What the hell did you do that for?" He jerked the ropes off.

"Look!" She pointed behind him. "Gus is hurt!"

He tossed the ropes aside and glanced back.

She cupped her hands together and shouted, "He can't swim anymore!"

Richard didn't move.

"Perhaps he has a cramp!"

A floppy brown head slowly sank into the sea.

"He's going to die!"

With a look that said he was not pleased, Richard swam back. Although it was only a few yards, it seemed as if he would never reach the spot where Gus had gone down.

She kept her eyes on the spot, hoping. Gus still hadn't come up. Richard searched and she kept her gaze locked on the surface, watching for a big brown lovable head to appear.

The seconds seemed like hours. With each tick of time the burn of tears in her eyes became stronger, the more anxiously her heart pounded and the more hollow she felt.

Finally Richard dove down, and she held her breath, waiting. He resurfaced, shook the water from his head, and dove again.

Oh Gus ... Oh Gus ... Please, God, please.

Richard's head broke through the surface. He gave a quick glance as he took in more air, then disappeared again.

She swiped at her damp eyes. Richard would save him. She knew he would. She knew it. She closed her eyes and said a quick prayer.

"Woof!"

Her heart stopped. She thought for a brief instant that she had imagined the sound. It was so close.

"Woof!"

Stunned, she leaned way over the railing.

Gus was merrily paddling in a small circle just inches from the ship.

At the sight of his canine grin, she sagged against the rail and took her first deep breath of relief. Then, remembering Richard, she straightened and turned back just as he surfaced again.

She cupped her hands around her mouth and shouted, "Richard!"

He shook the water from his head.

Ignoring Gus's familiar growl, she waved her hands to catch his attention.

He looked up at her.

Excitedly, she pointed down at Gus. "Look!"

Richard's gaze shifted.

"Woof!" A frisky brown tail poked through the water, and when Gus was right next to the ship he playfully slapped it with his paws and barked again, twice.

Richard swam toward Gus with incredibly determined strokes. She'd always known that Richard had superior strength. He showed that heroic strength now, wounded, yet swimming with such purposefulness. She sighed dreamily, and when she looked back she could see Richard's face clearer. There was a seething tenseness to his look, which he directed at Gus.

She blanched slightly. He looked angry enough

118

to make the sea boil. He really did not like Gus. At all.

Richard disappeared beneath the bow of the ship and she couldn't see either him or Gus without leaning over the rail again. She wasn't sure she wanted to look over that rail.

"Richard?"

There was a tight grunt she assumed was a response.

"Is Gus hurt?"

"Not yet."

"Remember, he's just a poor animal God placed on the earth to help mankind."

"I know exactly how I can help mankind."

A second later Gus growled loudly.

"Gus!" she called. "Be sweet. He's only trying to help you."

"Yes, Gus. Come here . . ." Richard's strained voice carried upward. "Let me *help* you."

She inched her head over the rail and peered down. They were separated by about four feet, Gus snarling and Richard reaching his hands out.

"He'll bite you if you get too near his throat," Letty warned.

"It might be worth it." After a moment's pause he asked, "If he's going to bite me, then how do you propose I 'save' him?"

"I hadn't thought about that. I mean, he was drowning and we had to do something. It was one of those instinctive reactions that just happens. And besides, you wouldn't let me save him, so naturally of the two of us that left only you to do it."

Treading water, he scowled up at her.

"You know, Richard, doing something heroic cannot possibly harm you. I have always known that you have a heroic nature beneath all that cynicism. You just needed me to come along and help you discover it.

"I keep telling you that, but you don't believe me. Saving Gus, especially considering how you feel about him, was definitely a heroic act. Heroes act instinctively. Without thinking, just like you did. I will always hold the memory of this close to my heart." She paused, waiting for his response. Nothing. "Richard? You're not saying anything."

"I'm freezing."

"Oh, I'm sorry!" She leaned over the rail again. "There's something else we forgot."

"What?"

"How are you going to get back on board the ship?"

"There's a ladder."

"Oh. Good." She scanned the deck, then thought of something and turned back. "Is there one tall enough on board?"

"What?"

"I said, is there a ladder that's tall enough on board?"

He didn't respond.

"How would one know the length of the ladder they'd need if they don't know how deep the water is? That doesn't make sense."

"It hangs off the side of the railing, Letty."

"Oh."

"The water is freezing. Toss the ladder over the side!"

She searched the deck again. "I don't see any ladder."

"There should be a ladder near the windlass!"

"What's a windlass?" she shouted.

"It's a hoist with a crank handle!" he shouted back.

She found the hoist and crank, but there wasn't anything resembling a ladder.

"I don't see any ladder!"

"It's made of rope!"

She chewed her lip, a sinking feeling of dread running through her. "Was it tied to the windlass?"

"Yes!"

"Did it have big knots in it?"

"Yes!"

She just stood there, a little helpless.

"Letty!"

"I'm still here."

"Then throw the blasted ladder over the side!" Richard shouted.

"Uh ... I already did."

An hour and a half later, Richard sat inside a small cabin, huddled in a thin blanket, shivering and looking blue. His hands were blue. He stared at his feet, which looked blue. He looked out the porthole at the Channel water, which was blue. He'd just spent over an hour in it, which would tend to turn one blue.

He shivered, in spite of the thin scrap of blue wool that served as a poor excuse for a blanket. At that moment he'd have given almost anything to see the blue-hot flames of a fire. But there was no fire, no coal braiser, nothing but the barren cabin of a smuggling lugger, which was, as he recalled, painted bloody blue.

He had never been so cold in his life. He was cold in places he hadn't known could be cold. Even his throat was cold. Probably from cursing the air blue when he realized the hellion had tossed the ladder into the deep blue sea.

He looked at her, sitting quietly in a corner, her

blue dress spread out so the hellhound could sleep on it. Her head leaned sleepily to one side.

In the last few minutes her blue eyes had drifted closed. Two pink smudges marred her cheeks, remnants of the sharp Channel winds, and her curly hair formed a tangled cloak about her.

Ironically, she wore the most peaceful expression.

It had been too long since he'd felt anything even close to peace. But he'd never been a peaceful sort. He looked away, scanning the small dingy cabin in search of a little blue ruin, the quickest method he knew to warm up and find a little peace.

No bottles around. No port. No brandy barrel.

For some inexplicable reason, he found himself staring at the hellion. She had asked him why he drank, the look on her face telling him she could never understand.

His life wasn't dreams and fairy tales. It was past deeds and mistakes. It was years of fighting to not conform to what his father wanted.

It was a world where nothing mattered because no one was left. It was empty, devoid of anything but the memories of every damn mistake he'd made. And all the pretending in the world wouldn't change the past.

He indulged because ... He paused a moment, truthfully asking himself if it was habit borne from the need to defy his father or from guilt. He came to the conclusion that, of late, the world was more livable through a haze of spirits.

But as he regarded her, he realized that here was one thing that looked better through clear eyes. The hellion.

Letitia Hornsby was no longer the pudgy, wide-eyed imp that had ridden a cow across a bridge and right into him. Time had changed her.

His sense said look away, but he didn't. He stared at her as she slept, strangely compelled to do so, and felt like a voyeur.

She was a woman with all of a woman's assets, white skin that was smooth and scented, a softness that seemed to hover about her, making him aware for the first time of her every feature: the full lips of youth, a small ear, the heart-shaped face a man could cup in one hand if he wanted to kiss her gently and with finesse.

There had been no finesse in the way he had kissed her earlier. He relived a twinge of shame and was surprised. 'Twould seem he did have a conscience.

Odd that she of all people could strike such a chord in him. The thought intrigued him, he who was interested in little and bored by much.

Her chest rose and fell slowly with each breath she took. From the edge of her dirt- and ash-smudged gown he could see the dark shadowed crease where her breasts met. He remembered the fullness of her in his hand, and his mind flashed with the memory of a glimpse of her cream-colored thighs as she tied her garters.

He felt a twinge of something much more elemental than intrigue. So much for his bout of conscience.

She shifted slightly, sliding her arms around that hellhound and resting her head on its neck. He was struck by the image they made: a big lumbering brown beast and a young woman who lived in a fog of idealism, who years before had childishly given her heart to an unprincipled rakehell she imagined to be some fairy-tale hero.

For the first time, instead of thinking of her as a nuisance, he thought of what her life must have been like with no friends, no place in society. She had always looked up at him as if he were her whole world. And it never ceased to annoy him.

It was little wonder that she thought of her beast of a dog the only friend she had. Perhaps he was. She clung to that dog in her sleep as if she were afraid to let go. It crossed his mind that she must have had some devastating loss to cling so desperately to that which she loved.

He clung to nothing but his own stubbornness. Yet clinging to nothing, needing nothing, didn't protect one either. He closed his eyes because that was the only way he could really see himself.

He supposed he did cling to something. He clung to bottles and bitter memories: a career that never was, an older brother he had worshiped, and a father who demanded things Richard could never give or be. All were gone now, as was any remnant of youthful idealism he may have had.

He forced his eyes open. Her face was the first thing he saw. Perhaps it was the way she held on to that blasted dog, perhaps it was the failures he knew she'd suffered, perhaps it was something he sensed in her, but there was an overwhelming aura of sadness about her.

Pity wasn't what he was feeling; quite the contrary. He didn't think she would want to be pitied, and for some reason he respected that. But when he looked at her asleep on Gus, her vulnerability was all he saw. She was a young woman who had nothing but a dog for a friend.

The thought was somewhat grounding. And here he was, a man who thought he'd witnessed every kind of human pain. He shook his head to rid himself of any feelings even remotely benevolent.

Not that there was anything benevolent about him. Thank God.

Still, he sat there, staring at nothing, thinking nothing, until he finally looked up. Odd, how his gaze was drawn to her once again.

Then seconds went into minutes with him just looking at her. He no longer counted the measure of time. Instead, he watched her sleep, realizing for the first time that he shared something kindred with the hellion.

Loneliness, it seemed, touched both of them.

Chapter

10

*T*he first cannon blast woke them both.

The second woke Gus, who, after sniffing the air and blinking once, began to howl to the whine of soaring cannonballs.

"Hush, Gus!" Letty started to stand up, but another blast shook the ship and she stumbled.

Cannon and dog continued in cacophony, and a second later a blue blanket sailed through the air and landed on Gus, who stopped in mid-howl.

Frowning at Richard, Letty reached for the surprisingly still blanket.

He answered her frown with a hard look. "You touch that blanket and I'll tie you in it."

"But—"

Another cannon blasted, and seconds later the ball hit close water. The ship, already barely seaworthy, rocked in unsteady cadence, creaking loud enough to be heard over the thunder of the running crew and the blast of return cannonfire.

Letty fell backward and Richard grabbed the bunk. "We need to get out of here. Now!" He shoved off the bunk and crossed the cabin.

The ship lurched again. He jerked at the door.

It wouldn't budge.

He spun around and scanned the room. "See if you can find something, anything, to pry open this door!" Then he stood back and kicked the door soundly.

The ship shook from another blast. There was a muffled howl. A loose-lipped brown snout wriggled out from beneath one edge of the blanket.

Gus sniffed the air, then sat, the blanket hanging from his big head like a wimple. He looked at Letty, grinning as if this were a delightful game. His tail responded in joyful thumps, making the blanket bounce. With the whistle of cannonfire he stuck his muzzle in the air and bayed once more.

"Shhhh!" Letty warned him, then turned and began to quickly search the cabin for anything that would help Richard. She moved from door to cabinet door, but there was nothing. She opened the last cabinet and found nothing inside but a piece of old rotten rope.

"Move, you son of a—" came a gritted voice.

"Woof!"

She spun around.

Gus sat blocking the door, his tail wagging as he nipped playfully at Richard's raised boot.

"Gus!"

Muttering, Richard swung his foot away.

"Woof!" Gus leapt up and chased the boot—and Richard's foot—as if it were a stick being dangled around for his amusement.

"Gus! Stop that! Richard's trying to be heroic!"

The look she got from Richard was enough to make her clamp her mouth shut. He jerked his boot from Gus's mouth and crossed the cabin.

She scampered back quickly and tried to be brave by not covering her eyes. She knew he wouldn't strike her no matter how angry he looked.

He strode right past her, threw the tick off the bunk, and tore out a wide bed slat. He crossed the cabin and raised the wood high over his head.

She screamed.

He froze.

"Don't hit Gus!"

Richard stared at her for a stunned moment. "Tempting though it might be in this case, I do not beat animals senseless." He turned back and stared down at Gus. "Anyway, this one's already senseless, else the beast would have the bloody sense to move out of my way!"

"Woof!"

"Here Gus! Here boy!" She patted her skirt and Gus happily trotted over to her, lips and ears flopping.

Richard slammed the slat down on the door latch. The wood splintered in half and the door popped open, the latch hanging at a bent angle.

"Come. Quickly!" He grabbed her hand and all but jerked her out of the room and up a short flight of steps.

Smoke hovered gray and shroudlike above the deck now slick with sea wash. She waved the smoke away and made a face. The air was heavy, damp, and it stank with the sharp taste of burning sulfur and sea brine.

"Can you see the other ship?"

"Barely."

"Won't they help us?"

"I can't make out if it's an excise ship."

"Oh." She peered through the smoke and caught glimpses of the rival ship. Another cannon sent gray smoke billowing over before she could see anything familiar.

Richard groaned. "It's a Yank ship."

"A what?"

He turned and looked down at her. "An American privateer. And what in the hell it's doing here I don't know."

"Oh. Wouldn't they help us if we told them who we are?"

" 'Privateer' is a drawing-room term for 'pirate.' "

"Oh." She winced as one of their cannons blasted, then waved away the fresh smoke. "Pirates? No wonder we were at war with Americans so frequently."

"The Yanks have a natural inclination to fight." He scanned the deck, looking for something, and muttered, "What they really need is a bloody king."

"We could give them ours."

He turned back.

She smiled. "I doubt if he'd be missed."

Richard barked out a laugh, but it was short. A cannon blasted and water splashed hard from the port side, rocking the whole ship. The crew scurried over the deck, shouting to be heard above the cannons' roar.

Phelim stood behind the closest cannon. She felt sure it was Phelim, because he was wearing the cocked hat of a naval officer and a Nelson eyepatch, which he had turned up so he could better angle the cannon. Philbert stood nearby, his arms crossed while he watched a crew member light one of the cannons, and Phineas hid behind a mast with his hands covering his ears and his eyes squeezed tightly shut.

"Keep your head down!" Richard shouted and pulled her along with him, Gus lagging close behind.

Richard stopped in front of one of the masts and

wrapped her arms around it. "I have to untie that skiff and lower it over the side. Hang on to this and do *not* let go. Do you understand? Do *not* let go for any reason!"

She nodded, not daring to defy him when he had that look on his wonderful, heroic face.

"Keep your head down and clear of the boom!"

"What's a boom?" she shouted back.

He pointed at a wooden crossbeam above her head. "That's a boom! It shifts with the sail! Understand?"

She nodded, and Richard moved toward the skiff. She stared up at the beam, her hands linked tightly to the fattest part of the mast. "What an odd name. I wonder why they call it a boom?" she thought.

Another cannonball splashed nearby, sending a shower of sea water over them. She turned and looked for Gus, worried.

She shouldn't have been. He had a new toy. He was lumbering after Richard, nipping playfully at his boots.

All around her was smoke and stench and spraying water. The ship rocked unsteadily, leaning more toward the side of the ship she'd damaged. The masts creaked and she looked up, just as the boom swung in a wide arc.

Breath held, she ducked, feeling the brisk wind of the beam as it passed over her head. Eyes looking upward, she watched the heavy boom swing, dragging a long rough hank of rope over her shoulder.

She grasped the rope, holding it tightly while she tried to find somewhere to secure it. There was no pin, no hook, nothing but a splintered set of holes where the securing device must have been.

There was a shout, a familiar gravelly voice. Letty turned.

Two sailors, their arms filled with cannonballs, were running toward her. One of them was Harry. His gaze met hers. His ruddy cheeks drained of color. He cursed.

She remembered his curses. She remembered Richard's orders.

The rope slid from her fingers as she hugged the mast a little tighter, waiting for Harry's face to flush with anger. Then she'd run. Even Richard couldn't blame her then.

But Harry stood frozen for an extra second.

The mast creaked.

She looked up.

The boom swung back.

She ducked and squeezed her eyes shut.

There was a whacking *thud*. A grunt. The rolling thunder of loose cannonballs.

She cracked open her eyes and winced. Both men were doubled over the swinging boom. Even over the noise of the opposing cannons she could hear Harry calling for his mother. With solid momentum, the boom swept both Harry and the other smuggler over the side, where they dangled for an instant before they slipped off the crossbeam like human raindrops.

A seafarer's lifetime of hearty curses echoed back to her as the empty boom swung back. She hunched down, still staring at the spot where the men had flown overboard. Their shouts faded into a splash.

Surely sailors could swim. She hesitated, then craned her head around and searched for help. Most of the crew were at the cannons. She called out, but no one paid heed. Everyone was too busy, too hurried. And the cannon noise was increasing.

Back on the other side, Richard was hunkered down behind the small boat, untying it. Gus was with him, his tail wagging and half his body wormed between Richard and the boat.

"Richard!" she called out.

His hand shot out from behind the boat to wave her quiet. He didn't understand.

"Richard!" she tried again.

He turned, scowling down at Gus's backside, then he finally looked at her, his face a mask of irritation.

She pointed toward the opposite side of the ship. "I ..."

He raised a finger to his lips and shook his head, frowning.

"But ..."

His narrowed eyes promised dire retribution should she disobey him.

She swallowed the rest of her words as he disappeared behind the skiff. She glanced around, wondering what to do. Then, with a break in the wail of the cannons, she heard Harry's shouts, seconded by the other man.

She took her first deep breath in minutes. Dead men don't shout. A deckhand moved from a nearby cannon and leaned over the side. He turned back, called and waved for help, then hurriedly threw a knotted rope over the ship's side.

With a sigh of relief, she laid her cheek against the damp smooth wood of the creaking mast. She clung tightly and watched the beam swing back around with a powerful *swoosh*. Cannonballs rolled past her, loose and abandoned, rumbling across the wooden deck like thunder. In her mind's eye she saw the strong arm of the wooden beam sweep through the air, the men flying off the deck. Finally enlightened, she nodded slowly, then muttered, "So *that's* why they call it a boom."

Richard gave the hellion a hard look. What he wanted to give her was a hard push. "I said ... *jump!*"

She stood on tiptoe and peered over the railing. "I don't think so."

"We are trapped on this ship, prisoners, in the middle of a sea battle, surrounded by smugglers—inept though they might be—who want to do God only knows what to us; and who just might succeed, although it would surely be by complete accident. This is our only chance. Now jump, or I'll throw you in!"

She shook her head.

"You were willing to jump for that dog. Now jump!"

Her hands gripped the rail even tighter. "That was spur of the moment. He was already in the water. It was instinct." She peered doubtfully at the water and muttered, "Besides, I knew you'd do it."

He paused. Intimidation wasn't working. He climbed over the railing and hung on the outside. "The boat's our only means of escape. It's down there, waiting."

"I know . . ."

"Come, hellion." He slid his hand over hers. "I'll hold your hand."

She paused for a second of doubt and stared longingly at their hands, then shook her head again.

He leaned closer to her, speaking soothingly and stroking her hand lightly, the way he would calm a frightened mount. "We'll jump together. You and I." He hesitated. "Kindred spirits."

She sighed. "You are so very brave."

"Yes, and you're going to be equally as brave and jump with me."

"No."

Jaw tight, he glanced around the deck, searching for her dog. In some desperate part of his mind he thought he might throw the beast in first so she'd go after it. But she would insist he play hero again and jump.

They had little time and almost no chance. Should he just pick her up and throw her in? He looked at the girl who claimed to love him, who swore he was a hero and had saved her life.

A devil of a smile played at his lips. He controlled it and took a step toward her, feigning what he hoped was a pleading look. Then he took another step. "Letty," he said slowly and reached for her.

Then he slipped and fell through the air, the wind whipping past him—a sensation he was beginning to instinctively associate with the hellion. Like pain.

The water hit him with a hard icy sting. Underwater, he heard her call his name, but he let the current slowly carry him to the surface, where he splashed enough to take several deep breaths of air, then grew still and floated facedown like a dead man.

She called his name again. And again.

He wondered how long he could hold his breath.

She sounded as if she were crying. But he justified his conscience by telling himself she sounded that way because he was underwater.

Another choked shout.

His chest began to ache for air.

Seconds ticked by.

Jump, dammit!

Sporadic cannons still blasted, splashing near the port bow or sailing over to the starboard, but this side was still clear.

His lungs swelled to bursting.

Jump! Jump!

Then she screamed so loudly she probably warned both ships, but the sound of it had a decided echo and grew louder . . . and louder . . .

She hit the water a good twenty feet away. When

the hellion jumped, she jumped. From the backwash, he'd say she did so with the same amount of grace with which she danced: none.

He hadn't known one could smile with one's face underwater. But he had, and was. She splashed around and swam toward him. He covertly turned his head to the opposite side and took in air, then floated very still.

Now, did he give himself away, grab her, and drag her to the waiting skiff, or did he continue his act and let her save him?

He spent about a second in thought. If the next cannonball landed on the port side of the bow, he'd grab her. If the next cannonball landed on the starboard side, he would continue to float.

Yes, that was it, he thought, gloating somewhat for the way he'd outsmarted the hellion, congratulating himself because, in actuality, he'd also outsmarted fate, fortune, and—feeling quite cocky—even God.

The next cannonball landed in the skiff.

Chapter 11

Not even in her wildest dreams did Letty Hornsby think she would ever be aboard a pirate ship. She amended that: a privateer. But here she was, captive again, yet more fascinated then frightened. With Richard at her side and Gus at her feet, she was surrounded by those whom she knew would protect her.

She'd proudly reminded Richard that she was not a female prone to hysteria as they were hauled out of the water. His only comment had been that innocence was a gift to protect fools. Then he'd mumbled something about fools losing their innocence and becoming idiots who made stupid decisions based on the whim of some bloody cannonball.

She hadn't understood what he'd meant then and she still didn't as she stood in a long human line across the deck: Richard, Gus, and herself; Phelim, Philbert, Phineas, and the remainder of the smuggling crew, except for Harry, who was unconscious.

136

At gunpoint, he had boarded with the rest of the crew, then immediately tripped over an anchor chain and hit his head on a nearby cannon. He had been going for her throat at the time.

Letty cast a timid glance at him and blanched, remembering him crossing the boarding plank and how quickly his face had changed when he saw her. His hands became clawlike and reached out. He never saw the chain.

Now, however, he looked rather peaceful, lying there on the deck. But the thought crossed her mind that she should have the good sense to be cautious should she happen to be nearby when he came to. He seemed to think her very presence a bad omen. Women on a ship and all that, she supposed.

She glanced up at Richard, who watched the pirates closely, his face unreadable. His inscrutable stare shifted to the man she assumed was the captain, a man with deep red hair and a reddish gold beard. He had just come above board a moment before and now silently stood before them.

He was striking at first glance, someone whose stature left no doubt that he would stand out in any room. A man not to be forgotten. The dark shirt and breeches were common enough, as were his tall black boots. But taken as a whole, the unrelenting dark of his cloth, the power of his build, and the long woolen coat, stark black, that hung from his wide shoulders, gave the man the sinister quality of the devil.

More ominous than his dark attire was the attitude he wore. He was a man who was used to winning, a man whose demeanor said he frequently toyed with chance, yet never lost. There was a subtle shrewdness to the way he examined them through a steely black-eyed gaze that said he knew each of them only too well with a brief glance, and subsequently found them vastly amusing.

Richard's stance showed he had come to the same conclusion. He was standing to his full height, straight, somewhat regal, a fallen angel facing the devil that had felled him. There was a wary respect in the look they exchanged, a kind of silent communication that one sees between two keen-eyed dogs who are challenging each other.

Letty looked down at Gus, who was uncommonly quiet, neither taking to nor advancing on the man. He seemed perfectly content to just sit at her feet. She had never seen him more controlled.

The pirate leaned languidly against the bulwark and picked a pinch of something from his shirt pocket and tossed it into his mouth. Before she could wonder what it was, he signaled to someone with a slight wave of his hand. She caught a glimpse of movement, turned, and saw another pirate wearing a red bandanna with a shock of white hair sticking out of it.

Despite the stark color of his hair, the man was not old. There was something about him that said he was untouched by time.

Perhaps it was his slender, almost fragile build, perhaps it was the way he ranged catlike through the crates and barrels of contraband that had been transferred from the other ship. But whatever, the slim man didn't fit her image of a hard, sea-bitten pirate.

"Gabriel." The captain spoke the name in a blunt statement, as if the fellow owed him his existence.

The sound of the dark captain's voice sent chills over Letty. It was calm and very lethal. And she had foolishly told herself she wasn't afraid. Something swelled inside her—fear, mixed with some emotion that threatened to run rampant. Hysteria. She, who had never succumbed to a fit of the vapors, was on the very edge of doing so.

Almost instinctively, she slid her shaking hand into Richard's and felt comfort from the firm strength of his responding grip. From the corner of her eye she caught a small flicker of something in his eyes, but it happened so quickly she didn't know what emotion she'd seen.

As if mentally commanded to do so, she turned back to the pirate captain. He didn't look up, but instead spent an inordinate number of tense seconds scoring a piece of wood with a deadly-looking dagger.

He flicked a shaving over his shoulder and asked casually, "What day is this, Gabriel?"

"Wednesday, Capt'n Hamish," Gabriel answered in a Gaelic purr.

"Ah, yes. So it is." Hamish paused in a way that was pure calculation, and the tension grew in the silence. One had the feeling that was exactly what he wanted. Another eternal moment, and he continued, "A dull day. *Dead*-ly dull day."

He shoved off the bulwark with a lithe push of his boot and slowly raised his bearded head, gazing down the line of captives with a bored look. He strolled past each captive like a merchant forced to examine damaged goods.

Pausing in front of Phelim, Philbert, and Phineas, he casually scratched a corner of his mouth with the tip of the dagger and examined each identical man with idle curiosity. "How odd."

He moved the dagger tip toward an already skittish Phineas, who watched the blade through wide frightened eyes and whose skin slowly drained of color.

The closer the dagger came, the paler the man got. Just a scant inch away . . .

"Don't!" Letty cried.

But poor frightened Phineas weaved slightly, then his eyes rolled back and he fainted dead away.

Hamish glanced down, vastly amused. "Interesting..."

Phelim bristled, and Philbert tried to grab him, muttering about his sanity, but it was too late. The gruff and bandy little smuggler puffed out his chest and spouted, "Who be ye to frighten the wits from me brother?"

"Wits?" Hamish frowned at Phineas sprawled on the deck. "Surely you jest." He pulled his gaze away and swept slowly over Phelim with an assessing glance. He stopped at neck level, where the eyepatch hung from a string around Phelim's neck. "Well now, what have we here?" He reached out and lifted the patch by daggerpoint. "Hmmm. An eyepatch?" He pinned Phelim with a wry look. "Wear this for effect, do you?"

He didn't wait for an answer, just turned. "I believe, Gabriel, that I've been sorely remiss in my attire." In an instant his dagger hand shot out toward Phelim.

Letty gasped and every conscious prisoner flinched or stiffened.

Hamish pulled back the dagger and the eyepatch dangled from it. "Why thank you, my friend," he drawled, giving Phelim a humorless smile. "Consider it shared booty among fellow thieves."

He stepped away.

Bristling, Phelim opened his mouth.

"One more thing." Captain Hamish turned back around. "Another word from you, only one word, and you'll have need of the eyepatch."

Philbert's hand closed over his brother's mouth.

Hamish gave the silent Philbert an amused look. "Odds were in your favor that one of you had to have some sense."

A moment later he stood in front of Richard and Letty. She caught the distinct scent of cloves. "My, my, look at this."

Richard's fingers tightened over hers.

Hamish stared pointedly at their clasped hands, then slowly raised his dark gaze to first Letty, then Richard. He waited for interminable seconds, then cracked a feigned smile of indulgence. "Sweet."

He walked around them slowly, and Letty could feel his every look. She stood stiff and still, perfectly aware of the quiver of real fear running through her, but just as aware of the reassuring squeeze of encouragement she received from Richard. Her fingers tightened around his.

She tried to think about him only and block out everything around her. She closed her eyes in an effort to concentrate. The warmth of his hand was her lifeline. Through the tips of her fingers she could feel his heartbeat. It was steady, not rushing and thudding like hers, and she took a deep breath.

The salty dampness of the cool sea air was an instant reminder of where they were. In the tense absence of any human voice, her senses attuned to the caw of the gulls, the rocking creak that seemed the constant call of a seaward ship, and she heard the slow, ominous tap of Hamish's boots as he circled them.

"Gentry if I've ever seen it. Now what do you suppose a toff like him and this little lady are doing aboard a smuggling lugger?" He stopped in front of Letty. "Suppose you tell me, my dear."

She raised her face and looked in his shrewd eyes. She couldn't utter a word.

"What do you think, Gabriel? Cat got her tongue?"

"Leave her alone," Richard said with deceptive quiet.

Hamish raised his eyebrows suggestively and looked at Richard, who returned his look with a cold stare.

"Ah," Hamish said in knowing tone. "A hero."

Richard's jaw tightened.

Hamish looked at Gabriel, then back to Richard, and he gave a wicked laugh. "I'd wager he's gotten her tongue."

Richard's hand crushed hers. She gasped in pain and looked up at him horrified when she saw him draw back a fist.

A pistol shot froze everyone.

"That's quite enough!" came a voice so commanding Letty had the odd feeling that she had just heard God speak. She whipped her head around.

The bright sun limned the slim black form of a man standing on the topdeck. He stood in the stance of one familiar with the sea, his back straight and his legs spread to absorb the ebb and flow of the ship's motion. His face, his features, almost everything was in shadow. All one could see was his lithe silhouette. He slowly lowered a hand with a smoking pistol.

"There you are, Dion," Hamish said in a bland tone. "I wondered how long it would be before you'd come and spoil my amusement."

The pirate Dion moved then, two steps, before he leapt down from the upper deck with lightning-quick agility. He handed the pistol to Gabriel and walked over to stand next to the captain.

"I see you cannot control your tiresome penchant for absurd melodrama, Hamish. I suspect you are the one cursed with a tongue affliction."

"Nary a lass has ever complained. One of my more tantalizing black arts. I'd prove it with this wide-eyed little gillyflower if I didn't think Galahad here would do something stupid and then I'd have to kill him."

Hamish moved his languid gaze from Richard to Letty, and he gave her a wicked wink.

She could feel Richard tense, and it was her turn to squeeze his hand in warning. He didn't respond, so she glanced up at him. His jaw was fixed tightly and his eyes were narrowed in challenge, as if he wanted the pirate to try.

Hamish laughed, apparently finding Richard's anger amusing.

"Stop taunting him," the other man warned.

"Ah, Dion my friend, as always you leave me no toys to play with." He leaned back against the bulwark, crossing his boots and tilting his hat back with the dagger. "What shall we do with them? Plankwalking? Keelhauling? Hmmmm, what are some other delicious pranks? Ah, yes, I remember now. It has been a while. Wenching, looting, and plundering." Hamish gave a lazy smile. "I feel in the mood for some plundering. Who goes first? You or I?"

"You do have a cruel streak."

"I try."

"Too hard at times," Dion said with subtle meaning, and he began to pace slowly in front of them.

Letty had the distinct feeling that this man was actually the one in command. There was intelligence in his manner and a smooth confidence that gave the impression he was in complete control. He turned, and she had the first good look at his face.

His features were fine, his hair long and queued and spun as golden as Rumpelstiltskin's straw. He paused and looked out at the smuggler's ship, listing but not destroyed. "Is the cargo emptied?"

"Every last crate and barrel, silks, lace, glass, and even more interesting than barrels of brandy"— Hamish paused before he added—"were three crates of gun locks."

Dion whipped around. "What?"

"Gun locks." Hamish flicked another wood shaving toward Phineas, who had come around and was being helped up by his brothers, then he casually pointed at them with his knife. "Hard to believe of those three."

Dion was silent for a few long seconds, then said, "Get rid of them."

Letty jumped forward. "No! Please. Don't hurt them!"

"Come back here!" Richard tightened his grip on her hand and tried to pull her back.

She stubbornly jerked her hand free and faced the pirate Dion. "I'm certain they didn't mean to do anything so terribly wrong. Did you?" She looked at the triplets just as Phineas hit the deck again with a loud thud. She gave Phelim and Philbert an imploring look. "Tell him you're sorry. Anything. Please!" She turned back to the pirates. "Don't kill them. Please."

Dion stared at her as if taken aback. Hamish burst into deep, wicked laughter.

She turned to Richard and followed the direction of his look. He was watching the pirate Dion with intense regard. She took a deep breath so she could brave the other beast, planted her hands on her hips, and glared at Hamish. "Murdering people is not amusing."

Hamish laughed even harder, and he turned to Dion. "And you accuse me of melodrama?" He chuckled as he sheathed his knife, then braced his hands on his hips and said, "Shall you tell her, or shall I?"

Dion looked at her through shrewd gray eyes that held a trace of a wry smile. "Foolish girl. I was talking about the gun locks."

And so it was that an hour later the smugglers had been escorted back aboard their listing ship, less gunpowder, cannonballs, and other such weapons. With an odd feeling of kinship that had nothing to do with familial blood and everything to do with spilled blood, Richard had watched two of the men lug Harry back to his own ship. He hadn't come around, to the hellion's good fortune.

The gun locks had been given a quick burial at sea, and the remainder of the plunder was stowed in the hold, except the human plunder: Richard and Letty, and the inhuman Gus.

With the prod of a pistol muzzle in his back, something that was becoming as natural a sensation as breathing, Richard walked past the pirate Hamish and through the ship's companionway, pulling the hellion along with him. Gus trailed behind in a floppy kind of half trot, half lumber, until the corridor ended at a large oak door and they stopped.

Hamish reached around him, pressing the pistol deeper into Richard's back, and opened the door. Then he straightened and looked at the hellion. With swashbuckling flair he waved his free hand, gave a slight nod of his head that was anything but polite, and his mouth quirked into an irritating smile that bordered on a leer. "After you, little gillyflower."

"She stays with me." Richard tightened his grip on her hand.

Hamish gave a thundering laugh. "I stand corrected After *both* of you."

Richard pulled the hellion inside after him. She looked up at him with true fear in her eyes. The chit had finally grown some sense. He kept a tight grip on her hand and instinctively shifted closer to her.

Dion entered the cabin, and Hamish pushed the door closed behind them and leaned against it, crossing his boots. He gave them a pointed black-eyed stare, then said with casual wit, "Perhaps they're Siamese twins, joined at the hand."

Scowling fiercely, the hellion tried to pull her hand away, but Richard held fast—his own volley to the challenge of the man's snide remarks.

Seeming to ignore them, Dion crossed the cabin silently. Meanwhile Hamish wore a droll smile that said he had expected Richard's response, then he raised the pistol sight to his squinting eye and slowly shifted the barrel from Richard to the hellion.

Instinctively Richard pushed her behind him and pinned Hamish with a look that said "go ahead and shoot."

"As I said . . ." Hamish grinned, looking from the hellion, who was peeking around his shoulder, then to Richard. "A hero."

Dion silently watched the exchange from behind a heavy mahogany desk, which stood in front of a bow of mullioned windows. Behind him was a vast view of the rippling gray-green sea and cloud-darkened sky where every so often a shaft of yellow sunlight would pierce through.

But he appeared unaware of the elements around, above, and before them. His intent was focused elsewhere. Exactly where was a mystery to Richard. He, who prided himself on gauging most men, couldn't fathom what this man intended.

Dion braced his slim hands atop the desk in a gesture of command. He gave Hamish a meaningful glance. "Behave yourself."

Hamish shrugged as if he could care less and leaned back against the door, his face filled with lazy amusement. Richard felt the strong urge to wipe that look off with a hard right cross.

"Sit." Dion gave a curt nod toward two chairs standing opposite the desk.

Richard guided Letty around to sit in one of the chairs, and Gus lumbered over and flopped down at her feet, resting his head atop his mammoth front paws. It seemed to Richard that the dog was most cheerful when they were caught in a disaster. The animal was completely devoid of any danger instinct. Completely oblivious.

But Richard wasn't. He stood behind Letty's chair, his hands gripping its back. He gave the man a direct look. "I'd prefer to stand."

"As you wish." Dion slid into his own chair and picked up a letter opener from the desk. He studied it for a moment, then leaned back and gracefully swung his boots atop one corner of the desk. There was but one sharp, precise click of his boot heels hitting wood. Silent, he coolly twirled the opener in his hands and stared out through the wall of glass.

Time grew slow in the silence, and the hellion began to squirm. The quiet was getting to her.

Richard slid his hands from the back of her chair to her shoulders and heard her catch her breath at his touch. He gave her another squeeze of encouragement and felt it when her gaze shifted up at him.

But he didn't meet it. Instead he kept his sharp eyes on the man seated across from them. Ever since this enigmatic man had joined the others above board, Richard had had an eerie feeling that he'd seen this Dion before. The name wasn't familiar, nor was his face, per se, but there was something.

His instincts were unusually keen—when they weren't dulled by drink. And though he knew he'd had nothing to drink, his senses were still muddled. It was unsettling, because for the life of him he couldn't figure out where he'd met this man or what it was he recognized.

There was no sound in the room except the natural

sound of the sea, the only movement the slight motion of the ship and the rise and fall of human breathing. But tenseness continued to hang in the room like fog, threatening, dangerous, almost palpable it was so strong.

And even the confining walls of a ship's cabin couldn't keep those caged within from reacting in primal challenge. Richard bristled with it, felt the strong need to hold his own against some force that was stronger than he.

"So," Dion said smoothly, never taking his gaze away from the sea, "what do you think we should do with them?"

"I opted for plundering."

He ignored Hamish and looked from Letty to Richard. "Suppose you tell me who you are and how you came to be on that lugger."

Richard could play his own taunting games. He said nothing, letting the silence hang around them for a change. The pirate didn't move, but he didn't take his shrewd gray eyes off him either. After another tense few seconds, Richard said, "I'm—"

The cold steel of a pistol barrel pressed into Richard's temple.

"Not you. Her."

Richard silently swore. He tightened his hold on her shoulders and hoped to God she understood what to tell them. No ... He had a second thought. What *not* to tell them.

He could feel her stare and looked down. Her head was tilted back, but her gaze was locked on the pistol at his head. The color slowly drained from her face.

Her shoulders shook under his palms, and he tightened his grip again and had the satisfaction of watching her worried look flash to his.

"We're waiting." The smooth voice was controlled, too controlled.

"I'm Letitia Hornsby and he's Richard Lennox."

Gus's head popped up and he snarled. For once the blasted dog had served a purpose. In warning, Richard quickly pressed his fingers into her shoulder. Her eyes flinched slightly, and she looked down. "Hush, Gus."

" 'Twas all my fault," she began quietly, speaking to her hands clasped in her lap. Her shoulders heaved with the force of the breath she took. She slowly raised her head and looked directly at the pirate with all the martyrdom of a burning saint. "I'm in love with Richard," she admitted, as if that explained everything.

Richard's first reaction was to groan, but he didn't. The pistol left his head and some of the tension flowed out of him. Then he heard a snort of laughter from behind him and felt his jaw tense.

"I've loved him for half of my lifetime." She sighed. "So I followed him to the cliffs near our homes. We're neighbors, you see, and I had hidden in the pantry earlier, on my way to snitch some honeybuns—I have a horrid sweet tooth at night—and heard Cook talking to one of the servants. They said he'd come home. Finally. He hasn't been home for over two years." She looked up at him. "Do you have any idea how long two years is when one is waiting?" She took another breath. "It seems almost a century.

"So I followed him, and then Gus barked and Richard fell off his horse and the smugglers snatched him. Naturally, I wanted to stay with him, him being—"

Richard tightened his grip on her so she wouldn't spill the tea about his title. Her mouth clamped shut. He had to give her credit because she didn't give his signal away and look up at him as he would have thought, nor did she ask him why he'd gripped her shoulders.

"Him being what?"

"Being so important to me," she said with a glibness he'd have thought impossible of her. He stared straight out the windows, schooling his expression to hide his reaction.

Dion continued to absently twist the letter opener while he looked directly at her.

She still stared at her clasped hands. "What are you going to do with us?"

"What do you think we should do?"

"Well, I suppose if I had my choice, I would say the best thing would be to take us home." She almost whispered the words.

"And where is home?"

"Devon," she said, before Richard could stop her.

"Fine."

Her head shot up, her face incredulous. "You will? Truly?"

Without responding, Dion rose and crossed the room.

There was something—Richard wasn't certain what, but something strange was going on. He felt mortal, manipulated, as if some giant hand were charting the course of his life, and it wasn't the course he wanted.

The pirate Dion opened the door and looked at Richard, then at her. "You'll go home." He gave Hamish a nod of dismissal. "Eventually."

The larger man strolled through the door after him, and just before he closed the door, he added, "After the ransom."

The door clicked shut. Letty sat frozen in the chair, her only anchor the reassuring warmth of Richard's hands on her shoulders. The only human sound was the distant thud of bootheels ascending the stairs.

She exhaled a breath that she hadn't even known she'd been holding. Her whole body began to shiver.

"After all this, surely you're not going to become hysterical now."

She looked up at Richard, unable to stop the shaking. Her words came out in a quivering choked whisper. "I—I think I might be."

He grasped her hands and drew her up, searching her face. To her absolute shame, tears spilled from her eyes and dribbled down her cheeks.

"Come here, hellion." He opened his arms.

She fell into them and sobbed against his chest. "I think I've had too much adventure. I'm ready to go home." Her voice trailed off and she shivered slightly, her clothes still damp from the water.

Her cheek rested against his chest, which was damp and warm, his shirt touched with the salty scent of the sea, and she closed her eyes, unable to do anything except curl against Richard. She felt the stroke of his hands on her back and she just let herself be weak for a moment.

"I've managed to mire us into this fix ..." She mumbled her confession into his chest. "I shot you. Gus bit you. You've had to jump into the sea twice and you've been half starved. Yet you're still being gentle with me." She gave a soft sigh. "Despite what you say, Richard, that is terribly heroic."

"Heroic? I don't think so." His laugh held a touch of scorn and self-mockery. "Perhaps recompense for the life I've led."

She stood there, letting him hold her and wondering at the kind of life he had led. He was so very different from her—worldly where she was sheltered. He was bitter and cynical. She had hopes and dreams. He had anger hoarded deep inside him like golden guineas itching to be spent, and she had a wealth of love just waiting to be freely given.

How odd they were, and how odd that it would be Richard—her opposite—whom God had fated to be hers. And she believed in the very depths of her soul that as surely as the sun would rise tomorrow, Richard was destined to be hers.

She didn't care that it was impossible for her to understand his experience. She could sense that it overwhelmed him, so much so that he didn't know how to let go of it. She could feel the taint of it, the cynicism and the bitterness, even if she knew not what it was that made him so.

And taint or no, it didn't change the way she felt about him. Love went beyond mortal sins. No matter how stained his past, her heart wouldn't change just because he wanted it to.

He hadn't lied when he said he didn't know what love was. Otherwise he'd have known that while love could change, grow, bend, and mellow, it would never die. Never.

So she took a moment to look up at him, to just let him fill her vision as he filled her dreams. She was aware of subtle differences in him. His skin was paler; the warm brown tan he usually had was starting to fade. The beginnings of a thick dark beard framed his mouth—lips that of recent years were too often thinned into a cruel line.

The thick, bristled dark beard covered his sharp-angled cheekbones and square jaw. His hair, which had been slicked back from the sea, now was drying with a slight wave, and it straggled even too long and unkempt for a rakehell.

But when she looked at him, disheveled and gruff and unmoving, he was as wonderful as he had been the first time she had ever seen him. Time had stamped his face with subtle changes.

The corners of his eyes crinkled slightly from excesses of weather and life. His brow had deeper lines, as if he spent too much time frowning. His face was more angular, thinner, and when one looked close, there were a few scattered gray hairs near his temples.

He looked tired. She studied him, looking for the cause and knowing it really wasn't physical fatigue that plagued him. He looked world-weary, as if he was tired of fighting so hard to be what he wasn't. Or perhaps he was tired of living a life with no direction. Perhaps he was tired of her.

He was looking at her with a look that said that he still didn't know what to do with her. She reached up to touch his cheek, because something inside her said she had to.

Or perhaps it was something inside him that called out to her. Whatever, she sensed the need to touch him. Her fingers drifted along his strong square jaw, bristled with a few days' beard. She started to touch his lips, but his hand whipped up to grasp her wrist very hard and still it.

The cynic was there, looking down at her, hard and bitter and reclusive. But there was something else; some of the brittle edge was gone, and she could sense that he was forcing it.

"There are times, hellion, when I look into your face and I'd wager I can see clear to Kingdom Come."

Her eyes grew misty and she tilted her head, so desperately wanting more from him than he appeared able or willing to give.

The mockery in his expression faded, a chink in the wall that showed a small snatch of what was behind it: utter and absolute despair.

"Please," she whispered, knowing she needed to

help him somehow but unable to know exactly what
it was he needed from her.

Neither of them moved.

"Please."

His hard look softened, as if hearing her plea was
more than he could handle. With a low moan of defeat, he gripped her head in both hands and covered
her mouth with his, and this time there was no violence to his touch.

His hands loosened their grip on her head and
combed through her hair to cup the back of her head
in his palms. His tongue traced her mouth, and she
opened to him. He stole her very breath the way so
many years before he had stolen her heart and given
her dreams and wishes and hopes.

Yet no dream, no fanciful wish, no bedchamber
door or down bed pillow could ever be as wonderful
as the reality of a kiss so intimate. She'd never have
imagined a more deliciously wicked thing than this
kiss. She could taste him, and his flavor was sweeter
than those honeybuns she always sneaked.

He tasted . . . male and necessary, as if he was something she must have to be fully a woman. It was a kiss
in which lips and mouths and tongues melded, while
his hands held her possessively—as if she belonged
to him.

A wish so great, so wonderful, so unimaginable that
she had never even chanced to dream of it. The ultimate fantasy: that he truly wanted her to be his.

She knew with her soul she would never again be
the same person, dream the same dreams. In her
whimsical mind she had wished for his kiss to be her
first. Now she wished for her kiss to be his last.

Warning bells went off in her head. *Watch what you
wish for . . .*

His claim sped to the very heart of her, and her

youthful yearnings—seeming so naive now—faded like yesterday's dream.

"Well ... well ..."

Richard froze. His mouth left hers with a lurid curse.

Letty peered around Richard's shoulder to the doorway, where Hamish leaned against the doorjamb with his arms crossed. He grinned wickedly.

"So you have gotten her tongue."

Chapter

12

Two days later in Wiltshire, England

*T*he Duke and Duchess of Belmore were at home, awaiting the birth of their first child, when a rider—a man with hair as bright as a ha'penny beneath his beaver hat—thundered through the iron gates of Belmore Park, clutching a handful of good-luck charms. In a breathless flash, he jumped two hedgerows and reined in his mount scant inches from the front stone steps of the manse.

For years the estate had been a somber, regimented cavern of a house, where everything was as rigid as Cromwell's laws, where love had never been, and probably never would have been, had not the Mac-Lean, one very powerful Scottish witch, stepped in and made a little matchmaking magic between her niece, Joyous MacQuarrie, an inept but endearing half-witch, and Alec Castlemaine, Duke of Belmore.

The rider dismounted and the massive front doors opened to a flood of footmen: one to take his mount, one to hold the door, and one to escort the Viscount Seymour directly into the His Grace's study.

Neil Herndon, Viscount Seymour, dubbed by his friends as the most superstitious man on English soil, tucked the amulets and charms back into his vest pocket and pulled off his gloves, tossing them and his hat to Henson, Belmore's head footman. Then he followed the other servant, his bootheels clicking across the marble floors.

He entered the study just as the Duke of Belmore rose to meet him.

"Alec." Seymour greeted his friend. "Your message said you've word on Richard."

"Come, sit. I received a ransom demand in the middle of the night."

"A ransom? Thank God." Neil sank into a deep leather chair, relief all over his face. He propped his elbows on his knees and stared at the design in the carpet for an emotional moment. He raised his head and sagged back in the chair, his look meeting the duke's. "At least he's bloody well alive."

Richard Lennox, Earl of Downe, was their closest friend and had been for over twenty years. His disappearance had only been noted in the last few days, when no one could locate the earl after he'd ridden away from his estate in the middle of the night. With no word, those left behind suffered the weak human reaction of imagining the worst in spite of their best efforts to do otherwise.

Alec handed him the note. "Here. Read this."

Neil scanned the letter. "It's written in Richard's hand."

Alec nodded and sat in a nearby chair. "I've read the thing a hundred times at least, looking for some code from Richard to give us an idea where he is.

Something ... misspelled words, anything. But there's nothing."

"It says I'm to deliver the money Saturday night on Lundy Isle. Do you suppose that's where they are?"

"I don't know. Could be. I've sent a message to the authorities but haven't heard anything. I'll send another messenger if I don't hear anything by tomorrow morning. They need to send an excise cutter over the night before the drop. It can sneak in under cover of night, anchor in a hidden cove, and surround the drop sight."

Nodding, Neil looked up. "He names me specifically to make the delivery."

"It has to be you. You have the sloop and always were the best sailor of the three of us. Also, I think he knows that I cannot, and will not, leave Scottish alone now." Not much more than a year before a look of tenderness would have never crossed the Duke of Belmore's face. But it was there now, and there whenever he mentioned his duchess.

Alec plucked a wedge of gingerbread off a nearby teatray and popped it into his mouth.

Neil eyed him a moment. "I thought you abhorred that stuff."

Alec shrugged and dusted the crumbs from his hands. "I seem to have acquired a taste for it of late."

"Curious. I was under the impression that females got cravings when they were increasing."

"Not if one's married to Scottish." Alec crammed some more gingerbread into his mouth and swallowed. "All of her cravings seem to affect me as well. Strange, but I'd have never thought to try pickled eel and clotted cream with strawberries." He paused thoughtfully, then seemed to recover himself and looked at his friend. "Your gills are turning green, Seymour. Read on."

While Neil read, Alec stood up and walked over to pour them both a brandy. He handed one to Neil, who glanced up from the page, a question in his eyes. "The girl? What girl?"

Alec raised his own glass in a mock salute. "Take a drink first, then read on."

It took only one minute for the Viscount Seymour to choke on his brandy. He coughed, and his eyes bulged slightly. He looked up and cleared his throat enough to say, "Downe is kidnapped with the Hornsby hellion?"

He and Alec exchanged identical telling looks. There was a brief moment of silence, then they both began to laugh.

Alec bit back his laughter. "You realize that if he saw us right now he'd use that punishing right cross of his on both our jaws."

"True, but that has never stopped us before."

"This is serious. We should—Seymour, stop crowing—make an effort to treat this with the concern it deserves," Alec said, trying to look serious and failing miserably.

"Yes, life-threatening ... considering who he's with." And Neil burst into another round of laughter.

While Neil still chuckled to himself, Alec reached out and gave the bellpull a quick jerk, and a moment later a servant knocked. He sent the gingerbread tray away, then paused and ordered brussel sprouts, buttermilk, and marzipan. He turned to Neil. "Do you want anything?"

His face took on a sick look. "I seem to have lost my appetite."

Alec shrugged, then crossed the room and hitched his hip on the edge of his desk. He stared at the note. "I wonder how he managed to get himself into this fix."

"More than likely he was foxed." Neil stared at his brandy glass with a distant look, then frowned and set it down. "Wouldn't mind being a fly on the wall so I could watch the goings-on, though. Downe and the Hornsby hellion." He shook his head, then looked at Alec. "Did you contact the chit's father?"

"I tried. He's gone on some Roman field dig in the north. He wasn't expected back for a few weeks. Seems the servants called in the local constable when the girl turned up missing, and messages were sent to both her father and to some aunt in London, but there's been no word." Alec braced a hand on the desk and leaned over to open a drawer. He took out a bulky leather money sack and dropped it on the desktop. "This is the money for both of them."

Neil nodded, then stood up and stretched. "I shall leave now. I doubt I could stomach the sight or scent of your next tray, and it will take a day to get to the coast and another to ready the sloop."

Alec rose. "I'll have the authorities contact the port officials at Bideford. I expect you shall hear from them in the next day or so. Let me know what they intend to do." His face showed he was torn between wanting to be there for his friend and needing to be home for his wife.

"Downe understands."

Alec nodded and looked for a long time at a huge portrait of his duchess that hung above the fireplace.

"By the time I get there, I daresay, I'll either have turned into a six-bottle man or he'll be sober as a nun. If it's the latter, that might be the best thing that's ever happened to him."

"Perhaps ..." Alec said, his voice fading into a thought. "But perhaps not." He stared at the portrait

160

for a long time, then added, "We seem to have forgotten something."

"What? Splints for his broken bones?"

Alec gave a slight smile but shook his head, then his look lost any levity. "I wonder what this will do to him."

"What?" Neil frowned. "The note claims he's not harmed."

"No, he's not. But the Hornsby girl's reputation is. She is undeniably and absolutely compromised." Alec looked at Neil's stunned face. "You know that he'll have no choice. He has to marry her."

Rising out of the Channel sea like the bruised arm of an angry Neptune was a stark gray rock called Lundy Isle. At first glance, Letty thought it appeared desolate, little more than a long, seemingly treeless plateau forced to bear the moods of wind and sea.

But as the longboat rowed closer to the southern tip of the isle, there were snatches of pink and mauve where wild rhododendrons huddled in the wrinkles of the rock, and a lone pine tree beckoned from a promontory point that was shielded from strong gusty breaths of westerly wind.

Behind them, anchored in a blue-green cove, sat the privateer, its sails battened and its masts little more than spiky fingers that bobbed against the afternoon sky. Gulls wheeled across that same sky, crying and diving, then lighting on a pebbly beach where they paced across a small ribbon of glittering sand like anxious hosts.

The pirate Dion knelt at the bow of the boat while a pudgy red-haired man with darting black eyes rowed. Letty and Richard and Gus sat between them, and Hamish lounged languidly at the stern of the longboat, his pistol drawn and his face in that perpetual droll smirk.

One final oarstroke and the boat rode a wave of sea wash into a sheltered cove where its bow thudded onto the beach. Gus shot over the rim of the boat and loped toward the gulls, kicking up clumps of wet sand and glossy ropes of kelp in his wake. The gulls cried in protest and flapped into the air, then tauntingly glided above him, just out of his reach.

Dion and Hamish exchanged a look that Letty didn't understand, then Dion gave a slight nod of his head.

Hamish leapt from the boat and waved his pistol. "Come, little gillyflower. As much as I would love to keep you, Dion won't allow me any toys." He leaned down toward her, that familiar scent of cloves following him. He chucked her under the chin with the barrel of the pistol. "Such a shame."

Richard looked ready to go for the bigger man's throat barehanded, and Letty instinctively grabbed his arm.

Lightning-quick, Hamish aimed the pistol at Richard.

Dion stood up quickly and pinned Richard with a cold stare. "Don't be a fool."

Letty could see the battle on Richard's face. Everything about him, from his tight jaw to his tensed stance, said he wanted to fight, that he didn't want to quietly succumb to whatever it was these men wanted. He was protecting her, instinctively, without even trying, and she doubted he even realized it. But she loved him even more for it.

She tightened her fingers on his arm, trying desperately to get his attention before he did do something utterly foolish. Slowly, Richard pulled his gaze away from cocky Hamish and looked down at her.

The plea in her eyes must have made him see reason, because he stepped stiffly from the boat and held out his hand to her, never once saying a word. But he didn't have to. His rigid silence was as powerful as words.

She stepped from the boat onto the beach and found herself pinned protectively against him by his strong arm, and they stood there on a lonely beach together, facing their captors.

Hamish gave the island a cursory glance, then said, "You and Galahad have your own little paradise." He placed his hands on his hips and laughed a big booming bellylaugh that was louder than the pounding surf, the crying gulls, and Gus's baying.

Then he stepped back into the boat, looked at the red-haired man, and said, "Row, Weasel."

"You're just going to leave us here?" Letty couldn't believe they would just abandon them on a deserted strip of an island in the middle of Bristol Channel.

Dion reached beneath him and tossed a bulky sack at their feet. "Once the ransom is paid, your friends will be told where to find you."

She tried to take a step, but Richard held her tightly against his side.

"Be still, hellion."

She looked up at Richard, confused. A part of her—her heart—wanted to stay close to him. Yet part of her wanted desperately to bring to an end this journey that she had foolishly imagined to be an adventure. At home everything might be dull and familiar, but in reality smugglers and pirates and ransoms were not as romantic as she had thought.

Like a young bird that has fallen from its nest, she stood there disoriented and bewildered. She looked from Dion to Hamish. "You promised to take us home. . . ."

Dion was silent as a stone.

As the longboat rocked through a wave, Hamish looked from Richard to her and shouted, "Perhaps, little gillyflower, you are closer to home than you know." He gave them a mocking salute with the pistol, then the boat cut swiftly through the surf.

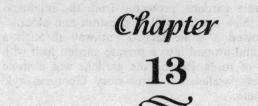

Chapter
13

The Viscount Seymour stumbled up the steep stony path that led from Lundy's dock to the residence of the island's owner and local magistrate, Sir Vere Hunt. Seymour paused to catch his wind and looked down at the harbor below. Five small outbuildings formed the only thing Lundy could come close to claiming as a village, and on the opposite side of the bay's small dock, an ancient fishing boat and a small sleek yawl were moored across from his sloop.

From his position on the high path he could see down Lundy's craggy northern coastline, a seemingly never-ending monolith of shale cliffs above white ribbons of seafoam and deep blue-green water. The wind picked up, swirling around him, ruffling his red hair and carrying along the doleful calls of sea auks and puffins that roosted in the cliffside cracks.

Seymour pulled up the collar of his coat and struggled up the last few hundred feet of the steep cliff. At its crest, the path led to a long carpet of rich lawn and elaborate gardens, protected from the relentless wind by a thick natural wall of chestnut and alder.

He followed a stone-flagged pathway through a hedgerow and around into a private garden lush with a rainbow of roses. Behind the gardens was a stone terrace that paralleled a three-story Georgian-style country home.

Sparkling in the late-day sun was a long line of white French doors that ran like a bright smile of welcome across the back of the house. Color bloomed profusely from the numerous flower urns that framed the terrace and stood guard near the stone steps. Unlike the dismally dark townhomes in London, Seymour's own included, this house would be filled with sunlight and color.

There was a warmth to a home like this. Every corner of the gardens, every nook, had something joyous and special, something there to make one smile: A statue of a woman lovingly holding her child was mounted near the rim of a small rock-edged lily pond. A fountain in the form of a frog with a crown atop his head spilled water into a pool, where ducklings dipped and fluttered and quacked. Trellises dripping in pink and red fuschias formed a welcoming arch at the garden's entrance, and beneath the lush shade of a sprawling English oak, larks and turtle doves frolicked in a birdbath until a shiny black crow swooped in with a loud caw and chased the lilting birds away.

In the sudden flicker of nature's silence he heard another song: the melodic voice of a woman humming Pachelbel. He turned toward the rose garden, where a tall thick bush shimmied like Prinny's chins. Seymour stepped beneath the tree, where he had an unobstructed view.

A young woman was bent over the other side of the shimmying rosebush, trimming it with a pair of garden shears. Every few seconds, as her song reached a high note, a branch of the bush would fly with lilting fervor over her shoulder, to land behind her in a haphazard pile of clippings.

Watching her tend her garden with such pleasure made him smile. She hit a high C, and a sucker limb plopped onto the clippings pile, where a basket of kittens tugged at a bright yellow ball of yarn and nipped at the lace on her bobbing hemline.

The top of her head wouldn't reach his chin, and she had glossy black hair that gleamed like crow's feathers in the late afternoon sun. Her face was in profile, beautifully sculpted, a cameo come to life.

As if coated with pearls, her skin had a subtle tinge of luminescence. Nature's kind hand had blessed her with a delicate nose and chin, full cranberry-red lips that rose into a slight smile when she cupped a lush silvery-gray rose and brought it close enough to revel in the scent.

It was a face that proved God's perfection.

"I say there!" he called out, impulsively eager.

The young woman stiffened, her gaze darting to his and showing sheer panic. She gasped and slapped a hand up to cover half her face, but not before Seymour saw the ragged red-violet scar that sliced diagonally across one otherwise perfect cheek.

Time stood as awkwardly still as they did. Finally she shifted slightly, so her scarred cheek was again hidden from view. She had moved subtly, smoothly, as if the protective motion was instinctive, then she let her hand fall away with a kind of resigned despair. "Who are you and what are you doing here?"

He took a step toward her and she took a step back, her eyes filled with doelike panic. All the *joie de vivre* that had been in her was gone, her stance wooden and stiff. Breakable.

He wanted to tell her it didn't matter, but he couldn't find words that didn't sound cruelly trite, words she had most likely heard a thousand times.

"Daresay, didn't mean to frighten you," he mumbled finally, shoving his hands in his coat pockets. "I'm Viscount Seymour. Here to see Sir Hunt on an urgent matter."

"My father is at the stables." She signaled by pointing the shears in the direction of the sun. "On the western side of the house and across the drive." She spoke to the rosebush, her face averted and never rising enough to again meet his curious look.

She was too lovely to wear shame so heavily. He felt her burden as surely as if his back were bent from its weight.

He wanted to speak to her, but his power of speech had abandoned him. The moment was eternal, empty, and strikingly harsh. Finally he turned away, a little sadder because he didn't know what else to do or say. He walked pensively toward the western path, but he hadn't gotten far when he heard the sharp click of a door closing.

He stopped and turned, wanting a last glimpse of her. Like a miracle one must see twice to believe. But the spot by the rosebush was vacant. A haphazard pile of rose branches, an empty overturned basket, and a pair of discarded garden shears were the only signs she'd ever even been there. Those lonely things and the memory of the sweetest song he had ever heard.

His hungry gaze followed a path of crushed flowers and leaves that scattered across the terrace and stopped in front of one of the French doors. He looked at the door for the longest time, then murmured, "I'm sorry."

As if in answer to his words, the drape inched back. A dark figure stood behind the door, the person's identity safely hidden by the piercing glare of sunlight on the glass. But her small silhouette was unmistakable. She watched him.

Heedfully slow, he walked back to the rosebush, bent, and plucked off the very silvery rose she had cupped in her hand. He lifted the flower to his nose, then ever so casually to his lips.

He carefully slid the stem through a buttonhole on his coat lapel. The subtle tang of roses filled his senses, and the whisper of a smile touched his mouth.

Out of habit, he fingered the well-rubbed good-luck charms on his watch fob. His thoughtful gaze lit on the rose, then shifted to the charms in his hand. Perhaps fortune shined down on him. His smile grew from a whisper to a shout, and he walked toward the stables, whistling Pachelbel.

"What's inside the sack?"

"I have no idea," Richard said in a wry tone as he stopped untying the wad of knots in the bag's drawstring. He slowly looked over his shoulder at the hellion. She knelt behind him in the sand, her small hands braced on his shoulders while she tried to peer around him with eager anticipation.

"Perhaps you should let me open it. You're not doing it very quickly."

"*Perhaps* if I didn't have to answer so many questions I could open it more quickly."

She cocked her head and gave him a gentle pat on the shoulder. "I didn't realize that you are unable to do two things at once."

He stared at her, trying to decide if she was being purposely obtuse. Her face was completely serious. He took an extra second to contemplate his answer, then a few minutes to contemplate her answer.

With a mocking wave of surrender, he sat back in

the sand and handed her the drawstrings. "Here, hellion. It's all yours."

She had untied the sack before he could rest an arm on his bent knee. "Oh . . . look!" Her voice was muffled because her head was buried inside the sack opening.

She sat up, laughing with delight, and pushed her tousled hair away from her eyes. Her face was flushed pink, and there was a sparkle in her eyes that almost convinced him there truly was treasure inside that old sea-stained hopsack.

A breeze drifted by and carried with it her fading laughter. But her smile lingered behind, bright and warm and refreshing. He had never known that a smile could carry so much power just because it was honest and unaffected.

Her charm held no artifice, and a thought came to him in the form of a revelation. What he beheld at that moment was true beauty; not beauty that was only physical—the perfect nose, the heart-shaped face, flawless skin, and a mouth that a man could die in— but something much rarer, so rare in fact he hadn't known such a thing existed until this moment.

She had beauty of spirit.

It was rather unsettling to realize that he, who reveled in his own worldliness, could be ignorant of anything. But he was sorrowfully ignorant when it came to her.

Such a foreign thing it was, deriving quiet pleasure from just watching her. But he did, and he smiled, because, for some reason he preferred not to analyze, he couldn't bloody well stop himself.

He sat there in the sand, taking in her expressive motions, her every look, through jaded eyes that were starved for something fresh and unknown.

He tried to remember how long it had been since

he'd enjoyed simply watching a woman be herself. And he wasn't certain he had ever known a woman who had been completely and refreshingly herself.

At least none of the women he'd known intimately—a thought that forced him to admit something he'd known for a while. His personal life had turned stale.

His gaze shifted to the hellion. She had her head buried in that sack one minute, and the next she was smiling with delight at some new treasure. He rubbed his chin thoughtfully, then wondered what it would be like to be with a woman who wasn't bedding his title.

His mind played with another unknown, something he'd never experienced or even contemplated before: whether there could be pleasure with someone who knew nothing of the sexual act. The women he had been with couldn't spell "virgin" much less remember when they'd been one.

Virginity was saved for marriage, and he had only one married friend, Alec, Duke of Belmore. His wife, Joy, was an original and a pleasure to be around, if one could avoid her pet weasel. And he supposed she was the only woman besides the hellion he would call refreshing.

But he didn't know Joy intimately. If he had, Alec would have killed him. He looked at the hellion. He didn't exactly know her intimately either. However, that could be easily corrected.

He watched her laugh and had the insane thought that he'd probably kill anyone who touched her, anyone who soiled the joy in that laughter. Anyone who would hurt her.

Except perhaps himself.

Odd, wasn't it, that when he looked at her now he saw the young woman, the female ready for a man. A body with lush curves and shadowed cleavage, a long white neck—the pathway to a mouth so sensual he ached from just looking at it. The memory of shapely calves, blue-ribboned garters, and soft pale thighs exposed in the sunlight—a sensual pathway of another more carnal sort.

Yes, he looked at the hellion ... and thought of seduction.

He'd sunk to a new low.

One by one she had pulled out a round of cheese, some dried meat, two loaves of dark bread, fruit, a tin of biscuits, a jug of cider, and other food similar to that which they'd been fed aboard the second ship.

The hunger he was feeling, however, had nothing to do with food.

She's fragile and you'll hurt her.

Yes, he could hurt her, and that thought told him he hadn't reached bottom yet. A long-lost remnant of conscience existed within his dark, bleak soul. Somewhere.

But he had to ask himself how long it would last. He had no answer. For the first time in days he felt the need to hide in the numbing effects of a barrel of brandy, rum, gin, wine—anything that would skew his world for a while.

But there was no drink to be found. Instead, he found himself looking at her again, because he had to. His gaze locked on her mouth. God, what a mouth.

Some sane part of him knew she was completely unaware of the battle going on inside him. She was too busy with her treasures, and even if she weren't, she wouldn't have known, because she was too innocent.

And she's too young.

She's nineteen. Old enough.

She's too naive.

She's ready, perhaps too ready. He cursed the scarcity of his morals—that he could look at her and think what he was thinking.

She carefully placed the last food item on her skirt and then casually glanced up at him. She gave him a smile, one that would melt a reserve made from granite. A soft look that would test the celibacy of a monk.

And he was no monk. He shifted to his knees and started to move toward her, his blood too hot and his eyes locked on her mouth, his mind buzzing an aching need.

Selfish bastard.

The hellhound came bounding up the beach, tongue lolling out his floppy mouth, his gait anything but graceful. He skidded to a gangly stop, sending a shower of sand over Richard.

The sand had the same effect as a pail of cold water. He froze and pulled his gaze away from her, shaking his head. Sand rained down around him. Sand was in the creases of his breeches. Sand was in the tops of his boots. Sand was in his waistband, and he could feel the grit of it.

He closed his eyes for a moment and took a deep, calming breath. When he opened his eyes he felt distanced, almost as if he were on the outside looking into a locked room for which he had no key.

Gus stuck his nose under her arm, sniffing, and stretched halfway to the closest loaf of bread. She grabbed it, holding it safely out of his reach, and frowned down at the hound, whose big head was still stuck under her arm while his bloodshot eyes peered up at her longingly.

"You couldn't possibly be hungry *again*," she said.

Aboard the second ship, Gus had managed to steal Richard's dried meat, some of his bread, all of his cheese, and an apple. Any food the earl had eaten consisted only of those things he could successfully hide from Gus.

"You've eaten plenty today," she said.

Gus whimpered and pulled his head out from under her arm as if she were a traitor. He took two hangdog steps, and as soon as he was out of her sight, he crawled around to her other side, slowly slinking toward the pile of fruit.

Richard reached for him.

The dog moved in a flash of brown, then looked up and grinned wickedly around a plump red apple. Warned by animal instinct, Gus darted a quick look at Richard and then took off down the beach.

Richard shot up and went after him, running faster and faster, kicking up his own trail of sand as he went. His speed had nothing to do with the dog. Or the apple.

It had everything to do with his conscience. He was running away from her and away from what he might have done, running away from his thoughts and what he was.

The cool wind from the sea went over and through him, but in spite of it his skin grew hot and clammy. Sweat began to pour down his face.

He couldn't remember the last time he'd run, if he had ever done so as an adult. He'd had a lifetime of running away—figuratively, not physically. But now he just ran, pounding down the beach as the waves pounded on the shore, his arms and legs pumping as fast as his blood. Harder. Faster. Rescuing her from himself.

His heart throbbed first in his ears, then in his burning chest, where air and breath were tight and almost nonexistent. But he ran on, laughing suddenly and painfully, for he had discovered the ultimate irony.

He was a bloody hero.

Chapter

14

Seymour leaned over the map atop a desk and watched Sir Hunt point out the location of the ancient chapel. According to the note, the ransom exchange was to take place there tomorrow night.

"The chapel is on the southwestern tip of the island," Hunt was saying. "About a mile from Beacon Hill."

"Beacon Hill?" Seymour repeated. "The port authority said there was no lighthouse on Lundy."

"There isn't. The foundations were laid for a beacon, but the merchants who funded it went bankrupt last year. Lost everything in a shipwreck off this very coast. We're still using cannons to warn approaching ships. The fog comes in and eighteen-pounders are fired every ten minutes off the three major points on the island."

"I see." Seymour stared at the map. He wondered if perhaps Downe and the girl were already somewhere on the island. "Is there any location you can think of where someone could keep them prisoner? Anywhere near this chapel?"

There are secluded bays and inlets all along the island's coast. There are too many caves to count, too many bays in which they could moor."

Seymour stared at the map, lost in thought.

"You did say the excise cutter would arrive tonight?"

"So they told me. The ship planned to leave the coast at Bideford with the midnight tide, cross the Channel, and moor in a secluded bay near the drop sight." Seymour scanned the map, looking at the bays near the ruins.

"There are three bays near that point." Hunt showed him the map. "Here, there, and this one called Devil's Slide. It's about a mile from the cannon gunpoint."

Seymour straightened and glanced at the tall clock. "I suppose there's nothing to do now but wait until tomorrow. The men aboard the cutter have instructions to surround the drop. I was told they would report to you first thing tomorrow."

Hunt nodded. "We have plenty of rooms. There's no need for you to stay on your sloop when you can wait more comfortably here."

The image of an incredibly lovely face flashed through Seymour's mind. She was here. Somewhere.

"I'm certain you'll want to talk to the excise militia when they arrive," Hunt continued. "It would be more convenient to use my home as your base. I don't relish these barbarians using my island as part of their schemes."

"Perhaps that would be more convenient." He gave Sir Hunt his first genuine smile.

"I'll send someone for your things. Do you have a crew?"

"Just two others. They'll be more comfortable on-board."

A discreet knock, and the library door opened to a butler who announced tea.

"Has Giana come down?" Hunt asked.

The butler looked pointedly from Seymour to Hunt and replied, "I don't believe so, sir."

"My daughter usually joins me for tea." Hunt paused and looked to be contemplating some silent inner battle. There was tension in his stance, a tightness in his voice that hadn't been there a moment before. He was a tall man, and yet he suddenly looked smaller and terribly weary. A man with a burden. Quietly he added, "I suppose I should prepare you to meet her. Usually makes things less awkward."

There was an eloquent pause, and Seymour had an idea what was coming. "I spoke with your daughter. She gave me your direction."

"You spoke with Giana?" Hunt straightened in surprise.

"Yes."

"Unusual." Hunt's face creased with a puzzled frown. "She normally avoids callers."

"I took the cliff path from the dock, and am afraid I came upon her in the rose garden quite by surprise."

"Then you understand that I needed to warn you."

Seymour looked him square in the eye. "No. Don't believe I do." He stood a little taller himself and said, "Your daughter is the most exquisite woman I have ever clapped eyes on." He heard the harsh element of challenge in his voice, and social etiquette forced him to add, "That is, unless you intended to warn me of her unique beauty."

Hunt looked dumbfounded for a moment, then he studied Seymour with a father's critical eye.

They stood in the elegantly appointed library, each

taking in and weighing the other's measure. The only sounds in the room were the ticking of a tall clock and the occasionally snapping of a dry log in the fireplace.

Hunt broke the tension with a bark of relieved laughter. "Yes, young man, I do believe you are right." He turned to the butler, whose cool aloofness had melted slightly. "Tell Giana I should like her to join us."

The butler left, then Hunt turned back and clapped Seymour on the shoulder. "Come along, Seymour. I do believe you should formally meet my stubborn Giana. Should be interesting. Very interesting."

Letty huddled deeper under the blankets wrapped around her shivering shoulders and glanced around the dark sea cave. It wasn't very deep, and it was cold and damp. Sand and rock formed the floor, and the jagged rock walls seemed to magnify every sound. A trickle of fresh water meandered like a vein of sparkling silver down one wall and pattered rhythmically into a small rock basin.

In the distance, she could hear the boom of the surf hitting the shore. It sounded loud as thunder and just as wild and untamable. She'd always thought the sea a power with which to be reckoned, but now, with nothing but rock and sand and sea around her, she felt as if she were just a drop of fresh water surrounded by the sea. Small. Inconsequential.

Pulling the blanket even tighter around her shivering shoulders, she glanced at Gus, who was sound asleep in a dark corner, his belly full of apples and half a loaf of stolen bread, and his body exhausted from harassing the island's bird population—and Richard.

For the hundredth time since the dense fog had crawled onshore, she looked at the cave opening with an uneasy feeling. There was nothing to see but white dense mist, clouds that kept the world away, nature's cold wet breath.

Richard was out in that. Somewhere. He was collecting driftwood for a fire, but he'd been gone a terribly long time.

So she waited quietly, cold and alone. Finally she closed her eyes and leaned back against a cave wall, trying to imagine she was home, in her room, with a warm fire and burrowed underneath down coverlets and sipping the rich sweetness of hot chocolate.

His curse was the first thing she heard. A stumbling footstep the second.

"Can't see a bloody damn thing."

She opened her eyes just as he materialized like some Celtic demon from a cloud of damp eerie mist. He seemed taller, somehow, perhaps because the cave ceiling was so low, or perhaps because the reality of him was so much more overwhelming.

Standing there with his arms full of driftwood, he scanned the interior of the cave, then stopped when he saw her. There was such isolation in the look he gave her, cold and bleak, as if he had been suddenly shorn of a heart and deserted by any kinder emotion.

His hardened gaze was on her mouth, and she parted her lips, taking a deep breath. He flinched as if he'd been hit.

"Is something wrong?" She frowned, not knowing how to respond to his intensity. The surf echoed in the distance, but it was calm compared to the way her heartbeat thundered in her ears.

"No," he said, his face like stone, nary a thing to be read there. He pulled his gaze away and closed the distance between them. He knelt, letting the wood fall from his arms, then he began to stack the wood for a fire. He used some flint and lit the wood, fanning it until they truly had a small fire.

"Here," she said and held out one of the blankets, feeling awkward and out of place.

He straightened to his full height and turned, looking down at her. In his wind-ruffled hair, droplets of water caught the glimmer of firelight and misty fog that was behind him, seeming to almost glow. A halo for an angel who had fallen from grace.

She shivered again—not exactly from the cold air, but the coldness she saw in his eyes. They say the eyes are the mirror to one's soul, but she'd never believe that Richard was the lost soul he thought he was. He had to work too hard at it.

He was staring now at the blanket in her outstretched hand. His look shifted to her shivering shoulders and slightly chattering teeth. He shook his head. "You use it."

"But—"

"Don't argue with me, dammit!"

She stiffened, caught off guard by the sharpness in his voice. "What have I done?"

He wouldn't look at her. Instead he stared at the fire. After an eternity he said, "It's not you. It's me."

"Can't I help?"

He looked at her and his eyes grew cynical, then he laughed. "If you knew what was bothering me, you wouldn't ask." He seemed so distant. He stared at nothing, at everything, then he looked at her and said, "Go to sleep."

She wanted to help, but she couldn't if he refused to tell her what was wrong. Huddling down into the blankets, she lay down on her side facing the fire and rested her head on one bent arm. She watched the flames lick the air, wishing she were warmer.

The fog drifted inside and mixed with the smoke to

make the air glow in an eerie, misty light that looked unreal. She closed her eyes and tried to get warm, to think warm. Even pulling the blankets tighter didn't stop her teeth from chattering, and her knees and shoulders from shivering. She was so cold, and lying on the bare ground made it seem even colder.

She knew the moment he looked at her. She felt him watch her for the longest time, felt it when he shifted and moved. His boots crunched across the pebbled floor of the cave. A second later he stood over her. She held her breath, then released it when he knelt beside her.

The next thing she knew he was lying alongside her, his larger and longer body providing a shield of human warmth. He pulled her against him, his arms holding her firmly, his warm breath in her hair. "Better?"

She only nodded, because she couldn't speak with her heart in her throat. And she lay in his arms, listening to the fire pop and snap, picking up the scent of wood in the damp air, watching the flames draw flickering shadows on the cave walls.

She might have been frightened from the shadows had she been alone. But she wasn't alone. For some reason his being there was almost as warming as the heat from his body. It was the most marvelous feeling, knowing he was there for her. She couldn't imagine what it would be like to have him there for her all the time, whenever she needed him.

She felt the rise and fall of his chest against her back, his hips cupping her, his legs along hers. She adored the feel of him, the closeness, taking in his scent, experiencing the thrilling whisper of every breath he took.

Her heart felt like a star inside her, burning so brightly she had the fanciful thought that she might glow from it. "Thank you," she whispered.

He grunted a response.

She shifted slightly, her body wriggling naturally closer to his warmth.

She sighed.

He groaned.

"Am I crowding you?"

There was a long silent pause, then his only answer was to slide his arm tighter around her waist. It was enough of an answer for her. She smiled, and her eyes drifted closed to the snapping of the fire, the distant pounding of the waves, and the soft silly sound of Gus's snore. But the last thing she heard was the most soothing: a voice as wonderfully sweet and smooth as hot chocolate.

"Go to sleep, hellion."

The fog was even thicker in the Bristol Channel, where a blue smuggling lugger listed to one side from a canvas-patched hole and limped through the dirty weather with no direction—except the same wide circle in which it had been sailing for hours.

"Can't see a bleedin' thing." Phelim stood on the bridge and turned the helm, completely unaware that he'd just steered the ship in a new direction. He scowled at the panorama of white fog and grumbled, "Turn yer eyes on the compass, Bertie, and give me some sense of direction."

"Give ye a sense of direction?" Philbert said low enough to escape Phelim's ears, then sniffed. "An' while I'm doing that I'll fly from the ship on fairy wings and tiptoe me way t' shore."

Phelim scowled at his brother. "Don't stand around like ye've cannonballs in yer boots!"

"Better than cannonballs in yer head," Philbert mumbled.

"Read the bleedin' compass!" Phelim paused, then added, "It always points north."

"I kin figure out how it works." Philbert stared at the compass in his hand as if it were growing a head. "The needle's spinning."

"The Devil take ye, Bertie. Hold the bloomin' helm and give me the blasted thing!" Phelim snatched the compass from his brother's hand and repeated, "The needle's spinning ... Hah! What kind of an idiot do you take me for?"

"Most likely the idiot ye be."

A mouthful of inventive curses drowned out everything but the sound of Phelim stomping across the cabin. He moved nearer the ship's lantern hanging from an iron hook above the door and held the compass up to the dim light, squinting at it.

The door flew open with a *thwack!*

Unfortunately, the *thwack* was Phelim's head hitting the wall.

Phineas froze, the door in one hand. He looked across the room at Philbert, who was wincing.

A brass compass hit the wooden floor with a loud *clunk* and rolled out from behind the doorway. With a look of dread on his weather-crinkled face, Phineas hesitantly peered around the door.

Phelim stood between the door and the wall, wobbled slightly, his face dazed, his eyes glassy and distant before they rolled back as he slowly slid down the wall.

Phineas looked at his unconscious brother and chewed uneasily on a fingernail, then gave a resigned sigh. "He'll be vexed over this one."

"Ye think so?" Philbert asked in a droll tone. "Can't think why bashin' his hard head with a door might vex him."

"What say we don't tell him," Phineas suggested,

then glanced at Phelim. "Do ye think he'll remember?"

Philbert shook his head.

"Do ye think he's hurt?"

"I'd wager an iron door couldn't hit Phelim hard enough to hurt him."

"True," Phineas agreed with a nod as he continued to stare at his unconscious brother. Then he turned to Philbert. "I come t' tell ye that Harry's taken lookout near the bow."

"Could he see anything?"

"T'aint nothing t' see but dirty weather," Phineas said. "Though Harry swears 'tis better to face fogs and storms, bloody pirates, and a hundred hungry sharks than that one female again."

The sound of thunder rumbled in the distance.

"Did ye hear that?" Phineas said. "Figure there's one corker of a storm brewing."

"Sounds like yer stomach again t' me."

"T'aint me stomach. Hain't had a thing t' eat. 'Tis a raging thunderstorm, I tell ye!"

"Then tell me something else, Brother. If there be a storm ... why isn't this ship rocking?"

Phineas scratched his head.

"Ye can't have fog *and* a storm." Philbert stared out the helm gallery at the foggy mist beyond.

The thunder rumbled again.

"Cannon t' the left of me!" came a shout.

Both brothers turned, caught off guard.

Phelim stood before them, one arm out of his dangling shirt sleeve and the other arm brandishing a grappling iron as if it were an admiral's saber. He squinted one eye. "Cannon t' the right of me!"

Philbert groaned. "Not Nelson again."

"God save the King and roast the frogs! Man

the gunports, load the balls, and fire the eighteen-pounder!"

"That does sound like cannonfire," Philbert said thoughtfully.

" 'Tis a thunderstorm," Phineas argued.

"No. 'Tis cannon."

"Thunder."

"Cannon."

The booming grew louder.

Two minutes later the limping ship crashed into Lundy's rocky coast.

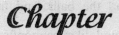

Chapter
15

The Duke of Belmore leaned against the open door to their sitting room and reveled in the pleasure of just watching his wife—the witch. Joyous Mac-Quarrie Castlemaine, Duchess of Belmore, stood in front a huge gilt mirror, frowning and making faces.

"No. That's not right," she muttered, tapping an impatient finger against her lips. "Let me see . . ." Joy threw her hands up into the air and took a deep breath. "Eye of newt! No . . . no . . . no . . . That's not right either." She lowered her voice an octave.

> *"Oh, powers that be,*
> *Please listen to me.*
> *I've lost my aunt,*
> *And find her I can't.*
> *Also missing is Beezle,*
> *My familiar—a weasel.*
> *And Gabriel too,*

186

DREAMING

A white cat with eyes of blue.
It's my wish on a star,
That I can see where they are!"

She waved her arms around in front of the mirror squeezed her eyes shut, then snapped her fingers.

The mirror fell off the wall.

"Oh, my goodness!" She stared at the fallen mirror for a moment, then scowled and gave her fists a couple of frustrated shakes. "I did it wrong again!"

"Good thing that mirror didn't break, Scottish. It would have given Seymour seven years' worth of gray hair."

She spun around, her hands covering her mouth. "Oh, Alec!" Her look turned sheepish. "I'm having a problem."

"I can see that." He gave the mirror a pointed look.

"Yes, well . . ." She paused, then quickly changed the subject. "Have you seen the MacLean?"

"Did you check the broom cupboard?"

"My aunt would fill your precious port bottles with ratafia for that comment."

"Before or after she stopped stirring her cauldron?"

"I'll have you know, Alec," she said, crossing her arms over her burgeoning belly and tapping a small foot, "there are times when I long for the days when you didn't have a sense of humor."

Alec crossed the room and stood behind her, sliding his arms around her and resting his hands on her bulging belly—the precious place where his future heir slept. He whispered into her ear. "No you don't, Scottish. I was a pompous ass."

She sighed. "Yes, you were, weren't you? But you were still a wonderful pompous ass."

He laughed a laugh that was no longer rusty, and

she leaned back against his chest and crossed her arms comfortably over his.

"Stephen's planting the new roses. I told him to plant the pink ones first."

She smiled.

"He's already begun to plant them, so I doubt we'll see him for a while."

"The garden will be lovely when he's finally finished," she said distractedly.

"I detect little enthusiasm in that response, Scottish. What's wrong?"

"I haven't heard one wee word from the MacLean in days."

"Knowing your aunt, I'd say she's probably out wreaking havoc on some poor unsuspecting mortal's life and future."

Joy sighed. "She does enjoy wielding her powers, especially if she can play Cupid. The only thing she finds as amusing are those silly wagers of hers."

Alec stiffened slightly. "I fail to find them as amusing as she does."

"That's because she goads you into them and you always lose."

He grumbled some response, then added, "Mary MacLean can well take care of herself. I doubt you have anything to worry over. She has popped in and out before."

"I know, but I suppose I'm more concerned than I would normally be because of this situation with Richard."

Alec was quiet for a moment, then said, "Seymour's taking the ransom to Lundy. He should be there by tomorrow."

She looked up into her husband's serious face. "I can hear the concern in your voice. You could go, Alec. I wouldn't mind."

He glanced down at her, his features unmoving. "I mind."

"I'm fine. Truly, I am."

"And I intend to make certain you stay that way."

"I wish the MacLean were here. She could get Richard back with just a snap of her fingers." Her voice trailed off as if she were uneasy. She added quietly, "I suppose I could try to cast my own traveling spell."

Alec cast a wary glance at the mirror. "I don't think you should, uh ... exert yourself in your condition, Scottish. It's going to take more than a magic spell to help Downe."

"You mean because of the Hornsby girl?"

He nodded.

"She loves him."

"I suppose she does. But Downe's not ready for marriage."

She gave a small snort of subtle laughter.

He looked down at her and frowned. "What is so humorous?"

"Alec. No man, especially one as stubborn as Richard, ever thinks he is ready for love, much less prepared for marriage."

In Alec's arms was the woman who had taught him what love was and who had loved him in spite of himself. He smiled down at her. "I suppose we need you women to knock some sense into us then, don't we?"

"Someone must do it. Left to your own devices, you men would never come 'round."

Alec began to laugh. "Then perhaps Downe could use some of your aunt's matchmaking magic. I can speak from experience when I say that if the MacLean and her Machiavellian witchcraft did become involved,

Richard would never know what in the bloody hell had hit him."

"Bloody hell!" Richard cursed, releasing the hellion. He shook his head in disbelief and sat upright. "Why did you hit me?"

"You told me to."

He scowled down at her, a distinct ringing in his ears and his head throbbing. He hadn't known one could go from sleepy passion to anger in the blink of eye—or, in this case, a bash on the head. His voice full of his disbelief, he repeated, "I told you to?"

"Yes, you did," she said in a stubborn tone. "On the smugglers' ship. I shall never forget it. You were very angry and told me I should have hit you for touching my breast that way."

He groaned and rubbed his sore head, his breath still passionately uneven. He'd been half asleep, her body pressed against his, and his touch had been instinctive.

She seemed to be searching his face for some answer. Hell, he had no answers to his own questions, much less hers.

"I didn't think hitting you was a particularly good idea," she admitted, still appearing to study him. "Now you look as if you want to hit something yourself."

"Where's Gus?"

"Richard!"

"Grrrrrrr." The low growl came from a corner of the cave. The beast was still asleep.

"I remember the Reverend Mrs. Poppit saying that violence breeds violence. If you strike someone, they'll strike back. It's instinctive ... human nature." She adjusted her clothing, then sat there in the uncomfortable silence plucking at her hem. Quietly, she said, "I would never have hit you if you hadn't said I should. You did tell me to do so."

"I know I did," he bit out in a terse voice, then picked up the piece of driftwood she'd dropped, scowling at it, because he didn't know what else to do. "I meant to slap me."

"You weren't specific. You said 'hit.' You didn't say what with."

"I didn't expect you to crack my head open with a piece of driftwood." He gave the wood one last look, then tossed it over his shoulder.

"You're angry with me again, aren't you?"

He sat there, his forehead resting on one hand as he stared down at nothing. He was angry, angry at himself, angry at his situation, angry at his past, but not truly angry at her.

"I'm not certain what I am anymore," he admitted, knowing he spoke the truth. He wanted her, yet he didn't want to want her. He felt things he didn't want to feel. He looked at her and saw in her his guilt, the poverty of his morals, and, even poorer, his inability to control his response to her.

"I only hit you to make you happy," she told him in that open, honest way she had, the one that made him aware that he was only using her.

She cocked her head, as if that way she could better understand him. He looked at her for a long time and had the grounding thought that perhaps she didn't need to understand him after all, but instead that what she needed was for him to understand her.

Half the time he didn't understand himself. And he wasn't certain he ever wanted to. He swore silently and looked away.

"The truth is," she said, "I didn't wish you to stop. I like it when you touch me that way. Makes my heart fly."

Unable to believe what he heard, he turned back to her.

She patted her chest. "In here. Actually I wish you'd touch my other breast because it feels so wonderful." She sighed. "As if I've swallowed warm butterflies."

Her dreamy words hit him like a pail of salt water. He pinned her with a hard look meant to quiet her. "Dammit! Would you stop that!"

She frowned, her face telling him that she didn't understand what she'd done wrong.

"God . . . Letty. Don't you have any pride?"

His words hung there, cruel and callous. The air grew stale with silence. There was raw pain in her expression, and it told him how completely he had just humiliated her.

As the seconds ticked by, his harsh words were an echo in his mind. He heard himself say them again and again. The only image he could picture was her face, and it was poignant with pain.

For the first time in his life he asked himself how he could have come to the point where it was easier to hurt someone than to care for them.

He looked at the hellion, searching for words that would win him forgiveness, the right words, but he was afraid that if he said anything at all it would only make things worse.

So he said nothing.

Instinct made him try to steel himself against the incredible and overwhelming sense of guilt he was feeling.

Her face crumpled and his chest tightened as if he'd been punched in it. She turned away, her bearing—the slump of her shoulders, her head bent in defeat—telling him more strongly than words that she could do nothing else at that moment but turn away, so great was her humiliation.

Bastard ... bastard ... bastard ...

Part of him, some humane part, wanted to go back in time, to swallow the cruel words he'd shouted at her. But it was too late. If there was one thing he knew, it was that words once spoken, cruel or not, could never be taken back.

She didn't look at him. He didn't blame her. He couldn't have looked at himself at that moment either.

When she spoke, it was softly, a voice barely audible for the wealth of her tears. "Yes, I have pride, but it really doesn't matter if I do or not." She took a breath, a deep breath that he heard shudder deep in her chest. It was the kind of breath that sounded as if her heart were struggling to keep its beat. She stared across the cave at nothing, her eyes sparkling with tears, tears he had caused.

"I think, Richard, that you have more than enough pride for both of us."

In the captain quarters of the privateer, Hamish leaned back in a chair with his boots propped atop the desk while he cleaned his fingernails with a dagger tip.

Dion stood in front of the bow windows, staring out at the channel seas. After a moment he turned and looked at Hamish, then gave a quick flick of one slim hand.

There was a flash of golden smoke. The puff of smoke slowly faded.

The elegant pirate had disappeared.

In his place stood a stunningly beautiful woman.

Long blond hair hung in a golden fall to her small waist. Her face was ageless: creamy white skin, perfect bones, and sharp gray eyes that appeared to miss little.

Five golden rings adorned her slim fingers, and she

wore a flowing white gown trimmed with matching golden threads. She also wore a devious and wicked little grin.

Hamish returned her look. "Ah, Mary MacLean, for a witch, you do that so very well."

She laughed. "To quote an infamous American warlock . . . I try."

The door opened, and Gabriel stepped into the cabin. The MacLean snapped her fingers, and he was suddenly transformed into a slim white cat. She picked up her familiar and gave him a stroke. "Where is that slothful weasel?"

The cat leapt from her arms and prowled over to rub against the door. The MacLean lifted a finger and moved it once. The door opened wide. A plump redhaired sailor was slumped against a wall . . . sleeping.

"Beezle!" she called sharply.

He twitched once, but didn't appear to wake up.

She snapped her fingers again, and he turned into a summer-red ermine weasel. The animal slowly opened one eye, then the other. He yawned, then slowly rose and waddled into the cabin only to plop down and fall back asleep next to Hamish's chair.

The MacLean stared at her niece's familiar and said, "Useless. Utterly and absolutely useless."

"Back to matters at hand." Hamish paused, then looked to the MacLean. "We've left them in the cove . . ."

"Aye."

"Taken care of the ransom note."

"Aye."

"Conjured up a little dirty weather."

"I must commend you on the fog, Hamish. 'Tis superbly thick. Weather has never been my strong suit."

There was a moment's pause, then he winked and

said, "I try." He sheathed the dagger and locked his hands behind his head. "What game is next?"

"We wait."

"I suspected as much. You never have told me why these two mortals."

"You wouldn't ask that if you would have seen them a year or so ago. Without a doubt my biggest challenge. Two more unlikely subjects you could not have imagined. Besides, I was bored at Belmore and, being friends of my new Sassenach nephew, they were handy." She flexed her fingers. "They were also English—a more hard-headed lot of mortals I've yet to meet. The perfect specimens with which I can keep my witchcraft sharpened."

"You should try your hand at wars, MacLean. I've always held fondness for them in my black heart."

"You can have your wars. I'll take romance."

"Must have been that Burns fellow. You've never been the same witch since you met him," he muttered. "But enough of the past. So what now?"

"We'll wait. No more games for a few days."

"I'd say Galahad looked about ready to succumb."

"He's a hard one, that earl. But if a few days stranded together in a deserted cove won't bring him 'round"—she smiled deviously—"only a little magic could."

Seymour stood in his host's drawing room, his hands locked behind him and disappointment on his face. He stared out the terrace doors at the thick night fog, then dismally shook his head. "The excise ship will never leave Bideford in this."

"No, I don't suppose they can," Hunt agreed. "There is the chance it could burn off by tomorrow night. But if not, I'll gather some of the help, and together we'll surround the drop."

Seymour turned around. "Are you certain you want to get involved in this?"

"As I said before, I don't relish anyone turning my land into a place for ransom exchanges, a haven for smuggling or kidnapping or any of the like. This is *my* home and my daughter's home. I need to know she's safe here. It's always been that way, and I won't allow that to change." Hunt joined him at the doors, a brandy in each hand. He handed him one.

Seymour took a drink, then turned back to the window. On the opposite terrace an eerie yellow light spilled from the windows above, where lamplight glowed through the mist, making the terrace look as if it were covered in golden clouds.

"I'm sorry Giana didn't join us for supper."

Giana, Seymour thought. He looked up and wondered which window was hers. Giana's.

"As I told you, she avoids strangers."

Seymour took a sip of brandy, never taking his eyes off the windows, then said, "This afternoon was difficult for her. Daresay I tried my damnedest." He gave a short laugh. "Felt like I was talking to the part in her hair."

"You were," Hunt said with a smile in his voice.

"I don't suppose she'll give me another opportunity."

There was a pause, then Hunt said, "Look. Outside."

A small figure walked out of one dark misty corner near the rose garden. She stepped into the golden light, wearing a deep midnight-blue cloak with a hood that hid her face.

Startled into action, Seymour set down the brandy and reached for the door handle.

Hunt stopped him with a hand on his arm. "I don't want her hurt."

"I have no intention of hurting her, and every intention of marrying her." Seymour returned the man's look. "With your permission, of course."

"You've convinced me, but most importantly, you must convince her. I won't force her."

A handful of good-luck charms clutched in one hand, Seymour opened the door and grinned. "You won't have to."

Chapter
16

*O*ut of the mist burst a familiar figure. The man paused in the cave entrance and brandished something that looked to Richard like a grappling iron.

"God save King George! Lead the way to ol' Boney!

The hellion sat up with the wide-eyed blank stare of someone startled from a deep sleep. Gus shot to his feet and barked a greeting. Then with his tail wagging, he trotted over to sniff around the man's feet.

Richard stared at the cave entrance, feeling both disbelief and a sense of doomed irony. It couldn't be, he thought. But it was.

Phineas? Philbert? Phelim? Yes ... that was it. Phelim.

Frowning, he watched a group of dripping-wet smugglers stagger into the cave from a cloud of fog. "Of all the seas, of all the islands, of all the coves, of all the caves ..."

"Let me at the scurvy snail-eater what blasted me ship with an eighteen-pounder!"

Philbert grabbed Phelim's arm and took away the grappling iron before it conked him on the head. "Put a clapper on it, Lord Nelson. Yer bloody ship's sunk."

"Oh! What a small world!" The hellion was awake.

The men stared at her as they would stare at a ghost. She was there, but no one could believe they were actually looking at her.

Smiling at them, she said, "You found us!"

"Not exactly," Philbert said with all the enthusiasm of a man about to be sent to Tyburn.

"We were waiting to be ransomed. The pirates left us here. Now you're here too. You can take us back home." She stood up and walked toward the group as if she were about to give them an open-armed welcome.

"The ship was wrecked on the rocks." Philbert gave a quick nod in the direction of the small cove.

"Oh." Her smile faded. "Was anyone hurt?"

Philbert shook his head, and a small dribble of blood rolled down his cheek.

"But you're hurt." She moved toward him and dabbed at the small cut with her sleeve. She started to say something and turned, then froze in midturn.

Harry stepped from the fog into the entrance of the cave. They looked squarely at each other. There was a full minute of stunned silence.

Frowning, Harry shook his head slightly and took another look at her. Then he screamed as if he just stared death in the face.

In the time it took to blink, the man was gone. The echo of his scream eventually faded and the cave was tellingly silent, every gaze on the vacant spot where Harry had been standing.

One of the triplets stared wide-eyed at the cave entrance. "Shouldn't one of us go fetch him back?"

"Ye'd best stay here with *the Admiral,* Phineas. Someone needs to keep watch on him. Might well mistake one of us for ol' Boney."

Philbert picked up a piece of driftwood and stuck it into the fire for a torch, then he straightened and signaled another smuggler. They faded back into the fog.

Ten minutes and as many grunts later, the two men dragged a reluctant Harry back into the cave. His hands and feet were tied with ropes of kelp, and the old bandanna he usually wore around his neck was tied as a gag across his mouth.

Small nubs of black hair, like whiskers, were beginning to grow back where his hair and eyebrows had been. And beneath them, his eyes showed a mixture of anger and panic. Despite the gag, Harry was talking. "Mmphf! Mmmmmfph!"

A winded Philbert dropped Harry's bound feet with a disgusted thud and stood there, his hand to his panting chest, his face bright red and beaded with a mixture of fog and sweat.

The other smuggler seemed less winded and said between gasps, "Found the bloke away down atop the rocks where the bleedin' ship broke up. 'E was tryin' to dive back in the water and swim out to sea."

"Mmmfph mmfph, mmmmfph mmmfph!"

Richard stared at Harry for a moment. He'd have wagered his best mount that the man was swearing behind that gag. Or possibly praying.

The hellion stood there chewing her lip, rocking a little on her heels and watching Harry with a tentative look that said she might bolt at any second.

It was a moment of sheer idiocy. Just one of many recently. And Richard felt the strong urge to laugh, but he was afraid that once he started he wouldn't be able to stop. So completely and farcically absurd was the mental image of Harry, sans hair, beard, and eyebrows, taking one look at the hellion, then screaming like a banshee and running for his life.

Pitiable, laughable, but absolutely understandable. If anyone could understand Harry's reaction to her it was Richard. He consoled himself with the thought that, should things get dull, he could go over and sit next to Harry. They could compare wounds, he thought, watching the scene with a kind of detached amusement.

However, there was one thing he couldn't deny. Not once since they'd been nabbed had Richard been bored. He had been shot, starved, drunk, half drowned, insulted; he'd been mad as hell, but he had not been bored.

Unusual. Very unusual. His memory held a life's log filled with dull and empty days. Even those wild ways that the Reverend Mrs. Poppit would deem wicked no longer held much in the way of amusement.

Yet this motley group held his wayward interest the way nothing had for so long, except perhaps a brandy bottle, and even strong drink had ceased to be the escape for Richard that it had once been. He had so few places to run anymore. Nowhere to hide.

Thoughts of running and hiding fled while he watched those around him. He crossed his hands behind his head, leaned against a cave wall with his legs comfortably outstretched, and just let himself be entertained.

He had nodded off for a while, yet he had no idea how long. Not that it mattered. He wasn't going anywhere. No pressing schedule.

They all sat in a quiet tentativeness around the small fire, Gus literally dogging the hellion's steps as she doled out food to a row of ragtag smugglers who sat between Harry and herself. Rather like a neutral ground between warring factions.

With a sharp bark, Gus leapt up and snatched a piece of cheese right from the hellion's hand, making her jump back in surprise. "Gus!" she scolded. "Stop pilfering the food! You be sweet!"

Philbert frowned, an expression that told Richard he too thought the idea of Gus being sweet more than a little farfetched. Richard immediately felt a sense of kinship with the man.

The beast had trotted gleefully over to plop down in a dark corner, where he seemed content to masticate the living hell out of that cheese.

Ignoring the smacking that echoed from that corner, Richard tore off a chunk of bread and chewed it, studying each person around him and asking himself if this could all be a nightmare—an in-his-cups type of nightmare. One drink too many. A bad hallucination from which he would soon awaken, hung over.

But nightmares didn't last for days. They either lasted one night or a lifetime.

He came to the only logical conclusion: He had actually died—yes, that was it—and had come back as part of a lost play by ... by Moliére.

Les Inadaptes. The Misfits.

That's what they were, he thought, looking at each man. Then his gaze shifted to the hellion. And suddenly *he* felt the misfit.

He doubted he had ever been that naive, that young, that filled with the ability to find good in everything.

One thing was certain: He knew he'd never been a dreamer.

Yet she was. A happy dreamer. With a bounce to her step she moved down the line of men, handing them hunks of bread and wedges of sharp cheese and acting as if it were the food of the gods, as if they were her bosom beaus, and as if this were the most delightful of moments.

When he watched her expressive face, he could almost believe that there was something special about today. Except he knew better. But on she went, smiling at each man, a smile that was warm and inviting, honest, a real smile that could move him more than it was comfortable to admit.

The past few hours had held no smiles. She had made that comment about his pride, then had quietly moved across the cave, curled up against the security of her dog—her only friend in the world—and slept while he'd sat there feeling like a puffed-up horse's ass.

He felt a sharp pang of guilt as he watched her. Because he remembered how pointedly silent she had been a few minutes ago. She had stood before him with her arms full of bread and cheese.

She had no smile for him. She stood there as if she couldn't bear to look at him, so instead she held out the food while staring at her shoes. Made him feel like the very devil.

He knew what she needed. She needed to be home. She needed to be away from him. She needed to learn reality—that dreams didn't come true. And no matter what she did, how hard she tried, he would never, could never, allow himself to be what she wanted him to be.

Her knight on a white horse.

He absently rubbed the thick stubble on his chin and stared at her a little longer. He supposed it was best to leave things as they lay.

She handed the other brother a wedge of cheese and some bread.

"Thank ye, Missy." Phineas looked up at her and paused, then added, "Ye was right, ye know."

"Me?" She smiled that smile. "About what?"

"On the other ship, when ye came to our defense. Ye said we didn't mean no harm. We didn't have the foggiest notion them crates were full o' gun locks until it was too late." He hung his head slightly and said, "Ye might be finding this hard to hold true, but"—he held up his right hand—"God's truth, we've never smuggled afore."

Richard didn't find that difficult to believe at all. In fact, he'd have wagered most of his fortune on it.

"Truly?" she said, then she darted a covert look at Richard. "Just as I had said. One doesn't feed people that one is intending to murder. That doesn't make sense."

Turning back to Phineas, she added, "Richard told me that people who are going to be executed are given last meals, you see." She lowered her voice. "He's a known rakehell." She stopped to give a huge dramatic sigh, as if the notion was difficult to bear.

"So he knows quite a bit—for an earl, I mean—about gambling, drinking, smuggling, debauchery, executions, even piracy. Did you know that he was the one who told me that the term 'privateer' was a more socially acceptable word for 'pirate'? I surely didn't know, never having been around pirates. Of course, now we all have, haven't we? But back to my point . . ."

In which lifetime, Richard thought, would she make her point?

"I believe that is why he—Richard, that is—can be so terribly cruel at times."

It was his turn to flinch. She'd made her point. Quite accurately.

"But you didn't intend to harm us, did you?" she continued. "And, as I was saying, I told him so, after I found out he'd lied to me about the little adventure to tell our—I mean, *my* grandchildren. But he said that the gun locks were the only reason you had to nab us." She took a breath and hugged the bread and cheese more tightly to her chest, then cocked her head. "So why did you take us?"

Phineas frowned, nodding his head every so often as if he were trying to recall everything she had said.

Philbert nudged Phineas with an elbow jab and whispered, "Forget all the blithering questions. Just answer the last one."

Both brothers exchanged a knowing look, then turned toward Phelim, who was sleeping against a cave wall.

Like the others, Richard found himself staring at the sleeping smuggler. He no longer had his admiral's hat or eyepatch, but one sleeve of his shirt hung empty, the arm that belonged in it resting in a long lump across his belly.

His burnt-brown skin showed his years on the sea and in the sun, and like the others, he had a shock of graying hair, which had dried and now sprang from his head in clumps of cowlicks. Richard stared at the man's head and had the sudden image of a red water jug with large handles. He'd be willing to wager the contents of both were the same.

Phineas and Philbert pointed at Phelim and in unison said, "He did it!"

Phelim's only response was a loud snore.

"Why did he do it?" she asked.

" 'Cause he lost his wits," Philbert muttered.

"Now, Bertie. Ye know Phelim wouldn't've done

that what he did if his head were right. Me brother hain't been himself, Missy." Phineas shook his head. "Not since he come home from the navy. He took a hit in the head. He was in Nelson's navy for twenty long years, while Bertie and me saw to the business. The whole time Phelim was off fighting the frogs, we took care of what were ours, we did."

The hellion looked at them. "So you weren't all in the navy?"

Phineas shook his head.

Philbert added, "We be milk hawkers. Buttermen."

Richard took a deep breath, rested his forehead in one hand, and stared at the cave floor. They'd been nabbed by cow farmers and shell-cracked sailors. God . . . He could almost hear Seymour crowing now.

"Our dairy farm be near the village of Dappledown," Philbert told them. "Phineas took the buttercart to the village every day but the Sabbath."

"Bertie here makes the finest cheese and the whitest butter in the parish," Phineas said with brotherly pride.

"Thank ye."

"Ye're welcome. I only spake what were true. I miss the life, Bertie, that I do."

"It be a good life," Philbert agreed.

"Aye."

" 'Til the bleedin' Parliament went an' passed the Enclosure Acts. Took away the common pasture and forced us to sell off all but two cows," Philbert explained. "Phelim come home just after. I knew we should've kept him with us. Should never've let him go off to London, Phineas. Should've never."

"He served in the navy fer a long while, Bertie. For England and God and King. 'Tweren't his fault what happen to him." Phineas looked at the hellion, his shoulders slumped in defeat. "We lost the farm, the last two cows, everything, we did."

The hellion had tears glistening in her eyes as she patted the older man on his slumped shoulder. "How?"

"He took off to London with Harry and the others." Philbert looked at them. "They'd all been t'gether in the navy and up and set a meet at the Fish and the Tail, a dockside tavern. Rough place it were too. Phelim didn't duck during a brawl and got hit on his head."

Philbert gave them a knowing look. "Ye've all seen what happens. He thought t' be Nelson bartering with the enemy for his stolen brigantine. By the time he came home, he had traded our small farm fer a ship."

"But it's obvious he's not well," Letty said. "No one should hold him to a trade, considering."

"We tried to explain, we did, both Bertie and me," Phineas added. "But the bloke what bartered it said a trade's a trade. He'd been looking to pension out on a farm himself, he had. So we was stuck with no home, no income, only that ol' lugger what was barely seaworthy before it wrecked. We be livin' aboard the ship when Phelim took it into his poor head to make a deal with some froggie émigré."

"The gun locks," Richard said, thinking aloud.

"Aye." Philbert nodded. "We was told all we had to do was ship some crates o' food, blankets, and the like to his family what were still in France."

"Claimed they was struggling to hang on to their home," said Phineas, picking up the tale. "Considerin' our trouble, ye can see why we were willin'. But there weren't no food in those crates, no there weren't.

"But we didn't know that. Bertie 'n' me was on the ship."

"Aye, an' one o' the crates fell when they was loading it on the beach," Philbert said.

"Then you two were there and ..." Philbert shrugged. "Phelim panicked. He told 'em to take you two along. Ye know the rest."

"And what were you going to do with us?" Richard spoke for the first time.

"I don't think Phelim thought 'bout that until ye scared him with the knowledge ye was an earl, and how nabbin' an earl were a worse crime than smuggling."

"We never broke a law afore," Phineas added.

Philbert glanced at his sleeping brother. "He don't think too clearly at'll now, whether he's notioning he's Nelson or just ol' Phelim Higganbotham."

"So what are you going to do now?"

Both brothers shrugged.

She turned to Richard, the first time she'd looked him in the eye.

He knew that look, and he slowly began to shake his head. "Oh ... no." He held up a hand. "Absolutely not."

"But surely you, as the Earl of Downe, could—"

"No!" He straightened, crossing his arms stubbornly.

" 'Tain't his lordship's fault, Missy. We got ourselves into this fix," Phineas said. "Surely cain't blame Phelim either. While we was all safe back here in England, Phelim gave all those years of his life—a man's best years—and his heart and, in the end ... even his mind fighting for all of us—farmers, sailors, ladies, the King, even earls."

"No." Richard would not give in. He would not.

They all hung their heads and looked at him through eyes that belonged on poor abandoned orphans instead of old farmers and sailors.

DREAMING

Gus lay in the corner, and he stared at Richard with those bloodshot eyes, then he sank his big head on his front paws and gave a quiet whimper.

And the hellion. She looked at him as if he held the moon wrapped up in stars.

"No."

"Please," came a soft female voice. "You can't possibly be that cruel."

"I said . . . no." His answer was stern, uncompromising, unmovable. "I told you before. I'm no hero."

Chapter 17

He was a hero. Letty just hadn't convinced him yet

And from her brief experience with men, she was certain of one thing: The sand outside would turn to gold dust before Richard would ever admit it. He sat against one wall of the cave, the rigidness of his shoulders, his tight jaw, and narrowed look telling her he was intent on being stubborn.

She looked at Philbert. "Isn't there somewhere else you can think to go?"

He shrugged, and both brothers shook their heads. "There be no ship, so there be no home."

She looked at the other two younger sailors, who sat guard on either side of Harry. "What about those two?"

"They was pressed in the navy when they be but street urchins. Not a one of them has any relations. Simon, the one on the left, was but eight at the time Schoostor don't know how old he is."

"Don't you have family anywhere in England?"

"We be all that's left of the Higganbothams."

"I don't suppose you have any money saved," she asked hopefully.

"Phelim took every last ha'penny to outfit the ship."

"An' then he forgot t' buy food," Philbert added.

"Aye," Phineas said, then glanced at Richard. "That one pot of stew be all we had, so there weren't nothing to give his lordship."

Letty cast a look to see Richard's reaction. He still sat there stiffly, and his jaw was clenched even tighter.

His profile was as hard as the rock walls around them, but one shouldn't have to work at being hard. It should come naturally.

He wasn't as unmoved as he was trying to appear.

"Well," she said, rubbing her hands together. "Shall we try to list each of your skills? Perhaps then we can come up with something you can do. Philbert makes butter and cheese, and Phineas can drive a cart, so I assume you can handle a team, which means you can handle a carriage or a wagon."

"A team?" Phineas repeated, shaking his head.

"You said you had a cart."

"Aye, that we did, but with one old ox to pull it. I ain't never driven anything but that ox."

"Oh." She tried not to let her disappointment show and added brightly, "Then I suppose driving a wagon won't work, will it?"

"Bertie an' me can milk and feed twenty cows a day," Phineas said with pride in his voice. "An' Phelim's been a helmsman, gunner, and first mate. Schoostor was a swabbie."

"Mmmphf mmmphf mmmphf."

"Oh, I near on forgot. Harry stood lookout and worked in the ship's laundry, and Simon can tie a hundred different knots and sew a sail.

"Anything else?" She looked at each man.

Simon sat a little straighter and volunteered, "Both Schoostor and me be street boys. We can pick a bleedin' pocket clean afore a bloke can blink."

The cave was suddenly silent, except for a choked snort from Richard's direction.

"Oh." Letty gave the grinning sailor a strained smile. "Uh ... That's not exactly the type of work I had in mind." She cleared her throat. "We should be able to find a job for each of you. I'm certain between all of us we can find a solution."

There was another odd noise from Richard's direction.

"We shall just have to put our heads together."

Seymour closed the door and stepped onto the fog-clouded terrace. The air was heavy with the scent of dampness and the spice of blooming roses.

Giana's roses.

He froze for a moment, torn between wanting to rush over to her and not wanting to frighten her away. He crossed the terrace slowly, quietly, until he stood between her and the closest door. A tactical move.

Yet she knew he was there. He realized it an instant later, something about the way she stood, her face shrouded by the cloak, as if the fog and dark of night were not enough to hide her.

If ever there was a time he needed luck on his side, it was this moment. This instant in time. He sensed that whatever he would say and do, here and now, would mean the difference between a life as he had lived—monotonously the same, filled lately with a nagging impatience for something else—or the life he wanted to live—fresh and new, alive with promise.

Something he hadn't known he wanted until today. A lifetime with Giana.

"I'm a viscount," he said with absolute stupidity.

He blinked once in disbelief, and a second later he groaned and slapped his forehead. "Of all the bloody words in the English language I had to pick those! 'I'm a viscount,'" he repeated, in a voice full of mimicry and sarcasm. "Well, bless me with four shillings and a ha'penny."

He jammed his hands in his pockets and began to pace in anger, his head down as he grumbled. "Here it is, the single most important moment of my whole featherbrained life. I'm standing in front of an exquisitely lovely woman—"

He paused in front of her and looked directly into her startled face. "You are, you know, the most lovely thing I've ever chanced to see." He turned and paced again, not hearing her indrawn breath.

"And what utterly brilliant thing do I say? 'I'm a viscount,'" He snorted with self-disgust, then turned and threw his hands in the air, sending his amulets and charms scattering across the stones of the terrace. "Perhaps I should just spit toads."

Water dripped from the edge of an eave and plopped at his feet. He stopped pacing and looked down in time to see his lucky shark's tooth roll into a small puddle near his boot.

Scowling, he rammed his hands back in his empty pockets. "Oh, hell. Those lucky pieces won't do me any good, unless they can find me a new mouth—one that won't say ... 'I'm a viscount' like some pompous braying ass."

There was an instant of pin-dropping silence. He stood there certain he was nothing more than a complete blithering idiot.

Giana burst out laughing.

He frowned at first, stunned by her reaction. Then he heard nothing but her, and he found himself smiling. Her laughter was charming, with a carillon-bell quality to it—clear and clean, almost lyrical. His smile grew in spite of the fact that a moment before he'd been so miserable that he'd wanted to cut out his own tongue.

Her head was thrown back, and the dark velvet hood had fallen around her shoulders, where her black hair was gathered in a cluster of springy curls. Her lips were parted, showing a line of perfect teeth. He remembered something Belmore had said once about checking a woman's teeth and withers—some bad youthful jest about there being no difference between choosing a wife and a good horse.

For Seymour, Giana Hunt was a thoroughbred. Her eyes sparkled brightly beneath perfect black brows that reminded him of velvet. He remembered from one short glimpse that afternoon that those sparkling eyes were a pale violet, almost lavender.

Hauntingly different.

Odd thing. When she laughed, her mouth wide with mirth, the scar faded somewhat, into a slight dark crease in her pale skin.

He wondered if she knew that. And something inside him wanted to keep her laughing until she never thought about what people saw when they looked at her.

Her laughter faded, but her smile was still there, making him want more from her than he should ask. He met her look. "What are you thinking?"

"That you are certainly a flatterer, my lord, and not someone who would spit toads." She averted her face.

He reached out and tilted her chin up so she had to look directly at him. "I'm not trying to flatter you. I meant what I said."

The laugh she gave this time held a wealth of bitterness. "I hate to be pitied."

"I'm not pitying you."

"Aren't you?"

"Why would I? You've looks to make every other English woman pale."

"Pale?" Her voice was even, but he could feel the anger in it. "Pale with fright? Pale with horror?" She shifted, turning her head so all he could see was her scar. "Look at this!"

The moment went on forever. Finally he said, "I'm looking."

"Don't be obtuse."

"I see the scar."

She said nothing.

"I also see the small beauty mark here." He touched the dark dot near her temple. "I see the beginnings of a laugh line here."

He ran his thumb over the tiny crease in her other cheek. He cupped her face in his hands and lifted it slightly, studying her. "I say, I do believe that . . ." He frowned. "Yes, I believe that one ear . . . this one . . ." He lightly flicked a finger over her left ear and felt her shiver. "Yes, it is." Then he paused purposefully.

"What?"

"It's slightly larger and higher than the other one."

Her eyes narrowed in suspicion.

He studied her face for a reaction. She didn't react, so he said with quiet reserve, "I noticed your other problem."

She looked at him long and hard. "What problem?"

"Your neck."

Her hand when to her neck and she frowned. "My neck?"

"Yes," he said seriously. "I noticed this afternoon . . . during tea."

Her mouth fell open.

"Perhaps stretching the muscles will help strengthen it."

She clamped her mouth shut. "There is nothing wrong with my neck." There was a distinct thread of indignation in her tone.

He tried not to smile. "Surely there must be."

"I don't know what you mean."

"I'd say it was weak neck muscles that keep your head down." He stared at her bent head. "That, or perhaps you like to stare at your toes."

Her head shot up. It only took a minute for the tightness around her mouth to slacken and the defensive tension in her stance to slowly drain away.

She gave him a small smile. "I suppose I asked for that, didn't I?"

"No. But I would prefer the luxury of looking at your face, rather than the top of your head. Not that it's not a perfectly lovely head. Although your part is crooked."

She laughed again, true and real, and he felt as if he'd won the first battle.

"So, my lord, you are a *viscount.*"

It was his turn to laugh then. "Yes, are you duly impressed?"

"Certainly, my lord." She gave a small curtsy.

"Indeed. Better than a baron, but less than a earl. However, I'm still considered quite the catch."

She laughed again and shook her head.

"Care to set your cap for being a viscountess?"

Her smile suddenly died. She looked at him with hurt-filled eyes, eyes that quickly turned cold. Her shoulders went straight, her chin a notch higher, and she started to turn away.

He grabbed her arm. "I'm not playing you false, Giana." He gripped her other arm and turned her back around.

She stared at the ground.

"Look at me."

She slowly raised her stricken face to his. The depth of her pain was unmistakable. He sensed what she had suffered with almost a lifetime of shame, scars that ran deeper than marks on the skin.

In her eyes there were no promises, no expectations, no hope.

He never wanted to see that look on her face again.

She didn't believe him. It was there on her face, as plain to see as her nose.

A hundred trite phrases ran through his panicked mind, none of which were the right things to say, so he went with his gut: He kissed her, softly.

He felt her breath catch in surprise. She stiffened, and he could feel her fists tighten against his chest. He could feel them shake. He hoped she didn't shake with anger or with fear.

He didn't want to frighten her. But she needed something.

The aura around her pleaded for help from someone. He was that person. And he hoped this was the answer.

She stood there stiffly.

His mouth whispered over her lips, to kiss her cheek and trace the scar with his mouth, gently, reverently.

She was like stone.

His lips moved on to her eyelids, her brow, back down her cheek. He worshiped her face.

He felt small shudders travel through her. *Don't be frightened. Please. Understand. I care.*

"No . . . please. Don't." Her voice was half whisper, half whimper. She pulled back.

He slid his arms around her and locked his hands, resting them loosely in the small of her back. She could have broken from his hold with almost no effort.

He gave her that freedom. The freedom to run away

and hide. The freedom to say no without speaking the words.

She didn't move.

He rested his forehead against the top of her head and just held her. They stood there in the damp fog, listening to the drip of water from the eaves, listening to their breathing slow, wondering if a heartbeat could be that loud.

He said it softly. "Giana."

"You have no right to do this. You cannot."

He cupped her face, that exquisite face in his hands. "I've spoken with your father."

"You have?"

"Yes."

"But you barely know me."

"I've known you forever. I knew it the first moment I saw you."

She took a deep breath and searched his face. She was looking for lies.

He gave her a direct look. "You know it too. Don't deny it."

"You spoke to Papa," she whispered, as if she needed to say it aloud to believe it.

"Yes."

He wouldn't have thought it possible, but she was more strikingly beautiful at that moment than when he'd first seen her in the garden. Her face was dazed and off guard, not a little wonderstruck.

The dark shadows of loneliness seemed to fade away. The look she gave him held a small bit of hope. The small ray of brightness said with more than mere words what he'd given her.

A grounding thought. One that gave him something he'd never had before: a purpose.

Perhaps he could make all of her darkness fade.

"I cannot believe that I'm standing here letting you

hold me and kiss me." She looked up at him. "I don't even know your Christian name."

"Neil."

"Just Neil?"

"Neil Charles Buford Herndon, Eighth Viscount Seymour."

"Neil Charles Buford Herndon." A small smile teased the corners of her mouth. "A *viscount.*"

He laughed, a hardy laugh, one that was filled as much with relief as happiness. He wanted to shout. He wanted to carry her off. He wanted to know this joy for the rest of his life. He wanted the world to share the moment.

Lifting her off the ground, he kissed her again, swirling her around and listening to the wondrous ring of her laughter. He slowed and set her gently on her feet. He took a step back, but he still held her hands.

They stood there a little awkwardly, both of them so filled with the bliss of each other that they didn't see Sir Hunt standing at the far window.

They didn't see the pride in his face as he looked at his daughter.

They didn't see the deep breath he took.

They didn't see his shoulders begin to shake.

They didn't see him cry.

He was her hero.

Oh, he didn't like to admit it, and he fought doing the honorable thing with almost every breath. But in the end, it hadn't taken Letty long to persuade Richard to act the hero again. It had just taken a little while.

She and the men had pointedly discussed every option from tinkering to highway robbery—the latter a suggestion by Simon and Schoostor.

It had been that final desperate offer of her mother's pearls that had broken Richard's resistance.

"Hell and blast!" The Earl of Downe would provide "bloody" positions for them, "dammit." He had groused that it was easier than having to testify at their trials.

She gave him her most thankful smile. He only stared at her lips for the longest time, as if there were something wrong with them.

After an uncomfortable few minutes, she began to wonder if she had bread and cheese crumbs on her mouth and ran her fingertips over them. His face took on the decidedly sick look of a man who had just been punched in the belly.

"Are you unwell?"

He didn't answer, just gave her that same foreign stare. He then seemed to realize what she'd asked and laughed that sardonic laugh of his. "Yes. I do believe I'm a sick man."

She had walked over to stand above him. He said nothing.

"Thank you."

He made some odd noise, then schooled his expression. "What changed my mind, hellion, was the mere thought of what could happen if the group of you put your heads together. Don't read any heroics into it."

But try as he might to deny it, she knew differently. "Well ... thank you anyway."

He grunted some response.

"Don't you suppose someone should untie Harry?"

"Not concerned for your safety?"

She glanced at the sailor. "Perhaps if I apologize ..."

Richard shook his head. "I'll take care of it."

She smiled and started to speak.

He held up a hand. "Good God. Don't thank me

again. I'm not certain the unscrupulous side of my ego can take that much boundless gratitude in one hour."

He went over and squatted down next to Harry.

She turned back smiling, trying so very hard not to laugh aloud with glee. She had seen emotion in his eyes.

Yes, she had. And with every part of her being she hoped, she prayed, that deep down inside, Richard cared.

Chapter

18

There was a full moon that Saturday night. But no one could see it. The fog was still too thick, and it seemed even more dense at the site of the old chapel ruins.

Figures moved with stealth along the rise where the medieval chapel had once stood. The nearby sea was strangely quiet. No wind. No chattering calls of the puffins that roosted in the cliffs. No thundering crash of stormier waves.

Just the muted crunch of bootheels on rock and dirt, the steps of Viscount Seymour, Sir Hunt, and five of his armed servants.

One lone lantern served as Seymour's only means of light. It swung like a pendulum from his hand and cast an eerie, wavering amber glow on the rocky ground and moorstones.

Seymour stopped to adjust the dueling pistol he'd stuck in the waistband of his breeches. He eyed the area. The rise grew steeper a few feet ahead, but a few feet ahead was all he could see.

It seemed they'd been climbing the rise forever, so slow was their progress. But he knew part of it was nerves. He had no idea what awaited them.

He only knew the instructions on the ransom note. He intended to follow them precisely for the well-being of Downe and the girl.

Without the support of the excise men, he and Hunt had discussed the possibilities of capturing the kidnappers, and both were loath to do so with only a few footmen, a butler, and a coachman. One of the younger footmen volunteered to follow whoever picked up the ransom. They decided that would have to do.

Seymour moved ahead and tapped Hunt on a shoulder. "How much farther?"

"I'd wager it's only a few more feet. Never seen fog so thick."

And true to his statement, they made the top of the rise a moment later. The group huddled around the lantern light, each man on guard.

Hunt leaned closer and asked, "What time is it?"

Seymour checked his pocket watch. "Ten."

"Two hours." Hunt turned and whispered, "You men surround the grounds. Find positions behind the walls, near rocks, someplace where you can watch the drop site but still have some cover."

The men faded like ciphers into the fog.

Seymour lifted the lantern and tried to see past the uneven stone wall that was in front of him. It was barely two feet high.

He shifted, holding the lantern higher, and moved slowly and carefully along one wall of the ruin. He could hear the soft crunch of Hunt's bootsteps following close behind him. They moved along the wall until they came to a corner.

From this vantage point there was a better angle of

the ruins. The fog wandered slightly, giving random glimpses of what lay beyond. He could make out the outline of the chapel walls. All but one had crumbled into a short pile of stones.

Although deteriorated, the moorstone walls seemed to form part of what he assumed was a rectangle. Within, there was nothing but a dark and soggy-looking plane of dirt broken only by a time-scattered stone or an occasional clump of heath grass.

"Do you see anything that looks like an altar?"

"Hold the lantern a little higher." Hunt paused, then pointed. "What's that over there?"

Seymour saw it. It was little more than a large stone block that stood in front of the only high wall left standing.

Hunt stood behind him, the other dueling pistol in his hand. He seemed poised, on guard and ready for anything. Quietly he said, "I'll stay back here out of the light. They could be nearby now, watching us."

"I doubt they could see us. There are moments where I can't see three feet in front of me. Dirtiest bloody weather I've ever seen."

"It does seem unusually thick. I can't recall seeing weather like this in the fifteen years since we moved here. But then I've never been out trouncing through the ruins in the middle of the worst of it, either."

Seymour pulled the other pistol out and cautiously moved toward the altar. Again the fog faded in, then drifted out. It almost seemed to move with each step, as if he stirred the air into doing so with his trespassing.

He could see a few feet beyond the altar, and a little above. But mostly there was just white misty fog with an occasional shadowed outline where remnants of some wall remained.

He set the glowing lantern on the stone altar and looked around him. Nothing but his shadow. He pulled out the leather sack and set the ransom on the altar, then he slowly moved back through the fog to where he took his watch position behind one of the corner ruins.

Hunt squatted down next to him. "Did you notice anything?"

Seymour shook his head.

"Nor did I." Hunt peered over the wall. "I suppose there's not much we can do now."

Seymour settled down into a better position and held his watch up in the dim light that spilled from the altar over the edge of the wall. He frowned and tucked it back in his pocket. He stretched his legs out and crossed his boots. "One hour and fifteen minutes. Nothing to do now except wait."

As dreams went, it was perfect.

A great stone castle, majestic and magical, reigned from a hilltop. The bright summer sun, high in the blue sky, peeped out from behind a cloud—the whimsical shape of which appeared to be a fluffy cotton unicorn.

Off in the distance the sea winked with silvery lights, as if the night before, it had been kissed by the stars, and the dank dark moors of winter were tucked snugly under a summer blanket of lavender heather.

Absolute perfection was the image of a knight on a white horse riding up to the castle, with Gus loping happily alongside. The helm of the knight's helmet was up, showing that Richard's loving gaze was only for her.

And Letty had titian hair.

An instant later it was as if someone had called her name. She opened her eyes, waiting for the golden edges of her dream to fade.

Richard was the first thing she saw. His look was naked, not clothed in that everyday coat of studied indifference.

She could sense some incomplete part of him reaching out, toward her, with a desperate sense of wanting and bleakness that said he thought he was locked outside in the cold and could never get in.

Seeing that overwhelming sense of isolation within him robbed her of breath. She had always looked at Richard as a symbol of her dream, her knight. Yet now she saw him as a desperately lonely man.

They sat there in the close confines of a cave with six other people and Gus, yet at that instant the two of them seemed to be completely alone. She glanced around the cave to see if anyone else saw it.

The others were busy talking around the fire.

Perhaps, she thought, it was because she loved him so much that she could see this part of him.

She stood up and closed the short distance between them, then sat down beside him, stretching her own legs out as he had his.

She said nothing.

She didn't look at him, but she knew he now stared into the hypnotic fire that flickered a few yards away. She laid her hand upon his.

It was cold, and larger than her palm, the skin seeming tougher than hers. Tough like the Richard he showed the world.

Yet from what she'd seen, a snatch here, a look there, she now knew that toughness provided cover for a man who purposely kept himself alone.

"I'm here," she whispered.

His hand went rigid. He slowly turned and looked at her, his thoughts masked.

She wondered what he was thinking.

He broke his stare and casually glanced down at their hands. With a droll laugh he looked up and said, "Trying to rescue me, hellion?"

Silently she searched his eyes, wanting to see some of the isolation fade, wishing ever so much that she could be a little necessary to him, even if it were only for a brief instant.

He reached out and ran a finger over her lips, then tapped her gently on the chin. "So very serious." He slid his thumb and forefinger under her chin and tilted her head up. "I can't be what you want me to be."

"I want to mean something to you. I'm not asking for much, just a small part of your life."

"My life, hellion? I thought you wanted my heart."

"I'll take either one."

He stared at the fire again, one arm resting on his raised knee. "We need more wood."

"Please," she whispered.

The fire crackled and snapped.

He blinked, then looked down at her.

Don't turn me away. Not again.

"You can't be part of my life. There is no part of it you could understand, or ..." He laughed bitterly. *"With*-stand."

He stood swiftly and brushed off his breeches.

His rejection hurt, but part of her had expected it. More painful, though, was the knowledge that he had to get away from her. It was there so plainly written in his expression.

She closed her eyes, half expecting to see him gone when she opened them. Finally her tears forced them open, and she looked up at him.

He was still there, standing before her in a tall blur.

"You want part of my heart?"

She nodded.

"I don't have one." He turned and left the cave.

"What time is it?"

Seymour looked down at his pocket watch sitting on the top of the ruined wall. "Five minutes 'til midnight."

Hunt edged up the wall and peered over it.

"See anything?"

He shook his head and edged back down. "The sack is still there and nothing."

Both men sat there, waiting, as they had for almost two hours.

"I suppose we'll hear them coming."

"I suppose."

There was utter silence. Time seemed to freeze.

Seymour nudged Hunt, then, raising his pistol, he nodded at the wall. Both of them moved slowly into position.

Pistols ready and aimed at the drop site, Seymour and Hunt kept their eyes on the ransom sack.

The fog drifted through the air, passing by as slowly as the seconds of waiting. Light from the lantern made the fog look like dense, wet sunlight.

Eleven fifty-eight. Nothing.

It crossed Seymour's mind for the first time that perhaps they wouldn't show.

Midnight. And still no sound.

The money sack sat on the altar, untouched.

He wondered if the felons had arrived before them. Perhaps they were watching them. And waiting.

Two minutes after midnight.

He asked himself how long the lantern would burn. A few more hours worth of oil. It could be a stand-off—who would outwait whom.

DREAMING

Three minutes after midnight.

Bloody hell. This was taking a toll on his nerves.

Hunt shifted. Seymour's breath caught, then he slowly exhaled. He glanced at his watch.

Five minutes after midnight.

The lantern went out.

Chapter
19

"**H**old! Don't anyone fire!" Seymour shouted.

There was a small flash of golden light behind the far wall. A flint. A moment later, light spilled over into the ruins.

One of Hunt's men held a lantern high in one hand, his gun in the other, as he stepped over a low wall. It was the footman who had volunteered to follow whoever picked up the money.

"Look!" Hunt pointed at the altar. "The sack is gone."

"What?" Seymour snapped his head around.

The money was gone.

"I didn't hear a thing," he murmured in disbelief as he walked toward the altar.

Hunt joined him. "Neither did I."

Seymour looked at the altar and spotted a single piece of paper that lay where the money had been. He reached for it.

"Seymour?"

"What?"

"Look." Hunt's voice was strained.

Seymour pulled his gaze, and hand, away from the paper.

"The fog. It's disappeared," Hunt murmured.

Seymour looked around him, and his jaw dropped.

The fog had evaporated, and the night couldn't have been clearer. The moon shone down on the water and the plateau. Chittering into the night air was the call of puffins from the cliffside, and in the distance one could hear the pounding surf against the rocks.

But there was no wind. Had been no wind.

If was almost as if someone had just snapped their fingers and the fog vanished.

"Do you smell something?" Hunt asked.

Seymour inhaled, then frowned. "What is that?"

"Some spice. Cider? No. Apples. . . . No, that's not it either."

"Cloves," Seymour said after another breath of air. He scanned the area. There was no one in sight but Hunt's men, and every last one of them looked as befuddled as he felt.

One of the men crossed himself. Another was whispering the Twenty-ninth Psalm. A chill ran through Seymour, and he felt the sudden need for those amulets he'd tossed away.

"Should we separate and try to find where they went?" the young footman asked.

Seymour looked at Hunt, who also stared in bewilderment at the clear sky. He frowned in speculation. "Odd. Very odd."

"Isn't it," Seymour agreed.

Hunt shook his head slightly, then looked at the footman. "If we didn't see or hear them, I doubt we'll find them now." He cast a glance at the paper still lying on the altar. "What does the note say?"

Seymour held it up to the dim lantern light, squinting. "Only two words." He turned back and met Hunt's worried gaze with a relieved smile. "Devil's Slide."

Letty sat quietly in a corner while Phelim, Philbert, and Phineas bickered over some source of amusement. Simon had busied himself by tying their only rope into a series of sailor's knots with odd names such as Eve's apple and slip of the tongue, while Schoostor practiced his sleight of hand by repeatedly plucking sixpence from the unknowing triplets' pockets. A canine snore wheezed next to her, where Gus slept peacefully.

And Richard was still collecting wood.

She felt someone look at her and glanced over to the quiet corner where Harry had just been sitting. Silent. Too silent.

A few times she had felt him looking at her, and once she'd braved the beast and looked up. He was no longer gagged or tied, and he didn't look as if he wanted to harm her.

Perhaps, she reasoned, that was because his hands weren't in claws reaching for her neck. Because he wasn't calling for his mother. And his eyes, while wary, weren't flashing with sparks of rage.

But somehow she wasn't quite certain that his antagonism toward her was so easily forgotten. Or forgiven. She chewed her lip, and her gaze traveled back to the cave entrance for the hundredth time.

No Richard. She sighed and stared out at the beach.

The fog had lifted. At least it appeared to have lifted.

One moment it was there, thick and wet, and, like smoke, it filled the entrance with a haze. The next time she looked she could see pearly moonlight glistening on the sea and stars sparkling on the horizon. A shiver ran over her, so she shifted to scoot closer to the fire.

On her left an odd shadow slowly crawled across the cave wall. She cocked her head and watched it move, asking herself what it looked like. A slug?

"A whale!" Phineas guessed enthusiastically.

Philbert snorted with disgust and dropped his hands. The shadow fell away.

"A whale? A *whale!* Ye be blinder than a bleedin' bat!"

"Looked like a whale to me," Phineas muttered. "And who be ye to jaw me dead over it. *Ye* were the one what called me rabbit a bleedin' rooster."

"If'n that were a rabbit, I be King George."

"Then don yer crown, Yer Bleedin' Majesty, and bonk Betty White a dame with yer scepter. 'Cause, blimey, if'n it weren't a rabbit!"

"Still looked like a rooster to me. Now see if ye cain't figure this 'n out." Philbert raised his hands, put one atop the other, and slowly rolled them as if they were floating on waves. The fire once again cast the moving humplike shadow on the cave wall.

"Phelim. Tell me," Philbert demanded. "What be that to ye?"

Phelim squinted at the wave. "It be the mighty bark the *Jenny Bee,* one o' the finest ships to sail the sea!"

"Looks like a whale," Phineas groused under his breath.

"It be a turtle!" Philbert was not pleased.

This was the third argument the triplets had had since the moment Richard left—the same moment time seemed to have stopped for Letty. It was no longer just minutes and hours, but forevers.

He had just walked away so coldly, as if it were

necessary, something he had to do. And now she realized he was staying away because of what she'd said, or what she'd admitted. Whatever the exact reason, he was still saying away because of her.

Oh, he had avoided her before, in the past when she'd made such a cake of herself over him—least that was how her papa had phrased it. Cake or no, she had just needed to be near him, to see him, to be a part of his life no matter how small the part.

There were times, only a few years back, when just breathing the same air he did was enough to cause her foolish heart to skip a beat. But what in her youthful obsession had always been a challenge, a game, was now something that hurt her deeply. She could have followed him, but she knew it wouldn't have done any good.

She stared at her tightly clasped hands. She could never quite say the correct thing with him. Do the right thing. A devastating thought, since he was the most important person in her life.

She asked herself if she could ever make him understand how she felt, if she could ever win even a small corner of the heart he claimed he didn't have.

No answers came to her.

She stood up and stretched. She could feel Harry's stare again. It made her a little cold, so she walked over toward the fire where she'd left their satchel of supplies.

The second Gus had noticed her direction, he was by her side, his ears flapping with his jostling trot like saddle flaps and his tongue lolling out to one side in anticipation of his obsession—food.

"Gus. You've had more to eat than any of us. Especially Richard."

He growled once, then whimpered.

"Now go back over there and lay down."

He sat back, then voluntarily flopped down and rolled over, his legs up, his head back, and his red-rimmed eyes giving her a hopeful pleading look.

"No."

He closed his eyes and flopped his legs, playing dead.

"I said no."

His eyes popped open and gave her one quick assessing look, before he sat up, then turned, his head hung down, and he plodded slowly back to his corner, where he lay down with his head away from her.

"Guilt won't work," she told him, then turned back, dropping the sack. She supposed she should wait for Richard before doling out more food. She stretched again, her muscles stiff from days of uncomfortable positions.

A second later Harry flew at her, his arms clamping hard around her and hitting her so hard with his body that they both fell to the ground. Pain shot through her back. Her breath flew from her lungs.

Dimly she heard him grunt from the impact before they rolled over and over the floor. He grabbed at her skirts, but she couldn't scream.

"You son of a bitch!"

Richard.

The next second Harry was off her. Her vision cleared to see Richard towering over her with one hand on Harry's throat.

He threw a powerful punch.

Harry broke from his hold and ducked, shouting in a hoarse croak, "Fire!"

Fire? Letty looked down.

One side of her skirt was charred. She touched it, and the fabric crumbled black and ashlike in her hand. She had turned swiftly. The fire had been directly behind her.

Oh God ...

Richard pinned Harry to the floor. The poor man couldn't speak with Richard's hands so tightly on his throat.

"Richard! Stop!" She ran over to them. "Stop! He wasn't hurting me!"

"I'll kill him! I'll kill him!" was all Richard was saying.

She looked back but the others sat shocked, immobile. She quickly looked for something to get his attention.

She picked up a piece of fallen driftwood and banged the ground next to him. "Richard, stop! My skirt was on fire! He was saving me! Stop!"

Richard was beyond hearing anything.

She whacked the ground again even closer to his ear. "Richard!"

Harry's face was red and he was making choking sounds.

"Stop! You must stop!" She raised the wood and closed her eyes.

At that same instant, Richard shifted. Unfortunately, he shifted to the left—to the exact spot where she brought down the wood with a powerful *thwack!*

Thwack! The dining-room door at Belmore Park burst open.

Startled, the Duke and Duchess of Belmore both looked up from their meal.

A plump red weasel waddled into the room.

"Beezle!" Joy shifted quickly, trying to move her chair back, which was impossible with the size of her burgeoning belly.

A slim white cat prowled in after the weasel, who had plopped down beneath Joy's chair, yawned, and promptly fallen asleep.

"Joyous, my dear." The MacLean sailed through the doorway like Queen Charlotte. Her long golden hair was piled high on her head, and the hem and sleeves of her white silk gown shimmered with golden beadwork that looked like rays of the sun.

"I've been so worried," Joy said, struggling to rise from her chair. "Where have you been these past days?"

"Och! Just a wee spot of charity work. I see we're in time for dinner," the MacLean said, deftly changing the subject.

Alec rose and helped Joy from her chair. "Unfortunately, MacLean, we are not serving eye of newt tonight."

"Hmmm, so I see." The MacLean eyed the course. "Brussels sprouts, sweetbreads, beets, buttermilk." She lifted a lid on a silver serving dish embellished with flying birds. "What is this?"

Alec stood a little taller, but it was Joy who spoke. "Duck liver."

"Duck liver?" The MacLean shivered.

" 'Tis one of Alec's . . . uh . . . *our* favorites."

"Looks perfectly vile. I do believe I would prefer newt eyes." She moved closer to another dish on the table and smiled. "Ah hah! I see something appetizingly familiar." She stuck one long slim finger into a dish of clotted cream and strawberries and took a small taste.

"Ugh!" Her face puckered. "What is in that? Pickled herring?"

Joy nodded.

"Is this what you're feeding my great-niece?"

"Nephew," Alec said stubbornly. "For hundreds of years, Mary MacLean, the firstborn Castlemaine has always been male."

The MacLean just smiled.

"Alec . . ." Joy warned.

"Would you consider making a little wager on it, nephew?"

"Certainly."

"Alec . . . please." Joy placed her hand on his arm.

"Now Scottish, this is between your aunt and myself."

"Aye, Joyous, listen to your husband. He is a duke, an Englishman, and thereby certain he is absolutely right."

Alec's eyes narrowed.

"If it is a lass," the MacLean continued in the same arrogant tone Alec had used, "you shall name her after me."

"And if it's a boy?"

"If, perchance, it is a laddie . . ." The MacLean tapped a finger against her lips thoughtfully.

"If it is a boy, you will swear to never again cast another spell, only for a jest," Alec said firmly.

"Agreed."

Joy shook her head and muttered, "Not again."

"And I would suggest," the MacLean added, "that you refrain from broom closet, cauldron, and eye of newt comments."

"I warned you, Alec," Joy said.

"You women seem to think I cannot control my tongue."

"Of course not, my love, but—"

"Care to add to the wager, nephew?" The MacLean smiled, and her gray eyes flickered with just a little wickedness.

"Add to your heart's content," Alec said, crossing his arms in a gesture of challenge.

"Fine." The MacLean gave Alec a direct look. "Should you make one of those comments again, then

I will add to the wager that you must name *every* lassie you have after me."

"Agreed," Alec snapped.

Joy groaned.

Alec looked down, sudden worry for her etched upon his handsome face. "Scottish. Are you well?"

"Don't panic. I'm feeling fine." She gently patted his chest. "Nothing is wrong with neither me nor the baby." She gave a small sigh. "I just wish you two would stop goading each other into these foolish bets."

"Mary, Mary," came a deep voice from the doorway. "Making those wicked wagers of yours again?"

They all turned.

Townsend the butler, who hadn't had the chance to do his job, announced quickly, "Mr. Mather H. Calvin."

Standing in the doorway was a strikingly huge man with dark red hair and a neatly trimmed beard. He wore a black coat and black trousers, and he handed Townsend his black caped coat with more flourish than the actor Keane.

"Mather Calvin?" the MacLean said with a laugh. "You are wicked, my friend."

The man smiled. "I try."

"Now I understand why I haven't seen you," Joy said to her aunt.

Alec placed his hands protectively on her shoulders.

"Little Joyous." The man crossed into the room and stopped in front of her. His darkly wicked gaze traveled slowly from her head to her waist.

Alec tightened his grip on her shoulders and stood suddenly taller.

"My my. Not so little anymore, I see."

She laughed.

"What's this? Now that you're a duchess you have no hug for your Uncle Hamish?"

Joy wiggled out of Alec's hold and went easily into the man's arms.

"Uncle?" Alec said.

Joy turned and reached out a hand to Alec. "Not truly an uncle. But a long-time friend of the family." Then Joy introduced them.

Each eyed the other assessingly, then Hamish turned to the MacLean and nodded. "He'll do."

Alec gritted his teeth.

Joy caught the look and quickly asked one of the footmen to add two more place settings, then turned back and said brightly, "Aunt, surely you would like a sherry. Uncle Hamish, please would you pour her one? It's over there." She pointed at the liquor cart.

"Uncle Hamish?" Alec said under his breath. "Who in the bloody hell is he?"

"He's a warlock."

"What!"

"Shhhh. Please, Alec. He's from America."

"Now why doesn't that surprise me?"

"Please don't be angry. Besides which, he always keeps my aunt very busy whenever they're together."

Alec stared across his dining room. A witch and a warlock were casually conversing in the corner, sipping his sherry, talking about . . .

What in the devil could they be talking about? The art of zapping? Cauldron stirring? Whatever in blazes a newt was?

Joy touched his arm and whispered, "I know what you're thinking."

Alec wondered if he would ever become used to this.

"Don't say it, or you'll lose your wager."

He glanced down at his wife, the little witch who

owned his heart. One look into that face and he knew what truly mattered in his life.

He was looking at her. And he continued to do so for a very long time. "Fine, Scottish, I'll behave."

She gave his chest a small pat with her hand as she always did, then said, "Thank you."

Sliding her arm through his, she started to lead him across the room.

"I'll behave," Alec muttered. "But who's to say whether or not they will."

After a few minutes, Joy managed to get her aunt aside and asked quietly, "What have you been up to?"

"Up to? Why nothing, my dear. What have *you* been up to?"

"You know what I mean. Why is he here?"

"Why is he here?" the MacLean repeated innocently. "Oh, you must mean Hamish." She glanced at the warlock for a moment, then, with a wee whisper of a smile, she looked down at Joy and said, "I haven't the foggiest notion."

It was a day that many a folk in Glasgow would never forget. In particular, one Angus MacFarland, a penny-pinching old goat who had just served eviction notice on the Glasgow Street Foundling Home.

No amount of tears or groveling had changed Angus's small mind. The orphaned lads and lassies of the home were not his problem. He walked past the lines of children, children who had been praying and wishing on first stars for weeks in the hopes that someone, somewhere, would save them. Angus never looked at a single teary little face. He just flung open the front doors and stormed through.

Yes, Mr. Angus MacFarland would remember that day. As would those who heard that penurious old Angus MacFarland had broken his leg on the very steps of the Foundling Home. Seemed he had tripped over a heavy leather sack filled with gold.

The supreme irony of a miser breaking his leg on a sack filled with gold did not escape many. People snickered for days.

The sack, it seemed, had carried a tag that said "To the Glasgow Street Foundling Home. Believe in the magic of wishes."

Now some called it God's hand at work. Some said that fate had stepped in. But to those children and to the women who ran the home, it was the magic of a dream come true.

Chapter
20

"**D**o ye think he'll come 'round?"

"Depends on how hard she hit him."

Way off in the distance of his hazy mind, Richard realized the voices he heard were talking about him.

"I'm so sorry. So, so sorry."

"There, there, missy. Stop yer crying. Ye didn't mean to bash him like ye did. Phineas, go fetch some water and we'll wake him up."

Richard slowly opened his eyes. A group of surprises faces, three of them identical, stared down at him. His throat was dry, so he swallowed and said roughly, "You throw water in my face again and the only work you'll have will be mucking out every filthy stable in Devon."

"You're awake," the hellion whispered with relief.

His head hurt like the very devil. He closed his eyes, flinching from the jab of a blinding headache. He took a deep breath and relaxed as the sharp jab of pain in his head faded.

A rock or two poked him in the small of his back, and the knuckles on his right hand felt bruised. He was aware that his head rested in the softness of her lap.

Something wet fell on his cheek and she quickly brushed it away. He opened his eyes and saw that worried face wearing the same dismayed and remorseful expression he'd seen so many times over the years, from that wooden bridge so long past to the ship's hold only a few days before.

Another teardrop fell.

"Don't do that."

"What?" she said in a choked whisper.

"Cry. I can't think when you cry."

"I'm sorry."

He closed his eyes and lay there reliving in his head what had happened. The whole incident came back to him swiftly with the throbbing of his knuckles, then the throbbing of his head.

Life's little ironies. Harry had actually been playing the hero. But Richard had lost control. Completely. Absolutely. He had wanted to kill the man for touching her.

He had walked into that cave and seen Harry on top of her, then he'd reacted on instinct, with no thought, nothing but pure red rage.

"I can't let you do this to me," he murmured, not realizing he'd even said his thoughts aloud until she spoke.

"I didn't mean to do it. I didn't hit you on purpose this time." Her words were rushed and threaded with a panicked need for explanation.

She didn't understand that it was too late, that what he had been speaking of had nothing to do with hitting

him on head, and more to do with the fact that she
had hit him where it counted—right in that heart he
claimed he didn't have.

Nor would he allow himself to have it now. Nothing
had changed, except that now their situation was more
complicated because he cared about her.

"I know these incidents keep happening," she ram-
bled on. "But I swear to you I don't mean for them
to happen."

"I understand," he said quietly, setting her up for
what he was about to do. Had to do.

"You understand, truly?"

"Yes." He paused, then opened his eyes and gave
her a cold stare.

She was very quiet, then said, "I would never hurt
you."

*Yes, hellion, I know that, but for your own good,
I'm going to hurt you.*

"I could never hurt you."

Although the others tried not to watch, Richard
knew they were all listening.

"You see, I believe you need me."

"Why?" He shifted closer until his face was scant
inches from hers. "Haven't you done enough damage?"

"I—"

"No, wait! Now I understand. Your purpose in life
is to torture me, and you're not finished yet."

It was her turn to flinch.

He could see he'd succeeded in humiliating her. He
didn't allow his expression to change. He tightened
one hand into a fist. It kept him from reaching out
and touching her.

"I'm sorry. I—" She stopped, her throat sounding
too tight to let her finish. Her head bent in defeat,

she stared at her tightly clasped hands, taking deep breaths that appeared to hurt.

She finally managed to swallow and whispered painfully, "As hard as I try, I can't seem to say or do the right thing." She slowly raised her eyes to his with a look that said she was afraid of what she would see.

And he didn't let her down.

He straightened and gave her a look meant to send her running. "Don't bother worrying about what you say to me. Just stay the bloody hell away."

Seymour spotted the smoke from the cave first. He jumped from the landing skiff and ran across a small strip of sandy beach. He stood in the cave entrance, his breath coming in hard shocks.

A small fire burned nearby, casting the interior in a flickering dim light. At the sight of a group of men, he drew his pistol, feeling the fool for not waiting for Hunt and the others.

But then he saw that none of them were armed. He scanned the interior, looking for discarded weapons. He saw none, but he spotted the girl.

She sat in a corner, her arm around that huge bloodhound and her body bent like that of a beaten child. Her hair hung in wild tangles that showed how long she'd been captive, and her clothing was filthy, her skirts charred black as if they had been burned.

But it was her aura of despair, her desolate sadness, that touched him more than anything. The chit looked as if she hadn't a friend in the world.

His gaze shifted to the opposite side of the cave, and he had to stop himself from shouting Richard's name. But something about the way his friend sat there stopped him.

Seymour felt a sudden jab of guilt. He'd sat in Belmore's study and laughed about Richard and the chit. What he saw now wasn't humorous.

Richard was as silent as the girl, his unshaven jaw tight and tense, and his head resting in one hand as he stared down at the ground. He wore no cloak.

His coat and shirt were torn and frayed. Both looked as if they had been for a swim with him. His garments showed the truth of what his friend had been through. He looked like hell.

Almost palpable was the tension from within the cave. The other men looked afraid to speak, awkward and out of place.

Everything about the Hornsby hellion screamed vulnerable, fragile. And Richard looked as if he had a wall as thick as that of Newgate around him.

Seymour could hear Hunt and the others coming up behind him, and he remembered how he'd intended to torment Richard with quips about his bad luck—their usual banter.

But it appeared that Richard had been tormented enough. All Seymour said was, "Downe."

Richard looked up quickly and winced, then shook his head slightly as if to clear it. His face was gaunt and paler than Seymour could ever remember seeing. "Seymour! Thank God."

Seymour felt the presence of Hunt and the others at his side but said nothing. His attention was on Richard. There was more emotion on his face than Seymour had seen in years. Gratitude, relief, and something else, something that troubled him. He saw raw fear.

Richard stood up, as did the others.

"Don't anyone else move!" Seymour warned, cocking the pistol.

Frowning for a moment, Richard looked from Seymour back to the group of men, then said, "They won't harm anyone."

"Aye," one of the men said, and they all spread their hands in front of them.

Richard took a step and faltered.

"Are you injured?"

"No." Richard cast a quick cold glance at the girl, who had not moved.

To Seymour, she looked as if she were afraid to, that if she did she might shatter. Then something flickered in Richard's eyes as if he too were going to break.

But as quickly as it showed itself, it disappeared behind that coldness Richard used to his advantage. He walked past Seymour. "All I want is to get the devil out of here."

Letty lit another candle, stepped over Gus, who was sleeping near the fireplace, and started to cross the bedchamber. A knock at the door stopped her. "Yes?"

The door opened slowly. A girl stood in the shadow of the entrance, partially hidden by the shadow of the half-open door.

"Miss Hunt?" Letty asked, feeling as tentative as the girl looked. She had no female friends. Never had.

Her papa's wealth had bought her one of the best governesses. But that same wealth didn't buy friends.

Her London season had been such a fiasco that none of the other girls wanted to be associated with her. There had been a few brave ones who tried to speak to her, but they were quickly shuffled off by mothers who didn't want Letty's hoydenish ways to soil their prospects.

The door opened wider and the girl stepped into

the candlelit room. "I've brought you some things to wear."

"Thank you."

"I'm sorry it took me so long, but I had to make certain everyone was settled. The men are staying in the outquarters near the stables," she said. Then in what seemed an afterthought, she added, "The earl is downstairs with Neil and my father. It's my understanding that you won't be leaving until some time Monday. You'll have time to rest."

Letty nodded.

"Here." The girl stiffly held out the clothing.

Letty took a step.

She tripped on the edge of the carpet and landed flat, facedown.

On impact, the candle flew from her hand. She looked up, horrified as hot wax and flames spilled across the beautifully polished wood floor.

The carpet fringe in front of her was on fire.

In a flash, the girl knelt beside her. She pulled Letty away from the carpet. "Are you all right?"

Still stunned, Letty nodded and rose to her knees.

Gus loped past her, barking at the flames.

The girl shot upright and grabbed the silk pillows of the nearby divan. "Here!" She tossed one to Letty and then quickly bent down and began to beat out the small fire.

Letty was on her knees beside her, swatting as hard as she could, tears of embarrassment streaming from her eyes.

It only took a minute and the flames were gone. They both knelt on the carpet, panting a little, pillows resting in their hands. Gus ran in circles, his instincts still raw from the fire.

Letty wiped her eyes and stared at the burned carpet, at the wax on the floor, then she slowly raised her head and saw the small cloud of smoke hovering above them.

She choked slightly, then said, "I'll pay for the damage. I mean, my papa will. I . . . he . . ." She paused, searching for the words that would make things right. There never had been any, and she couldn't find them now, either. "I'm sorry. I have . . ." She took a deep breath and spit it out as best she could. "I'm afraid I'm rather a disaster."

"But it was just an accident," the girl said.

"I have a reputation for a great number of those accidents," Letty admitted, staring at her lap.

"Truly?"

Letty nodded. "London society and I don't mix. I was sent home after only half my season."

The girl said quietly, "I never had one." She turned her face so Letty could see the long scar. "This doesn't make people very comfortable."

"No, I don't suppose it does," Letty said with candor. "How did it happen?" The question was out of her mouth before she realized what she'd asked.

"I was taking a fence when I was ten," the girl answered with the same forthrightness. "My mount missed, and I fell before he had cleared the jump."

"It must have hurt terribly."

"The scar it left behind has hurt me far more than the accident." She began to pick up the clothing she had dropped. "People look at it and either feel awkward and hurry away, or they stand there gaping in horror and thinking they are glad they don't have it."

Suddenly Letty's problems didn't seem so grim.

"But what's worse yet is when they try to say something to make it better. They don't understand that there is nothing they can say."

"Do you still ride?"

She nodded.

"My papa won't allow me near the horses," Letty said wistfully.

"Whyever not?"

"Well, not the horses ... the stable, actually."

"Why?"

"I flooded it."

"You did what?"

"I flooded the stables. I was trying to build a replica of the Roman aqueduct. My papa's most interested in Roman antiquities. For as long as I can remember he's been off on digs or speaking somewhere. He has always been gone more than he's been home." She sighed. "I think I realize now that at the time all I really wanted was his attention." She chewed her lip. "I got it too. Draining the entire lake into the stables would tend to make one sit up and take notice.

"I didn't do so on purpose, of course. And none of the horses were harmed, although they were skittish for weeks. His stallion would never again take a water jump, and all the tack and feed was ruined. Papa wasn't pleased with me."

"I understand. The first year after my fall I kept my head down so often that I broke almost every valuable vase and bric-a-brac in the house. I kept running into everything."

"You did?"

The girl nodded. "By the time I stopped running around like a mole there were quite a few less Chinese vases and rare porcelains. There still aren't many in the house."

Letty glanced around the bedchamber. It was a beautiful blue room with imported wallpaper and rosewood furniture. But there was no bric-a-brac, no vases, only a few paintings on the wall. And even more telling, she remembered that the only mirror in the room was behind a Chinese screen. She turned back and they stared at each other in silence, as if neither could believe the other truly existed.

"Of course, now that I think about it," Letty finally said in a philosophical tone, "perhaps the stable incident wasn't so horrible after all."

"How is that?"

"I might not be allowed near the horses, but I suppose the end result was a success."

"It was?"

"Papa did stay home for over two months after that. I had what I'd wanted: his attention." She shrugged and gave a small smile.

The girl smiled back. "I have the opposite problem. My papa was been here too much. He has no life of his own because he spends his time with me. After the accident he tried too hard to make me happy, to make our life the same as it had been before. It took him awhile, but he finally realized he couldn't make things the same as before, that people would always make it difficult for us no matter what he did.

"It was then that he bought the island and we moved here. Since then it has been only the two of us." The girl paused, then added as an afterthought, "My mother died when I was three."

Letty looked at her and knew in that flash of an instant that she had found a friend. "I was seven when we lost Mama."

It was very quiet as each girl became aware of how very much they shared.

"I'm Giana."

"I'm Letty. Well, actually, my name is Letitia." She paused, then added, "Letitia Olive Hornsby."

Giana made a face. "Olive? How horrid!" Then her eyes widened when she realized what she'd just said. She covered her mouth with her hand. "I'm sorry."

Letty burst out laughing.

Giana blushed.

"Don't feel badly. I'm sorry too. Sorry because it's my name and it *is* horrid!"

And they both laughed.

Two hours later the sun slowly awakened, turning the eastern horizon a brilliant red-orange, and while Gus slept at their feet, both young women sat on the bed, laughing and talking, two lonely people who had been starved for friendship.

"Look!" Letty said, pointing to the sunrise. "Isn't that incredibly beautiful?"

Giana nodded. "I have roses that same color."

"You do?"

"Yes. They're called Titian."

"Titian," Letty said with a sigh.

They looked at each other and in unison said, "I've always wanted titian hair."

Chapter

21

Some fourteen hours later in Sir Vere Hunt's elegant dining room, Letty sat in the worst possible place—across from Richard. She had looked at him only once, and that had been after their host had let her into the dining room.

She had been just about to sit down when she caught his eye. She had seen no emotion, only Richard looking through her as if she didn't exist.

She picked at the food on her plate. She wasn't hungry and she was glad, because every time she thought about that look her stomach tightened.

There was nothing but cold rigidity in his manner. And other than his discussion with the men regarding the swift disappearance of the pirates and the ransom, he said little and drank much. She watched a footman refill his wine goblet for the seventh time. It was only the second remove.

Only the second remove, she thought, knowing the meal would be one of the longest she'd ever endured.

Seymour's laughter rose over the table, and Letty turned. Every time the viscount looked at Giana, his face almost glowed. For her friend she could sit here and smile and pretend. For her friend she could watch Richard drink himself into the man he tried so hard to be. The drunkard. The rake. The man with no heart.

She glanced at her friend. Giana and the viscount exchanged a covert look that communicated something personal and made Giana blush slightly. He smiled at her then, and she could see the love in her friend's eyes. Yes, it was a love match.

There before Letty was a dream come true: a man who looked at a woman as if she were his world. For some reason she chose that moment to look back at Richard. Perhaps she foolishly hoped that some miracle would strike him and he'd be looking at her that same way.

He too was looking at his friend over the rim of his wineglass. He watched Giana as if he were measuring her merit. Then he looked back at her, and she couldn't tell what he was thinking.

He watched her for a long time.

She would have given anything to see a promise in his eyes.

He took another drink, and she wanted to go and take it from his hand. Whatever he thought or was feeling had been sufficiently dulled by the wine he drank so freely.

She had thought he drank because he was a rake, and rakehells drank. A simple reason. A wrong reason.

He had claimed he drank to destroy himself.

She looked at him squarely and realized he had lied. He didn't drink for destruction. He drank so he wouldn't care about anything. He drank to hide who and what he really was: a man with too much of a heart.

Perhaps it was because she'd slept most of that day, perhaps because it was because she was finally going home tomorrow, but whatever the reason, sleep escaped Letty. She tossed and turned, punched one down pillow until it was puffy. She hugged another. But nothing worked.

She tried counting sheep, counting the shadowed outlines of leaves on the wallpaper, counting images of Richard's face. She tried everything, even dreaming, and she was still awake.

Her dreams had left her. She couldn't find one that would give her respite, a perfect fantasy in which to hide from an imperfect world. It was an odd, empty feeling.

She closed her eyes, then opened them, looked around the dark room, then closed them again. Finally she gave up and rose from the bed, slipping into Giana's wrapper. She stepped around Gus and crossed the room to stand by the French doors that led to a balcony running along the east side of the house.

Crossing her arms, she leaned against the doorjamb and stared out at the dark night sky. She could hear the waves crashing in the distance but little else.

There was something still and a little sad about the night, as if perhaps all the lonely people of the world were doing as she did, looking out at nothing but a vast black sky.

She wondered if there was even one star out. Or was the night sky as empty as her girlish dreams had been?

She started to turn away, but some distant memory

made her stop. There was a little game she played as a child, a game in which fate became her playmate.

If there is one star shining, then don't give up on Richard. If the sky is dark and empty, well, then so was her future.

A little wistful, she opened the door, stepping out onto the balcony. It was cold, and she hugged herself as she crossed the few feet to the carved balustrade.

Despite the cold and damp, the air was filled with the rich full scent of Giana's roses. So she leaned back and craned her head, searching for even one elusive star. An empty black sky stared back at her.

Please . . . just one star.

An instant later she heard music and turned, cocking her head to listen. Yes, it was music. Lovely music.

Using the dew-moistened handrail for support, she leaned over the edge, trying to pinpoint the source. Off at the very end of the lower floor, dim honey-colored light poured from windows that wrapped around the corner of the mansion.

She slipped back inside, picked up a candle, and left the bedchamber. Within minutes she was softly padding down a long corridor at the northern end of the house. Once in that hallway she could follow the distant sound of the pianoforte.

The hallway ended at a set of polished rosewood doors. Though the music had drawn her here, now she stopped before those doors and felt a moment's hesitation. She wasn't home, where she could roam from room to room freely.

But so entrancing was the sound from behind those massive doors, she knew she could no more turn away than she could stop breathing. With her hand on the door handle and her eyes closed, she let the music carry her.

The piece ended. She stopped the swaying of her

head and opened her eyes. She found herself standing in the open doorway.

A second later came a concerto, played softly at first, then it grew and swelled into the room. She didn't move, just stared at the broad back of the man playing with such power and beauty.

It was Richard at the pianoforte.

A dark blue coat and white cravat were flung on the marble floor, leaving him in a white shirt. From atop the piano a candelabrum glimmered next to a crystal decanter, and the fabric of his silk shirt caught the light reflected from the flames and facets of crystal, shimmering when his hands moved fluidly over the keys.

She stepped inside as the second movement ended. With only a breath of a pause, the music began again, new and quiet at first, then building and building, until the notes grew into a powerfully dark crescendo that made the air vibrate.

She stood back a bit, watching him. His intensity was breath-catching. Richard was bent over the piano as if the music was a physical part of him. He seemed lost in it, in the sound and notes and the mastery of what his touch brought from that one small instrument.

Across his back, the candlelight flickered like blinking stars and made his shadowed silhouette dance over the floor. The music had changed again. It was dark and mournful, and she felt as if it were calling out to what was inside her heart.

The music stopped as suddenly as it had started.

His back and shoulders grew tense and tight. He sat a little straighter, then reached for the half-empty liquor decanter and poured a glass, drinking it down in one long swig.

He set the glass down, then began to play a light

little tune. "How long have you been standing there, hellion?"

"I don't know."

"It's late."

"I couldn't sleep." When he didn't reply, she added, "The concerto was lovely."

"Ah. So that's how long you've been there."

"I didn't know you played."

"Just one of many things you don't know about me." He stopped playing suddenly, hitting hard on the final chord. And he poured another drink, then spun around on the bench and leaned back languidly, resting his elbows on the keys with a discordant screech of misnotes.

Her gave her a mock salute, then threw back another glass, closing his eyes and raising his chin as if he was savoring the burn of liquor down his throat.

He lowered his head and opened his eyes, pinning her with a dark stare that traveled insolently down her person, stopping with purpose and a wicked smile on the parts that were most private to her.

Her blood rushed to her neck and cheeks.

He laughed and poured another drink.

She flushed with embarrassment first, then guilt and confusion, unaware that what she was feeling was not something she could control.

He lifted the glass to her. "Since you are so hellbent on destroying yourself, come. Have a little destruction."

She shook her head.

He stared into the glass.

The air swelled with words neither of them could nor would speak, then grew cold in the silence.

He twirled the glass, seemingly fascinated by the liquid within it. "I warned you."

"Warned me?"

"I told you to stay away."

"I tried."

He slowly raised his head. His face told her nothing.

In one long, lithe motion he rose and walked toward her. There was a hint of purpose in the way he moved. She wanted to run as she watched him close the distance between them.

But she knew it didn't matter. She could run to the far ends of the earth and he would still be with her, in her heart, in her memory, in her being. And when she looked into the face of the man she had dreamed of for so long, she wasn't certain if she wanted to run away from him or to him.

His hand was the first thing she felt. It slid behind her neck, cupped her head, and pulled her face close to his. She could smell the wine and brandy, but she caught his scent, the one she remembered from her first ball: the scent of sandalwood. This time there was no clean scent of rain.

And there was no dream hero. Only the man.

What she felt for him was more powerful than a dream of love. A frightening feeling. No mind could imagine the power that she felt, nor the confusion of it.

The intensity of his look was as hot and blinding as if she had stared into the full sun. He held her with more than his hand. He held her with his mind, with his look, with something that was so necessary to her being that what passed between them at that moment was almost magical.

But not magical like a fairy tale, with clouds and pretty endings tied up in soft silken ribbons. The magic was black and dark, and so very powerful that she felt in it her very morality.

The air around them vibrated with that magic as it had with the power of the music. His hand on her cheek made the skin on her arms break out in goose-flesh. Her breath came in small wispy pants, and her heart drummed loudly in her ears.

Slowly he turned her and they stepped back, one step, then another, and another. His touch was both her damnation and her salvation. Like swallowing the brightest star in the heavens. Once it's halfway down, you cannot stop even should you want to.

"Richard . . ."

His mouth was close, so very close, his look lazy and expectant. His hands stroked the sensitive skin of her neck and ears with sensual expertise.

She wanted his kiss as badly as she had wished for that star to be in the sky. His lips moved softly, whispered across her brow. Her eyes drifted closed.

His thumbs stroked the skin behind her ears while his hands held her head at the angle he desired. It seemed a lifetime before his mouth brushed hers. Just brushed hers, softly, like a whisper of love.

She moaned, then took a deep breath. "I love you."

His mouth kissed hers again ever so lightly. Against her lips he said in a breath, "No. Not love. It's more elemental than love. You should have stayed away, hellion."

He slid his arm around her and pulled her up against him firmly, quickly. Her breath caught, and she gripped his shoulders. He walked her back to the piano. His free hand swept the top clear.

With a crash of breaking glass the room went dark.

He pinned her between his body and the piano. As if he were filled with an aching hunger impossible to control, he drove his fingers through her hair and gripped her head.

Her eyes adjusted to the darkness.

He didn't move, his mouth didn't stroke hers again. His hands, which had gently cupped her head moments before, were inexplicably tense. "I'm not your wildest dream. I'm your worst nightmare."

He watched her and saw she didn't understand. Through eyes dulled by liquor, he looked down into her face. He saw too deep a chasm separating the two of them. He didn't know if he could do this again.

Someone needs to save her.

His mouth closed over hers, hard and demanding. She didn't fight his hold nor fight the hand that fondled her breasts. She didn't fight when he slid his hand lower.

All she did was thread her fingers through his hair and then gently stroke his neck. He knew she would let him do what he wanted.

He pulled his mouth from hers and rested his forehead on her shoulder. This hadn't worked the last time. It didn't work this time either.

Foolish girl. You should have stayed away.

He took a deep breath, then loosened his tight grip, cupping her head in one hand while the other reached up to gently stroke her jaw and ear. He kissed her this time with gentleness, finesse, seductive kisses along her eyelids, her cheeks, her mouth.

He ran his lips and then his tongue over her ear, down her neck again and again, until she was shaking. She gave a breathy sigh and said, "I've wished for this, dreamed of this ..."

"This is what you want?" he whispered against her lips.

"Yes, please, Richard. I love you."

He kissed her with his tongue for long languid minutes, tasted her over and over until he had to force himself not to give in to the passion he felt and his need to make love to her. He paused to get control, then slowly kissed a path to her other ear. He stroked it once with his tongue, then again. "I love you, Letty."

"Oh God ..." She hugged him so tightly it was all he could do not to break then and pull away.

He closed his eyes; his lips still touched her ear. "Is that what you wanted?"

Her answer was a passionate, breathy "Yes."

He pulled back. "Open your eyes and look at me."

She stared up at him from lazy eyes filled with her heart and her soul, her every thought.

"You want this, love?" He stroked her then rubbed one finger over her swollen lips. "You want me to love you?"

She nodded.

He leaned over and kissed her, some small latent spark of decency rebelling in him and making his motions slower and more awkward because they were forced. Before he could change his bloody weak mind he looked down at her, his mouth a breath away from hers. "Look at me, hellion."

She opened her eyes.

"I don't love women. I use them."

It took a second for his words to register, then her dreamy expression disappeared. Her mouth fell open and she raised her hands to cover it.

"I can say the words. Easily. I love you, Letty. I love you, Emily. I love you, Charlotte. I've said them before to get what I wanted." He forced himself to laugh. "They are only words, and they mean nothing but an easier path for a man to get between a woman's legs."

She twisted away as if she couldn't bear to have his hands on her. Her face was filled with disillusionment and disgust.

Seeing her like that almost broke him. He stepped

back and stumbled slightly. But from somewhere within him he found the strength to draw himself up. He squared his shoulders when he saw her tears.

Her expression was no longer so naively innocent. Like a piece of paper he had wadded up in his hand and tossed away, her face was crumpled in hurt and pain and humiliation.

Tears spilled from her eyes so freely he almost cried himself. His own throat tight, he had to turn around and take a deep breath, then another, to overcome by sheer stubborn will what he was feeling.

He cursed that weakness in him, that he cared when he was trying so desperately not to. He fixed his gaze on a wall sconce and didn't move. It took a few seconds for him to speak in the hard, dispassionate tone he needed. "You wanted my love." He gave a shrug. "And you got what there is of it. Words with no meaning. If you want the act that goes with it, stay there. I can play the lover for you."

There was an odd choking sound, and she began to sob.

Pitiable and aching, each sound she made was a fist in his belly. He started to turn around, telling himself he could not go to her no matter how hard she cried. Then he saw her.

She was bent over as if she'd been whipped, hair hanging freely, a curtain to hide the devastation on face, her arms wrapped around her waist, and her shoulders shaking with each breath she tried to take.

His hands tightened into fists and he wanted to drive them through something, anything. He forced his head up and stared at the dark ceiling. "Next time you get it in that idealistic little head of yours to tell some man you love him, remember this night."

He heard her breath catch, then stood there waiting

for her to leave. He needed her to leave. He didn't know how much longer he could do this.

"I did love you," she finally said in a voice as broken as her dreams.

"So you keep saying. You should thank me for the lesson, hellion. Don't waste your time telling people you love them."

"You think I don't know what love is. You appoint yourself God, Richard, to teach me a lesson. To let me know that speaking of love is foolishness. I learned a different lesson long before I ever knew you.

"I was seven. A servant came to my room and told me my mother wanted to see me. She had been ill for so long and I had hardly seen her in weeks. I was so excited I ran down the long hallways. I remember someone opened a door for me and I charged into her bedchamber. But once inside I stopped.

"The room was dark and eerie in its quiet. It smelled of camphor and sulfur and medicinals. My papa stood nearby. At first I thought Mama was asleep and he would scold me for entering the room like a hoyden, but when I looked to him, he gave a nod of his head, a gesture that I should go to her. He didn't smile, didn't say a word."

She took a breath, then continued. "I walked to her bed, confused, because something was different about the room and about them. Mama lay against the pillows, and she looked so tired and pale, and smaller than I remembered. I had always thought of her as tall and regal. She looked as thin and barren as the winter trees outside. Then she turned to me and smiled, brilliantly, as if she weren't ill, but instead was healthy and calling me over to see some special thing for just the two of us to share.

"She patted the bed next to her, and I remember

crawling up there. She only held me, and for the longest time. I felt safe, and it had been so very long since I'd been held by her or felt that security. It seemed too short a time when my father cleared his throat and said I should let her rest. I kissed her goodnight and started to climb down, but she stopped me and held my face in her thin hands, then she just looked at me as if she wanted to memorize my face."

She had to stop then because her voice cracked. He heard her take two long breaths that labored in her chest.

"Papa walked with me to my room afterward. He was still quiet. I got into bed and I can remember lying there in the dark and I suddenly thought, what would I ever do if she died? She had been ill for so long I suppose I had accepted her illness as part of our life. I hadn't thought about it as being a part of death. But I lay there shaking and afraid to think about it because by doing so I might make it happen. So I tried to think about something else. I remember that I listened to the mantel clock in my bedchamber. I concentrated on each of the nine chimes.

"The next morning I was told Mama died at nine o'clock." She paused and in a choked voice added, "In my excitement the night before, because the child in me needed to be held, I never had the chance, once more, to tell her that I loved her.

"I can't walk away from someone I love without saying 'I love you' one last time. I've known how very much I've loved you for a long time. You think I'm a child and I know nothing about the world or about love. But I know about love. I know about loss. And I know about loneliness, and goodbyes, and about never being able to voice those feelings again.

DREAMING

"Perhaps you've said those words, Richard, and don't mean them. But I never have."

The door clicked closed, leaving him standing alone in the bleakness of the music room. He still stared up at the ceiling, his shoulders straight, his back stiff. And tears streaming from the corners of his eyes.

Chapter
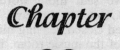
22

*T*he next morning, Seymour found Richard in the music room. He was sitting on the bench, his head resting on his arms which were atop the piano keys. He was sound asleep.

"I say there. Rough night?"

Richard slowly lifted his head. "God ..." He squinted at the room in general, then rested his head in his hands. His eyes felt as if they were filled with sand. He groaned, waited a few minutes that seemed like hours, then asked, "What time is it?"

"Ten."

"What time do you want to sail?"

"Noon." Seymour stared at the floor, where shattered pieces of the decanter lay beneath the candelabrum. "Won't be keeping hours like this soon, I'd wager. We'll have better things to do at night." He laughed. "Who would have thought we'd both be legshackled in the same year? Could have won a monkey on that one, wouldn't you say?"

"What the devil are you babbling about?"

"Us."

"What about *us?*"

"The vows, of course. Hanging our ladles, so to speak. What did you think I was speaking of? We'll dock the sloop and ride to London to fetch the licenses. I assume you'll want to be married by Special License, considering the circumstances. No doubt her papa will agree, and Giana doesn't need a spectacle, although both Hunt or myself would cough up the blunt for whatever my angel wanted."

"I think I might cast up my accounts." Richard mumbled into his hand, then slowly lifted his head and scowled at Seymour. "What in God's name ever gave you the idea that *I* am getting married? You're the one besotted."

"Don't see how you intend to get around it, my friend. The chit's compromised. Surely you realized . . ." Seymour's voice faded, then his jaw dropped. "Good God, man! It didn't cross your mind after all those days alone with her?"

Richard couldn't move.

"And you call me a slow top," Seymour murmured.

"Hell and blast . . ." Richard sagged back against the piano keys. They screeched a messy chord that rang through his teeth and throbbing head. "You're bloody well right."

" 'Course I'm right. Actually, I suppose I need to give Belmore credit. He was the first to bring it up when we were working out the details of the ransom drop. You look green at the gills."

"You don't know what I've done," Richard said quietly. He took a deep breath, then closed his eyes and gave a cynical laugh. "And all for naught. Damn."

"What's this? Remorse? Never thought I'd see it.

Downe remorseful. Belmore ought to be here," Seymour said under his breath.

"I'm a stupid ass."

"True, but we tolerate you in spite of it."

"Aren't you the wit this morning." Richard stared dismally at the floor. "I hurt her."

"Tell her you didn't mean to do it."

"She knows it was intentional. What she doesn't know is that I did it for her own good. I've found I have no taste for crushing hearts."

"Hmmm. Is that all hearts or just her heart?"

"I don't know," Richard said sharply.

Seymour was abnormally quiet.

Richard glanced up.

Seymour was staring at him from an eyeglass that hung on a chain around his neck.

"What are you looking at?" Richard snapped.

"I can't believe what I'm seeing. Are those scruples coming from the infamous Earl of Downe?"

"What you're going to see are the knuckles on my right hand if you don't drop that bloody monocle."

Seymour dropped the glass and held up his hands in mock surrender. "I'm going. I'm going. Giana said to tell you breakfast is in the morning room. Third room down the hall."

"Is the hellion there?"

Seymour shook his head. "She wasn't feeling up to snuff."

The news only made him feel worse.

Seymour clapped him on the shoulder. "It's good to have you back, Richard."

He looked up then. "Have I thanked you for all you did?"

"No need. You'd have done the same."

Richard stared at nothing.

Seymour stopped at the doors and turned. He eyed

him speculatively. "Look at it this way: You'll have the rest of your lives to resolve whatever's wrong." Then he left.

The rest of my life, Richard thought. After what he'd done to her, he wasn't certain that a lifetime would be long enough.

The carriage rattled over the gravel drive to the Hornsby home. With one arm slung around Gus's wrinkled neck, Letty peered out the window. She was coming home. It seemed a year since she'd been there; so much had happened, so much had changed.

To her clear eyes it was the same three-story stone house, with the same alder and chestnut trees along the drive. A blanket of grass spread as it always had toward the east, and those old familiar craggy cliffs lay just past the moors on the sea side of the house.

Auks and gulls flew through the sky and cried their everyday cries. The crunch of carriage wheels along the gravel was a sound she had heard more than a thousand times.

Everything was the same. Nothing had changed.

Except Letty. For her, nothing was the same.

In a matter of days her world had become different. She could remember looking at the moors so many times and imagining Richard riding across them, coming home to her. She and Gus had spent hours over the years running along the beach below those cliffs, where she had dreamed that someday she and Richard might walk hand in hand.

On lazy summer days she'd lain beneath a chestnut tree and painted a mind's-eye portrait of their children playing on that blanket of grass. And deep in the night, when she was alone in her bed with nothing but those dreams of hers to light her thoughts, she had the fantasy of Richard's carriage crunching over the drive on the day he came to speak to Papa of marriage.

Yes, she came home a different person. Her heart was emptier, and her dreams were dead.

The carriage halted in front of the doors.

"We're home, Gus."

The dog barked and panted, and his tail battered the leather squabs of the Viscount's carriage. The door opened, and she looked into Richard's face. He stood before her, one hand on the carriage door and the other held out to help her down.

She hesitated.

Some elusive emotion flickered in his expression.

She averted her eyes, gathered her skirts, and, cloak in one tight fist, placed her other hand in his. His long fingers closed over hers, and she fought to keep from responding with a soft gasp or from raising her eyes toward his—an old habit she intended to break.

The moment her foot touched solid ground, she slid her hand from his and walked toward the front steps with her head held high.

During the two-hour voyage back to the mainland, she had avoided him by staying in one of the Viscount's cabins, claiming a headache. Heartache was more to the truth.

She had stood at the dock when they'd reached port, her head held defiantly high. She refused to let Richard see how badly he had truly hurt her. She watched as the smugglers left the Viscount's sloop and climbed into the wagon that would take them to Lockett Manor. They were off toward a brighter future, working for the Earl of Downe.

Richard had opted to ride alongside the carriage that would take her home, and this had come as welcome news. She didn't think she could manage to sit across from him in such close quarters and not cry.

For protection, she didn't want to look in his eyes because she wanted to remember his expression as it had been last night. She didn't want to see anything but that icy-hard stare and the satisfied look he'd worn when he made a fool of her. It would always be there to remind her that she had been foolish.

She started up the steps and the door opened. Her papa was waiting in the doorway. She was in his arms in three quick steps and she began to cry—from relief, from hurt and stress and exhaustion.

"Letitia, Letitia." He just held her.

"Papa," she whispered, her head buried against his shoulder.

"Downe," her father said, and she felt him give a sharp nod.

"Sir."

"Come inside now." Her father guided her through the doors. Her movements were stiff, her body a sudden traitor, giving in to the exhaustion she had suffered for so long. "Let me look at you." Her papa gripped her head and tilted it up. "You are exhausted."

She nodded.

"Do you want a physician, anything?"

She shook her head. "I think I should just like to go to bed."

"Go on, then. We'll talk later."

She slowly walked up the stairs, weariness overtaking her body, her heart, and her mind. But as she turned on the first landing, she heard Richard say to her father, "We need to talk."

The sound of his voice stopped her. She just stood there. Then she sagged against the wall for a moment and buried her face in her hands.

Cruelly, her mind's eye held a vision of Richard's face and what she had seen so clearly last night: that she would never be his world. He wouldn't let her—a painful realization that had settled where her bright hope used to be. She would never be his world. Never. And that thought was the end of hers.

A knock on her bedchamber door woke her with a start.

"Letitia? May I come in?"

"Papa?" She slid off her bed and opened the door. Her father stood there. "I need to talk to you, child."

She opened the door wider and averted her eyes as he walked by her. "I suppose I have truly made a muddle of things this time, haven't I?" She waited for him to agree.

He stood staring at the fire, his arm resting on the chimneypiece. "I believe I am the one who has made a muddle of things. Not you."

"How could this have been your fault, Papa? You weren't even here."

"That is the very problem. I'm afraid I haven't been here enough, have I?"

"Oh, Papa. I told you I understand."

"Do you, child? I wonder if you do. Your mother was my world, Letty. I didn't know what a weak man I was until I lost her. I shudder to think what she would say about all this. About my running away on digs and leaving you on your own."

"I think perhaps she would be angry with me, not you."

"No, child. No." His voice faded. Then he appeared to shake off his thoughts, and he looked down at her. "I have something else to ask you." He paused, then asked, "Do you have any idea what the earl wanted to talk to me about?"

She shook her head.

"Yes, well, he said he hadn't spoken to you."

"No," she said quietly. "He hasn't spoken to me." We haven't exchanged a word since last night, she thought.

"Downe has offered for you. And considering, he was quite kind and generous with your provisions. He has assured me that you will want for nothing and—"

"Offered for me?" she whispered, then turned and repeated, *"Offered* for *me?"*

"Yes, well, under the circumstances there was nothing else he could do. He just left a few minutes ago to ride straight to London today."

"Why?"

"To get a Special License. You will be married tomorrow afternoon."

"I didn't mean, why did he go to London? I meant, why did he offer for me? Richard doesn't love me."

"Letitia. The two of you were alone together for days. A terribly compromising situation."

"But nothing happened."

"I'm very pleased to hear it."

"Nothing but a few kisses."

Her father froze. "He kissed you?"

She nodded. "But that was because I asked him to." He groaned. "Letitia . . ."

"And he touched me, privately—now that was his idea, but—"

"He did what?"

"He touched my breast," she admitted honestly, then chewed her lip as her father's face colored. "But I hit him on the head with a piece of wood," she added in a hopeful tone.

Her father's jaw dropped.

"Oh, that was his idea too. He told me I should hit him if he ever touched me that way again."

"Again?" her father said weakly.

She nodded.

He sagged into a nearby chair and shook his head. "God, how I wish your mother were here."

"Me too."

Her father rubbed a hand across his eyes for a minute, then rested his elbows on his knees, his hands dangling in between. He stared at the carpet. "I think, considering what has gone on between you two, that marriage is the best thing. How do you feel about that?"

"He doesn't love me."

He looked at her, then said, "Wasn't it you, my dear, who spent over an hour one day raving about how I didn't understand you and that you had loved Richard Lennox forever?"

"Yes and no. I said half a lifetime, not forever. Almost forever. But that was before." She stared at her hands. "I understand now that when only one person loves, that isn't enough."

Her father was suddenly quiet. He seemed to be a million miles away.

"Papa?"

He blinked, then said, "Come, sit by me."

She crossed to the chair and sat at his feet like she had when she was little.

He placed his hand on her shoulder and said, "Your mother's marriage to me was arranged."

"It was?"

He nodded. "I adored her the moment I laid eyes on her, but she didn't want anything to do with me. She told your aunt I was too stuffy."

"You're not stuffy. A little preoccupied, perhaps," she admitted honestly. "But not stuffy."

He smiled then. "Your mother thought I was. It took a long time to win her over."

"What finally did win her?"

From his face, she could tell he was remembering. He looked down at her, then said, "I took her on a dig with me."

"I remember she liked those trips, didn't she?"

He shook his head. "Not at that time. She did later, but she didn't want to go that first time. In fact, I rather think you'd have to say that I abducted her."

"Mama?" She sat a little straighter. "You kidnapped her?"

"Not exactly. I had your grandfather's permission. He was in favor of the match and was tired of watching her lead me a merry chase. He thought that if I compromised her, then she'd have little recourse but to marry me." He paused.

"So what happened?"

He smiled a private, distant kind of smile. "She came 'round. And that's one of my points. Perhaps that was why her death was so hard to take. I felt as if I had been fighting to hang on to her forever."

She leaned her head on his knee. "I told you that I understood."

"I know. You've an acre of forgiveness in that tender heart of yours, Letitia. And that's why I decided to tell you this. There are not too many parents who would confess to their children that their marriage was a forced one. Sometimes, child, when only one person loves it *is* enough. Sometimes it takes one person with strong faith and a tender heart to teach the other one what love is.'

Letty stared at the floor. "That might be true in most cases, but Richard is rather pig—uh ... strong-willed."

"He didn't seem too unwilling when he spoke to me, Letty."

"He was being noble," she said miserably. "He's a hero on the inside. He just doesn't know it."

He was very quiet, then he finally said, "I'm not certain I should tell you this."

"What?"

"I told him I wouldn't force you."

It was her turn to be surprised. "You didn't."

"I did."

"And would you force me?"

He shook his head.

"So I don't have to marry him, then?"

"It's your decision."

"What did he say?"

He gave a small chuckle. "Said I was a ramshackle excuse of a father and that you'd bloody well marry him if he had to drag you before the parson."

"He said that?"

He nodded. "He has quite the temper."

"Oh, he doesn't mean all that blustering. He just likes to think he's right."

Her father laughed then. "He said he has some things to say to you. I believe he called it 'a lifetime's worth' and that he was going to make 'damn well certain' that you heard him."

"Oh."

"I don't believe, Letitia, that those are the words of a man being forced into marriage."

And so it was that Letitia Olive Hornsby spent the remainder of that afternoon and evening preparing herself for a wedding. A whirlwind of hours that gave her little time for thought, until she was alone in her bedchamber.

She pulled tight the belt on her wrapper and walked over to the dormer window. She sat on the chintz-covered windowseat as she had a million times in her nineteen years, and it wasn't but an instant later that Gus leapt onto the seat and settled next to her.

She leaned her head against his wrinkled neck, her arm resting over his huge back. He laid his big muzzle on top of her head and they just sat there, looking out the window.

"Oh, Gus, do you think it's truly going to be fine?"

He gave a choked whimper.

Letty stared up into the dark night sky, so vast, so unknown. Just like her future. It wasn't long before a cloud seemed to weaken and grow wispy; then it just faded away. In its place was a single star, winking down at her. And the mantel clock chimed nine times.

Chapter

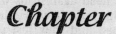

23

*N*o one left an earl waiting at the altar.

Richard paced the small vestibule with the same long strides as he had for the last ten minutes. The Hornsby carriage would arrive any moment.

However, the hellion wasn't just anyone. She didn't care a fig for his title. He stopped. What if, after chasing him for years, she didn't show up at the church? That worried the cynic in him. Rang too true to life, ironic as the thought was.

And he couldn't blame her if she did exactly that after what he had done to her. He ran an impatient hand through his hair, then checked his watch.

Damn ... Damn ... Damn ...

He tapped the bouquet he held in his other hand against his thigh. Her father would have sent him a note if she had refused to go through with this.

However, Hornsby wasn't known for his sense of responsibility. The man had said that he wouldn't force her. Only a loose screw of a father would refuse to force a compromised young woman into marriage.

Richard paced some more, then slowed. His own father wouldn't have hesitated to force any child of his to do whatever he wanted.

At that thought Richard ground to a halt.

A small voice of reason asked him if he would force a daughter of his own into marriage. Truthfully, he didn't know the answer to that. He supposed it would depend on the man.

Odd, how once Seymour had said the word "compromised," things had changed for Richard. It had seemed so simple. He had already ruined her; therefore marriage was a way of saving her.

He shook his head, frowning. He'd been around the hellion too much. His thinking was beginning to sound like hers.

A carriage came to a halt in front of the church.

Richard froze, then stretched his neck and straightened his cravat. He patted his right pocket. The Special License. He patted his left pocket. The ring.

The small room suddenly dimmed and shadows bled across the floor. He looked up. She stood in the doorway on her father's arm. He couldn't see her face. The two figures were limned in the afternoon sunlight. He knew, however, that she was looking at him, and he wondered if she could sense his nervousness.

God, he thought, my hands are shaking like a green lad. I should have taken a drink.

No, he amended that thought. No drinks.

"Downe," Hornsby said, and they stepped inside.

Richard nodded to her father and stepped forward. "Giana Hunt sent these. She said they were for you. For today." He held out the flowers, feeling as if he were sixteen.

"The Titian roses," she said with soft awe and lifted the bouquet to her nose, breathing in the scent.

Her face broke into one of those wonderful smiles—

similar to the kind that used to be for him. He had to admit that he missed those smiles. What he didn't miss was the awestruck quality of them. They had always made him feel as if she thought he was God.

Not a comfortable thought for a man old in the ways of sin.

He could never hold up to an image like that. He had fought long and hard to be what he was, not what someone else—either his father or even an awestruck girl—imagined he should be.

Richard was just a man who made mistakes, a man who needed her to see him as a man, not a god.

She lowered the bouquet. He saw that she wore pearls. Perfect pink pearls. Her mother's pearls. They looked like teardrops lying on her neck, and they reminded him of that night when she was bent and sobbing.

He drew himself up and said more sharply than he intended, "The reverend is waiting.'

She looked up at him, and her smile died.

Damn.

He opened the doors and watched her pass. Then he whipped in behind her, placing a hand on her shoulder.

She froze and looked up at him in surprise.

"I can be an ass sometimes."

She searched his face, then said, "Yes, you can. But you don't have to be."

Her father came through the doors and took her arm before he could say anything more.

The Reverend Poppit looked up from his pulpit. "Oh, fine, the bride has arrived. Yes, yes. Time to get started. Mrs. Poppit! Mrs. Poppit!"

A head covered in a mousy shade of brown hair popped around the sanctuary door. The expert on rakes, Richard thought as he joined them at the altar.

The woman looked at him and her eyes grew wide. He had the sense that, had the woman been Catholic, she would have crossed herself. Or perhaps she would have just held a cross up in front of her.

"Come, Mrs. Poppit. Hurry! Can't keep the earl and his bride waiting now, can we?"

Richard turned toward Letty and held out his hand. Hornsby placed his daughter's hand in his. The symbolism of the gesture wasn't lost on Richard. He paused for a second. He was marrying not only for the sake of family and heirs, for his pride and because of compromising positions. He was accepting a lifetime of responsibility for her.

Marriage became more than a ceremony, or something to avoid. He was taking a wife. He looked down at her, frowning slightly. His wife.

The permanence of marriage hit him square between the eyes, as surely as if she had bashed him with that driftwood again. This small brown-haired woman would be the mother of his children, the woman he would grown old with.

The look she gave him was as dazed as he felt. He gently pulled her hand through his arm and covered it with his own. He didn't know why, he just did. She stared at their hands for the longest time. He felt her fingers tighten slightly, but she didn't look up at him. And he knew then that she was afraid to look at him, because of what she might see.

He wanted to say something to put her at ease. But it was important that he say the right thing. He leaned over and looked at her until she had to look up at him.

"So how do we go on from here?" he whispered.

Her brow furrowed slightly and she murmured, "I don't know."

He was struck by how she looked, frightened and flawless. No more dirt smudges after long hours of being locked in a hold. Her dress wasn't tattered from their ordeal. Her dress was blue. The same icy-blue color of her worried gaze when she would look at him after some disaster.

She had small pink flowers of some kind woven through the brown curls gathered high on her head. For some reason that struck him as solemnly as the pearls had. Today was special to her. He remembered that first ball. He had the same sense of chivalry that he'd felt then, as if her happiness were dependent upon what he did.

After a moment she gazed up at him through curious eyes.

While the reverend fumbled around, searching for his Bible, he stood there, trying to think of something he could give her to make the moment special. He leaned down again and said, "I forgot to ask you something."

"What?"

He leaned down so that only she could hear him. "Will you marry me?"

Startled, she looked up at him.

He shrugged. "Something to tell our grandchildren."

She smiled, then gave a weak laugh.

"I take it that's a yes?"

Before she could answer the reverend began the ceremony.

As quickly as it had begun, it ended. Richard stood there somewhat disappointed. Somehow that didn't seem the way it should be. After so many years of avoiding the altar, it seemed to him that the wedding should have been more reflective of the fight to finally get there. But it wasn't.

They went through the motions, signing the book, the standard congratulatory comments from the reverend and his wife, everything as mundane as the day seemed to be.

In the vestibule they stopped. He watched as Letty looked at her father. The man had damp eyes. He opened his arms, and the hellion was in them. The older man held her as if he was loath to release her.

Richard turned away. He couldn't look at them right then because he felt some odd, piercing twist of emotion. It was confusing as hell.

He didn't understand. From what he knew, Hornsby was forever off in the North Country, looking for some broken piece of Roman pottery, while the hellion spent years running wild.

Yet what he saw pass between them was sincere. She loved the man in spite of his neglect.

He heard her say it: "I love you, Papa."

Perhaps you've said those words without meaning them, Richard. But I never have.

He spun back around and watched her, remembering her words. She never left someone she loved without telling them how she felt. She turned around then, her hand going to the pearls at her neck.

He stared into her face. The small room was silent and seemed suddenly oppressive with the multitude of questions in her eyes and the jumble of words on the tip of his lips.

His wife was looking back at him. His wife. He exhaled a breath he hadn't known he'd been holding.

He knew what he had truly been nervous about. He'd been afraid. Not that she wouldn't show up at the church. But that she wouldn't be able to forgive him.

Silently they left the church, and he lifted her into his open carriage. If his hands lingered a little longer on her waist, he didn't notice. If he sat a little closer to her than was necessary, he could not say. If no words passed between them, then that too was fine by him, for now.

Letty looked around the room and felt even more nervous and out of place. Since the moment she'd stepped into the church it seemed that nothing had passed between her and Richard except half a day of awkward moments.

Oh, there had been a look here, a touch there, but none of those things had alleviated the tension. She stood near the fire, rubbing her hands nervously and just listening.

Above the crackle of the burning logs, she could hear sounds coming from the next room: a drawer closing, the murmur of a servant's voice, the sound of their adjoining door clicking open.

Richard.

Her head shot up.

He closed the door behind him and turned around. He wore a long velvet robe the color of dark wine.

She looked down quickly and saw his bare feet. Slowly her gaze rose to stop at the vee of his lapels, where skin and a dark mat of hair gave a clue that he wore nothing else.

"You look frightened, hellion."

"I am."

He laughed quietly.

"What are you laughing at?"

"Life's little ironies." He walked toward her. "I find it vastly amusing that when I am trying to frighten the wits from you, you have more courage than Wellington. Yet on our wedding night, you look as if you'd faint if I so much as touched you."

"I feel . . . different. I can't explain it, but I do."

His wry smile faded. "Would it help if I said I was sorry?"

"I don't know."

"I am sorry. Very sorry." He paused, then added, "We both know I said those things to hurt you."

"You did frighten me," she admitted quietly.

"You were supposed to be frightened. I was saving you from yourself. The great self-sacrifice. I was playing the hero for you, hellion."

She looked at him then, unable to believe how differently they thought. "That's not the kind of hero I see in you, Richard. There's no courage in hurting people. I think it takes more courage not to hurt someone."

He seemed to think about that. Then he searched her face as if he would find the answers in it. "When did you grow up?"

She couldn't answer.

He seemed to sense that. The room was quietly tense, then he said, "I'm not certain I know how to do this."

She looked at him and her mouth fell open. "Surely you've done it before."

He frowned, then gave her a puzzled look. A moment later he laughed. "I wasn't speaking of lovemaking."

"Oh." She felt her cheeks color. "I suppose I should have figured that out, shouldn't I? You've probably done this a million times."

He looked as if he was holding in a laugh. Then he reached out and cupped her cheek in his hand. "I think perhaps there are some surprises waiting for me."

"I don't see how," she muttered, feeling suddenly gauche and young. "I don't know how to do it."

"Perhaps we'll both be surprised." He slid his knuckle along her cheek, down to her jaw, and slowly ran his fingers over her skin. "It's so soft. I don't think

I've ever felt skin so soft. I remember being afraid to touch it, afraid I might bruise you." His hand whispered down her neck, ever so softly and tentatively. He tilted her chin up so she had to look at him. "How do I touch you when I'm not trying to drive you away?"

She felt his lips touch her brow, and there was that wonderful light feeling again. "You're doing just fine."

He smiled and lowered his head, his mouth gently touching her eyelids, then drifting to the bridge of her nose and on to the other eyelid.

There was such gentleness in the way he held her, in the way his hands moved over her. It was the tender and gentle side of him he usually hid from the world with a veil of cynicism.

He kissed her temples, then threaded his fingers through her hair and held the back of her head, tilting it up so his mouth could capture hers. He stroked her lips with his tongue, once, twice, then parted them gently and laved her mouth thoroughly.

Her hands slid up his chest, pausing to feel the beat of his heart. Its beat was in time with her own. She slid her hands up and around his neck, her fingers busy toying with the hair that touched his collar.

His mouth moved onward to her temple, then to her ear. "Open your eyes when I kiss you and touch you, keep them open while I love you. I want to see what you feel, and those eyes of yours talk to me."

Her eyes slowly opened, and she stared at him from beneath a thick feathering of lashes. She watched his head lower, his gaze and hers locked together. She tasted his flavor, rich and male and exciting.

His tongue was in her mouth again, giving her his honeyed taste. His eyes burned into hers. Her lids grew heavy, but she didn't close them. Instead, she leaned against him for support. His hands left her head and slid over her shoulders, feeling every muscle, every curve, until his hands moved over her bottom and pressed her against him.

She moaned and he lifted her, walking back to the bed. Her feet dangled freely and she reveled in his kiss and his strength, the feel of his body against hers. He set her down, and she felt the side of the bed against the backs of her thighs.

But she cared not where she was because Richard filled her senses: his scent, his touch, the gentle rasp of his breath, his taste, and the sight of him, tall and beautiful, the face that could fell an angel, the golden hair and dark smoldering glint in his eyes as he stepped back to just look at her.

It took a moment for her to realize that they weren't touching. And she wondered if he was leaving her, now, when she most needed him. "Richard?"

"Wait." He walked around the room, putting out first a wall sconce, then a lamp, another and another, until the only light in the room was from one small candle and the burning fire.

Then he was standing before her again, the amber light spilling like gold dust behind him. He reached out and untied the belt on her wrapper, drawing one long finger along the opening until that fingertip drifted over the side of her breast.

Her breath caught, and she felt a jab of fire that jolted to the center of her body.

"You like that, hellion?" He pushed the satin wrapper off her shoulders with a flick of his hand, and the gown glided off her like falling water.

Her nightrail was of thin batiste, white and too sheer. His gaze drifted over her like a lover's touch, stopping where the crest of her breasts showed through the fabric, down lower to where there was a telltale shadow between her legs. His gaze grew pleasured and heated as it shifted lower, down to her feet.

Then just as slowly, his gaze traced the outlines of her legs, hips, and waist. He stepped closer and bent his head, kissing the tip of one breast through the fabric, then used his tongue to rub the fabric over the hard tip again and again.

Small gasps came from her lips and he moved to the other breast, giving it the same gentle touch. His hands slid over only the sides of her breasts and moved slowly down to where they settled on her waist. He lifted her to sit on the edge of the bed and stood between her knees.

"Lie back," he told her, and she did. He stood there watching her for so long she almost wanted to cover herself. He seemed to need to look at her, as if it were as necessary as breathing.

Then he bent over her, bracing his forearms on the mattress, his mouth on hers, his eyes hot and demanding, and his tongue exploring her mouth thickly. His hands held her bare shoulders tenderly, rubbing over the ribbons that held up her gown.

His mouth shifted to her ear, where he told her of the sweetness of her flavor, then his lips scored a damp path down her neck and over her shoulder, where he gathered the end of the ribbon between his teeth and pulled out the bow.

With his rough chin he nuzzled the soft skin across her collarbone, and his lips and tongue moved to the other ribbon. A second later it too was undone.

His head moved down to again lave her breasts, then each rib through the batiste. He suckled slightly, the pleasure of his mouth driving her eyes closed so she could savor each sensation.

Her skin was alive and fiery. He buried his head in her belly, then his lips gently kissed the mound where her legs joined, and she moaned as the rubbing fabric became a rasp of sensation against her most sensitive point.

She felt damp and her knees went limp, hanging from the bed on either side of his hips. His hands followed the lines of her body, down and down until he tugged on the lacy hem of her gown and slid it downward.

Cold air hit her breasts, waist, and belly, then cooled the fire between her legs and the batiste feathered over her thighs, knees, and calves.

His hand followed the air. A caress of a breast. A fingertip down her belly to stroke her mound and then inch between her most intimate place.

Her pent-up breath came out in a rush and instinctively she grabbed his wrist, ceasing the touch as she stared into his hot eyes with panic.

"There is no part of you that I don't want to love, need to touch." His hand stroked her breast. "You are beautiful, so beautiful. Here. Lovely." He touched the tip of the other breast. "And here." He spread his hands out over her waist and massaged down to her hips. "Here." He paused.

"And here, especially here." His finger slid along the moistness between her legs, and he rubbed ever so slowly and gently.

Her breath caught.

He looked into her eyes. "Don't be afraid. This is loving. This is right. Let me teach you."

He moved back up her body but didn't move the hand that caressed her so intimately. His lips touched hers in little sips, and then he filled her mouth with his tongue, while his finger stroked her in long, slow caresses that made her point throb and her knees widen.

His mouth moved to her ear again and he told her

how soft she was while his finger fondled her, flicked over her, and her knees began to quiver. He straightened quickly and shed his robe, then he lay over her, his chest touching hers and his damp hand still between her legs.

"Open your eyes."

"I can't," she whispered.

"Open them," he said more firmly.

"I can't," she said in a cry.

He pulled his hand away.

Her eyes shot open and she cried out.

He shifted and pulled her knees up so her feet were flat on the bed. He moved his hips closer, rubbing against her slowly with his hardness, making her writhe and call out his name.

No dream could ever have been like this. No wild wish, no fairy tale was as wonderful as the reality of Richard touching her, kissing her, loving her. Through lazy eyes she saw his body outlined in the dim backlight. With one hand she reached out to touch his chest and felt the thatch of hair that covered his chest, ribs, and belly.

Her hand brushed lower and skimmed across the hard thickness that made him male. She pulled back.

"Touch me, hellion. Touch me, please."

Tentatively she moved her hand back and stroked him. He groaned and flexed his hips, sliding his length over her nether lips.

It was her turn to groan.

He took her hand and placed it on top of him while his hips slowly shifted back and forth, creating the friction that had her moving with him until she was crying.

He leaned over her and kissed her. "You feel so good." He thrust his hips forward so he could slide along her, allowing her to know his size and smooth hard texture.

Stirred into motion, she sat up on her elbows and kissed him back, mimicking his motions, his lips and the path of his tongue. She scored his ear and he moaned. She bent her head slightly and began to lick his chest.

His hand reached between their bodies. She felt the wide tip of him barely going into her, pushing wide her lips, as his tongue had done to her mouth. He moved out again, teasing.

Her body was nothing but sensation, pleasure, and *his.*

Over and over he repeated the motion until her hands went to his buttocks and gripped them, wanting something, anything, that would quench the fire burning through her.

His hips and maleness kept teasing into her, slowly, barely; each time a little more of him slipped inside. Either minutes or hours later—she knew not which—he deepened his penetration and he froze, unable to go in any farther.

"Hold on to my shoulders, hellion." She obeyed. He began the gentle thrusting again and again, slowly pressing into her, then out. She felt as if she were crying, there between her legs, the tears flowing wet and moist.

She could barely get her breath. She arched so that her chest rubbed against his with every small stilted thrust he gave her. Then she raised her hips higher and higher until the place where the tip of him lay began to pulse.

She couldn't see. She lost her breath. Through a haze of pulsing pleasure she heard his voice.

"I'm sorry, hellion." He pulled out again. Then, just as she contracted, he pushed into her.

Pain burned up into her belly and shot down her quivering legs. She thought she might have screamed, but his mouth was on hers.

She tried to shove him off and out of her. "It hurts! Please ... it hurts."

"God ... Hold still." He grabbed her hips and forced her to lay there. Their breaths came in tattered bursts, and tears rolled from her eyes, over her temples and into her hair.

He looked at her as if he too was in pain. "I'm so sorry." And he kissed her cheeks, her eyes, her temples. His lips went to her ear and he whispered, "I would take the pain myself if I could."

His hands left her hips and tenderly held her head as he kissed her softly again and again. He still filled her, deeply, fully, but he didn't move and she didn't feel the sharpness of pain, only a dull ache that was fading and distant.

They kissed for long minutes, tasting and tonguing and savoring being one.

"Does it still hurt?"

She shook her head.

"Try to lower your legs."

She slid her feet down alongside his thighs, knees, and calves. Her pointed toes only touched his ankles. She was thinking about how long his legs were when he moved slowly and she thought he intended to pull out of her. She exhaled, but he slowly sank back inside.

"Does that hurt you?"

She shook her head.

He did so again. Her breath caught.

He froze. "I don't want to hurt you again."

"You're not hurting me."

He began to move, shifting and flexing, raising himself up on his forearms. She slid her hands up those arms and over his shoulders, her palms measuring the hard feel of his muscles and tendons, the powerful strength in those arms.

Her hands slid back down, a little awestruck at the rough feel of the hair on his arms, and she touched his wrists and the bones beneath his skin. Then her hands rubbed over his. She rested her palms on top of his splayed hands, feeling his hands flex with each thrust of his lower body.

He moaned her name, then pulled himself up higher, changing the angle of his penetration so that when he was completely within her she could feel the rise of that wondrous thrill again, the flames that licked inside her. Soon he was moving faster, deeper, and her name was a litany from his lips.

She raised her knees instinctively, and he arched his back with a deep motion and grasped her hips in his strong hands. Still he moved and moved, but his chest was atop her now and his head was buried in her neck, while he thrust and his hands gripped her thighs so he could move her body with his.

He said things, incoherent things, about heat and tightness and the feel of her. His words grew more graphic, the images they painted elemental and earthy, and she grew flushed listening to him, her body sweating as his did, and the core of her felt as if she were melting.

Her gasps grew again, and though her eyes were open, she saw nothing. She moved her head faster and faster and he held her hips hard, pulled her closer, moving quicker and building things inside her she could never describe.

His urgent words told her to come again, but she was beyond thought. There was only sensation, only the feeling he was stirring so deep inside her, the melting, the fire, and, finally, a burst of something beyond pleasure.

It went on forever, a lifetime of beating hearts.

He shouted once, then arched his back, his groin wedged solidly against her. And deep inside she felt him pulse as his life flowed into her.

She gazed up at him. His head was thrown back and his neck muscles strained, his eyes were closed and his mouth spread wide with a moan of release.

Time passed in glacial minutes. He lay atop her, his body limp, his possession complete. His head buried in her neck, she could feel his breaths sharp and static against her ear. Their hearts beat together, fast at first, then slower and slower, as their breathing became normal.

Beneath her palms his back muscles were hard and the skin damp. All around her was scent and sensation. The tickle of hair on his body. The musky odor of their loving, mixing together in a scent that was like wood smoke and heather, with an exotic touch of sandalwood.

She lay there, staring up at the dark ceiling, feeling the quietness of her husband breathing and the weight and breadth of his possession.

Richard was no god, no young girl's idol. He was a man, flesh and bone, yet his hold on her was more powerful than if he were a deity. She knew with a surety that from this very moment in her life there was no turning back to the past.

The reality of what they'd shared, their bodies coming together, made every dream she'd ever dreamed, every wish she'd ever wished, every foolish thought in her youthful head pale in comparison.

She had come to him as a child and thought herself in love. She had come to him as a young woman and thought she'd found the other half of her soul. But now she came to him as his wife and found something so far beyond love and souls that there were no words for it.

Time and thoughts seemed to drift away and she closed her eyes, not opening them again until he stirred slightly. She wondered how long they had lain there. She knew she could stay like this forever.

She lay there savoring the memory of what had passed between them. After a few minutes she said, "Richard?"

He muttered something into her neck.

"Where did you want me to go?"

"Hmmm?"

"Where did you want me to go?"

"When?"

"A while ago."

He lifted his head and stared down at her. "What are you talking about?"

"I didn't understand where you wanted me to come."

He actually flushed slightly before he groaned a curse and buried his head in her shoulder.

"Never mind," he said into her neck.

She was quiet again, listening to the crackling fire, the utter quiet that surrounded them. After a moment's thought she said, "Richard?"

He groaned. "Yes?"

'How many times have you done this?"

He was quiet.

She turned her head. "Richard?"

"Be patient. I'm counting."

"Oh." She waited. The seconds turned to minutes, and still he didn't answer. "Are you still counting?"

"Shhh. You'll make me lose count."

She frowned, and waited.

She sighed, and waited.

She sighed again. "Aren't you done yet?"

He gave a direct look. "Yes."

"How many?"

"A million and one."

Her jaw dropped.

His shoulders began to shake. He was laughing.

"You wretch!" She squirmed.

He grasped her hands and held her in place, looking down at her with amusement. "No. I miscounted. Not a million and one."

He threaded his fingers through hers and shifted his body so they were firmly joined. He lowered his head, his mouth a breath away. "A million and two."

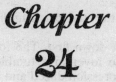

Chapter 24

*T*he minute she heard Gus's bark Letty was out the front door and down the steps. Gus made a flying leap from the driver's box and thudded to the ground, then he ran around the wagon three times, to the annoyance of the driver and the footmen, who were trying to unload Letty's trunks. The wagon team shifted and sidestepped while Gus sped around them, stirring up dust and gravel and trouble.

It took Letty about five minutes to calm him down, then he was happily trotting by her side as she remounted the steps to introduce him to their new home.

She entered the house and a second later there was screech. Gus bolted past her, running after one of the kitchen cats.

"Gus!"

The cat shot up the staircase with her dog close behind, heading straight for the landing, where a footman struggled with a trunk that was hiked on his shoulder.

"Gus! No!"

He bounded after the cat, running right between the man's legs.

The trunk went down first. The footman second.

Sprawled in the foyer in a tumble of green livery was Harry, his expression dazed and his stubbled head half covered in a crooked periwig. He was still sporting the faded bruise of his black eye.

Letty rushed over to him. "Are you hurt?"

Harry raised himself up a little, blinked once, then shook his head. "No harm done, my lady." He gave her a crooked grin, the first one he'd ever given her. "As ye know, I've got me a hard head."

"I suppose you needed one around me, didn't you?"

" 'Tweren't so bad. Never cared much for eyebrows, and I can swim. Besides, ye and the earl, well, your lord gave me a position and a warm bed. Said I had them for as long as I wanted. Never had no one be kind to me afore. I'll be the best bleedin' mother of a footman ye'll ever see."

He started to get up.

"Oh, Harry, you poor sweet man!" An apple-cheeked maid came running down the stairs. "Beg pardon, my lady." She knelt beside Harry, who was suddenly lying flat again, and she pulled his head to her bosom. "Are you hurt terribly?"

Harry went limp.

"Speak to me, Harry," the maid pleaded.

He gave a low moan.

"Oh, you'll let Gertie take care of you, now won't you." She looked up at Letty. "Never you worry, my lady. I'll keep good care of this poor sweet man."

Letty peered over the maid's shoulder. The maid held Harry's stubbled head to her breast and was stroking his brow. He opened one eye, the black one; the other, along with his nose, was buried in the wom-

300

an's ample bosom. "Oh, you're awake. Can you move, my poor dear man?"

"Not fer a minute or two," Harry said weakly, his words muffled against her breast.

The maid cooed, pulling his head higher up her chest, and Harry looked right at Letty. He gave a wicked wink, then closed his eyes and groaned another low moan.

Letty bit back a smile. Now she understood Harry's appreciation of a warm bed.

She turned and went after Gus. Richard had told her at breakfast that the men had all been settled into positions. The estate was sorely in need of employees, since no one had lived there for over two years.

Like Harry, Simon and Schoostor were employed at the house, except that Richard had given strict orders to keep them away from the family silver.

Phineas, Philbert, and Phelim were repairing cottages on the estate until a small herd of dairy cattle could be brought in from Jersey. The brothers would lease a section of land and repay Richard from their profits once they had the dairy up and running.

It seemed that everyone was settled in but Gus. She could hear him thundering down a hallway. At the top of the second floor she turned left, past the hallway into a section of the house she hadn't yet explored.

"Gus? Gus!" she called. He answered with a bark.

She moved down a wide hallway into a large receiving area. The room was shaped in a hexagon, with doors on only three walls. Medieval armor stood like guards between each door, and along the walls were old tapestries and weapons.

She stood before a suit of armor, imagining Richard as a knight carrying her favor. She smiled. He would have made a wonderful knight.

She turned and looked at each of the doors. Curious, she opened one and saw a sitting room, the furniture within still in covers. The room was dark and dank and smelled as if it hadn't been used in years.

Wrinkling her nose, she shut the door and moved to the next set of doors. Inside was a dining hall with a table that stretched to forever and a line of high-backed chairs along one wall. It too hadn't been used recently, from what she could tell.

At the next door she paused, for a suit of armor lay on the floor as if it had been knocked down. She stepped over it and moved inside. This was a man's study of some sort. The room was richly appointed with massive chairs near the fireplace and a huge mahogany desk that sat thronelike in front of a set of tall mullioned windows.

A small bookcase had fallen facedown on the floor, and books and bric-a-brac had spilled haphazardly across the room. She took a step and her toe crunched on something small and hard. She bent down and picked it up.

It was a toy soldier, the kind of expensive German toy she'd seen on display in the London shops. Beneath the bookcase was a crushed box with more iron soldiers spilled about it.

The sparkle of broken glass glimmered from near the fireplace, where the ashes of a dead fire still remained and a large leather chair had the dustcover laying next to it, as if it had been tossed to the floor. A brandy cart sat on one side of the chair, the stopper missing from one of the decanters, and an ottoman was turned on its side as if it had been kicked.

She turned around slowly, taking in the room in its impressive entirety. There were high ceilings that went up past the third floor, and at their crest they were rimmed in elaborate bold mouldings. The size and deep oxblood color of the leather furnishings gave the room a sense of unspoken power.

On the opposite wall above the desk was a massive portrait. She walked toward it, compelled to do so by the image of the figure in the portrait. It looked like Richard, but the clothing was of an older period.

She remembered the old earl, Richard's father, but she hadn't remembered their resemblance. Perhaps because she'd only seen the man on a few occasions and his hair had been gray, with no sign of those gold streaks.

In the portrait, however, he was younger, perhaps even younger than Richard was now, and he had the same dark hair with golden streaks, the same strong angled features and firm mouth and jaw. And like Richard, he was a tall man, but he looked leaner.

"What are you doing in here?"

Letty spun around at the sound of Richard's voice. It had a decided edge to it.

"I hadn't explored this section of the house yet."

Richard walked into the room, and the moment he was inside he seemed to distance himself from everything around him, including her.

His gaze was on the portrait, and there was that old sense of despair in his eyes. Isolation. He looked as if he were a lonely stranger in his own home.

She walked to him and placed her hand on his arm. He seemed to tear his gaze away and he looked down at her.

"Are you all right?"

"I always hated this room."

"Why?"

"Take a breath."

"What?"

"Take a deep breath. What does it smell like to you?"

"It's stale air, musty with old tobacco and ashes and the like. What do you smell?"

"Autocracy. It smells of my father."

He was quiet. It seemed to Letty that time had gone backward for him. He turned and looked around the room, and every so often something painful would flicker across his expression. When he spoke it was to the room in general. "Every fight we ever had was in this room."

He grew silent again, then he turned around, and she had the feeling it was the first time he was really looking at her since he'd joined her. "You love your father, don't you?"

She nodded.

"I saw that. In the church yesterday."

"You sound surprised."

"I was. I thought your father wasn't around much when you were growing up."

"He wasn't.'

"You don't resent that?"

"I don't know if I did sometimes or not. I tried awfully hard to get his attention, but it wasn't easy for him after my mother died. I think perhaps I might have reminded him too much of her." She shrugged. "I don't know. I've never asked him exactly. I know he has regrets. But I also know he loves me." She looked at Richard, trying to read him.

She slid her hands from his arms to his chest and around his neck, then laid her head against his shoulder. "Wish I could take your pain away, Richard."

He looked down at her. "Don't cry for me, hellion."

"I can't help it. You're hurting, and I don't know why."

Richard looked around the room. "The last time I saw my father alive was in this room."

He looked back at her. "Did you know he wanted me to enter the Church?"

She shook her head.

"For as long as I could remember I had wanted to be a soldier, even as a child."

She pulled back from Richard and opened the hand that still held the toy.

He picked it up and looked at it.

"It was on the floor," she said.

"I remember. I came in here that first night I came home, before I rode out on the moors. I'd been drinking and continued to do so, until I was so drunk I didn't feel the guilt anymore."

"Why do you feel guilty?"

"Because my father and brother were coming after me when they were killed. If I hadn't been so bloody stubborn, if I hadn't waved that commission under my father's nose, they'd both be alive. I might as well have pulled the trigger myself." He sagged into the chair. "There have been times in the last two years when I felt so guilty I tried to force an end to it. I felt as if I were a coward for living."

"But you're wrong. There is no strength in dying, Richard. It's much harder to find the strength to live your life when those you love are gone."

He said nothing; he seemed to need to fight his demons silently. She walked past him and stood at the tall mullioned windows behind the desk. She leaned against a wall, staring out at the land and hillsides beyond. "How do you see the world around you, Richard?"

He was quiet for a long time. "You and I see it through different eyes. You see delight. I see despair."

"I think you see the past and I see the future. I think perhaps we'll have to do something about that. You need to see the future."

"I believe, hellion, that you would have made a better soldier than I."

"Why do you say that?"

"Because you are relentless. You never give up. I think that I gave up years ago."

"I think you are the bravest man in the world."

He laughed. "And you know so many men."

"I'm serious. I think you are brave. But you have your flaws. You're also stubborn, pig-headed, opinionated, autocratic—"

"You are describing my father."

"Am I? Well, I wasn't finished. You also try too hard not to care about things when deep down inside you do."

He seemed startled. He studied the portrait for a very long time.

"I think you were alike in more ways than you know," she said quietly. A few minutes passed and she started to leave, thinking he needed to be alone.

He grabbed her hand. "Don't go." He pulled her into his lap and rested his chin on her head. He stroked her hair, her back, and just held her. After a time he said, "When I look at you I see everything good in the world, and it scares the bloody hell out of me. You know why?"

She shook her head.

"Because when you look at me you see what I could be."

Letty followed Richard through a tour of the west wing of the house. They entered a gallery, and there before her stood an entire line of medieval knights. Banners were displayed above each piece of armor, and three medieval tapestries hung high on the walls.

"Isn't this wonderful?"

Richard studied an ancient battle axe mounted beneath a tapestry. "Looks painful to me."

"I think it's terribly romantic. Knights and ladies, armor and pageants."

Frowning, Richard raised the helm visor on a sixteenth-century suit of armor and looked inside. He let go, and with a loud creak the visor slammed shut. "Makes one thankful chivalry is dead."

"Richard!"

"Grrrrrr."

She spun around.

Gus was snarling in the doorway.

"You stop that!" She turned back toward Richard and froze. "Why are you swinging that mace?"

"I thought I might try throwing it in the moat for Gus to fetch."

"We don't have a moat."

He glared at Gus. "I'll build one. A very deep one."

"Someday you two are going to have to get along," Letty said, looking at the complete collection. There were at least twenty-five different suits of armor, a wall of shields, banners, and a case filled with chalices and golden platters. "Did you ever play in here when you were children?"

"No. My father hadn't started the collection until after I was at the university. Truth be told, until now I had never really seen it in its entirety."

"Well, I think it's wonderful. Look at this." She held up a bowl edged in jewels. "Can you imagine actually using these?"

She felt his look and gave him a smile. "I remember my mother reading to me the most wonderful tales of knights and castles and dragons. I spent so many hours dreaming up tales of knights and princesses and mad ogres. I used to wish I lived back then because I couldn't imagine anything more romantic than having a knight ride up and carry me away."

"Off to his stone castle with vermin-infested rushes, greasy mutton, and cold garderobes?"

"Where is your sense of romance?"

He was quiet for a moment, then he said, "Do you want to see what I think is romantic?"

She nodded.

"It's not in here." He grabbed her hand and pulled her down another hallway, then another, and up a small flight of stairs. He opened a door that led to a dark corridor.

"Where are you taking me?"

He lit a candle and pulled her inside. "You'll see."

They walked along a narrow warren of passages until finally he stopped. "Here, take the candle."

He reached above them and pulled some kind of latch, and a door slid open. "Now, this is what I find romantic. Close your eyes."

She did.

He took her hand and slowly led her through the hidden doorway. "You may open your eyes now."

She did, then she blinked once, twice. "This is our bedchamber."

"Why, so it is." He gave her a feigned look of surprise, then spoiled it with a grin. "Now where were we?" He pulled her back on the bed with him. "Ah yes, I remember. A million and sixteen."

Chapter

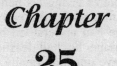

25

Richard stood on the rise and leaned against an old elm tree, watching the land spread before him. Over the past few days he had seen his home through his wife's eyes and realized that he was actually beginning to like it here.

He scanned the horizon, the hills around him, the river and moors, the cliffs and the ocean beyond. There was a permanence about the land, the house, and all that surrounded it. He began to understand the wealth he had, the earldom, and not in monetary units but as a different kind of wealth.

The land had been here long before he was. And it would be here long after he was not. It was a heritage—his past—but it was also his future. He found an odd kind of comfort in that, the idea that something could give pleasure that was not fleeting.

The swift breeze carried on it a gay laugh, and his heart. His wife. He'd always imagined that he was somehow immune to love. He'd thought of himself as someone incapable of giving his heart to another. But then he hadn't understood the emotions within him, any more than he had understood his father.

With his marriage he had learned that love was something one gave unconditionally. To love someone in spite of their weaknesses. The hellion had given him that, a better understanding of himself and of who and what his father was—a man with weaknesses like Richard.

He turned toward the dell, where Letty tossed a stick and played with that beast of a dog. Her wild hair blew out behind her as she ran through the tall grasses, her skirts molding to the soft lines of her body. And she was barefoot, her stockings and shoes tossed off somewhere on the hillside.

He who had cared about so little cared about her. As he walked toward her he could feel the pull of her, the awareness that she was more than just his wife, more than a woman he desired.

Yes, he wanted her with his body. But he also wanted her with his mind, with everything he was. With his being.

She was sitting on her knees when he reached her and he lay down alongside her in the grass. She looked at him with a sudden and welcome smile. "I love it here."

"I can see that."

"I have a surprise for you. Wait here." She stood up and ran over to her dog, who had his muzzle buried in a rabbit hole.

He would have liked to have buried that dog in a rabbit hole.

For the past week they'd had to close the beast out of their bedchamber or suffer him leaping upon the bed and growling and snarling in Richard's ear while he was making love to his wife. As of last night, Gus had learned to use his muzzle to open doors.

She walked back toward him with Gus loping alongside. Her smile was bright and excited, as if this were the most wonderful of moments. Her eyes sparkling with some secret, she stopped in front of him, her hands clasped behind her back. "Are you ready?"

He leaned back on his elbows in the grass, crossing his boots, and he let his gaze rove slowly over her. "I'm always ready, hellion."

She flushed. "That's not the surprise. Now be serious."

"I am serious."

"Richard . . ." Her hands flew to her mouth.

"What's wrong?"

She dropped her hands and pursed her lips slightly before she muttered, "Nothing." She spun around and her skirt belled out, giving him a glimpse of a slender foot and perfect ankle.

"Gus."

He barked, then loped closer, searching her hands for the stick. She clasped her hands behind her and rocked slightly on her toes.

"Sit."

The dog plopped down and looked up at her.

She looked at Richard. "Now listen."

"I'm listening."

"No, you're talking."

He was silent.

"Richard." She looked at him. "Richard . . . Richard . . . Richard . . ." She stopped. "Notice anything?"

"You know my name."

She planted her hands on her hips. "Gus didn't growl!"

Richard looked at the beast through suspicious

eyes. He waited a moment, then snapped a sharp "Richard!"

Silence.

"Richard!"

Gus just sat there, his tongue lolling out of the side of his lips and wearing that silly-looking grin.

"How did you manage it?"

"Bribery." She sat down beside him and hugged her knees to her chest.

"Such as?"

"Three apples, a beef bone, two chicken legs, and a plate of honeybuns."

"Ah, perhaps we're going about this bedchamber thing all wrong. Instead of locking him out at night, we should lock him in the pantry."

She laughed. The wind caught the sound and carried it to the crown of the nearby elm trees, shaking loose a few doves. He loved the sound of that laugh. It had melody and joy and life.

He experienced the pleasure of just letting his gaze wander from her head to her bare toes curling in the grass. He reached out and ran a finger over the top of her foot.

"That tickles!" She pulled back.

"Does it?" He grabbed the other foot and she tried to slither away, but he was stronger. Laughing, they rolled in the grass, tussling like children, free and happy.

Then he pulled her under him, capturing her hands at the sides of her head and pinning her legs with his. He threaded his fingers through hers, palm to palm, and she shifted, one leg lifting slightly between his.

The laughter died on their lips. He drank in the sight of her as a man who has thirsted forever.

He kissed her, worshiped her with his mouth. Her

name was a prayer on his lips, his name a whisper of love on hers.

Their clothing fell away easily, naturally. And he came into her, lost himself in her.

It was good, so bloody damn good. Like cold clear water running over him, washing away the dirt of his past, a baptism, the cleansing of sins and the bonding to a future that was only her.

In her—in this girl that he'd known so long yet had understood so little—he'd found something he'd never known was possible, would have bet every last ha'penny that such a thing didn't exist, and surely didn't exist for him.

But he'd been wrong.

It did exist, and nothing in his entire life had prepared him for what he'd found in the arms of an innocent young woman who loved him in spite of himself.

Richard slowed the motions of his body and gently cupped her head, turning it so that she had to face him.

"Am I hurting you?"

She shook her head.

"Then why are you crying?"

She tried to catch her breath and couldn't. She lifted slightly and pressed her lips to a small scar on his upper arm. "I shot you."

He gave a short laugh. "Yes, you did, and I probably needed to be shot."

"I can't laugh about it, Richard. I want so badly for everything to be perfect."

"I say this is about as close to perfect as anything can be. Good God, hellion, I don't think I could take much more perfection and live through it."

"Every time I see that scar I think about it."

"You've healed more deep scars than you could ever give me."

Her voice barely above a whisper, she asked, "Are you happy?"

He lowered his mouth to hers. "No, I'm not just happy. I'm in love."

The Duchess of Belmore gave birth to a daughter on the last day of summer. Some two weeks later the Earl and Countess of Downe and Viscount and Viscountess Seymour stood as godparents to the only firstborn female in the history of the Castlemaine lineage.

"I say, Belmore," Viscount Seymour said, peering down into the Belmore cradle, "looks like she has Joy's nose."

Mary MacLean, maternal great-aunt to the newest Castlemaine, breezed by with the comment, "One can only hope little Lady Marian inherits *all* of her mother's traits."

The Duke of Belmore choked on his wine.

"Careful, nephew, one must sip fine wine, you know." Mary thumped him on the back, a wicked gleam in her eye.

"I wouldn't know." Alec scowled. "Every bottle I've opened for the last two months has tasted of ratafia."

"Really? How odd."

Joy stood in the doorway. "Come, everyone. Richard and Letty are leaving." She started to cross to the cradle, but Alec stood up.

"I'll take her, Scottish." With surprising ease he bent down and picked up his daughter, then joined the others in the foyer.

So they all gathered to bid farewell to the earl and countess. Richard said his goodbyes, then stopped and gave the MacLean a long and thoughtful look.

He joined Alec on the front steps and said, "Joy's aunt looks more and more familiar to me every time I'm around her, but I can't place where I've seen her."

"Have you seen Macbeth lately?" Alec asked under his breath.

Richard looked at him, then smiled. "Worse than a mother-in-law?"

"A real witch," Alec said, knowing Richard wouldn't understand how true his words were.

A few minutes later Richard had joined his wife and the carriage took off down the drive.

The MacLean sighed as the front doors closed and she joined the Seymours on the stairs while Alex and Joy took the baby back to her cradle. "I suppose I should be off myself. I have a gathering to attend tonight."

"We'll be leaving shortly, Mary, if you'd care to travel with us." Giana gave the MacLean a full smile.

Mary patted Giana's hand. "Thank you, my dear. You go on and ready yourself and don't worry about me. My nephew has graciously offered to loan me a conveyance."

Alec rounded the corner of the reception room and muttered, "My broadest broom."

"Alec . . ." Joy groaned as he placed the baby back in her cradle.

"She couldn't have heard me." Alec straightened.

A minute later the MacLean strolled through the double doors, a piece of paper in her hands. She handed it to Alec.

"What's this?"

"A list of girls' names." She smiled wickedly as she crossed the room and sat down. "Marianna, Marietta, Mary Elizabeth, Rosemary."

Alec stared at the paper. "I think I need a drink." He turned to look at his duchess but froze midturn. His wine glass was floating slowly across the room. "Scottish."

She was tucking a blanket around the baby and

glanced up. She looked at the wineglass, then at the MacLean. "Aunt, you know Alec doesn't want us doing those things while there are guests."

The MacLean turned. "Doing what, my dear?"

"That," Alec gritted, glaring at the wineglass hovering near his nose.

"I didn't do it," the MacLean said truthfully.

He looked at his wife. "Did you do it?"

She shook her head and her eyes grew wide. She looked at the baby and muttered, "Oh my goodness." Hands to her cheeks, she turned to her aunt.

The MacLean was grinning with delight. She clapped her hands together and hurried over to the cradle. "Oh! How wonderful! And at only two weeks. Joyous, you didn't levitate anything until you were two months."

Alec snatched the glass out of the air, drained it, then sagged into a chair, resting his head in his hands. "Bloody hell . . ."

The earl's carriage rumbled down the road. Letty leaned her head on Richard's shoulder and sighed.

"Tired?" he asked.

"A little."

"I know," he said, putting his arm around her. "You always fall asleep in the carriage."

"It's the motion. Rocks me to sleep every time."

He reached beneath her chin and tilted her head up, then gave her a lazy look filled with promise. "Not every time." Then he started to kiss her.

There was a shout. The carriage suddenly ground to a halt. Letty slipped from Richard's grip and flew across the seat. He grabbed for her, but the door wrenched open.

"Get out!"

Letty looked up into a pair of rheumy and hateful eyes glaring at her from behind a black mask.

A pistol was pointed at her head.

"Easy, yer lordship, or I'll blow her head off."

"When I say 'now' move behind me," Richard whispered, then grabbed a small pistol as he slowly helped her up and then out of the carriage. He kept her in front of him as he slipped the gun inside his coat.

Two heavily armed bandits, one on horseback and the other on foot, faced them.

"Just give us yer money and jewels and ye can be on yer merry way. Move wrong and she's dead." One bandit waved a pistol at her.

"Take it out real slowlike."

Richard took out a purse of guineas and tossed it on the road, then stepped a little away from her.

"Now yer stickpin and watch, rings. Hers too."

Richard tossed everything on the road. "Give them your jewelry," he said to Letty.

Letty took off her rings, a bracelet, and earbobs and handed them to Richard.

"Don't ferget the pearls, yer ladyship."

"Not the pearls," Richard said in a gritty voice.

Letty looked at him. The look he gave the man was livid.

"Them pearls too."

"I said . . . not the pearls."

"Ye ain't got a say in it. Take off the pearls."

"Richard, I don't mind—"

"I do."

"Give over the necklace or—"

"Now!" Richard shouted.

Letty shifted.

The guns went off.

She flinched. Something burned through her.

Richard called her name.

She reached for him. And the world went black.

Chapter

26

Richard stumbled down the road, his wife in his arms, his breath in hard shocks from running.

He slowed. He knew he couldn't fall. Not with her like this.

He glanced down at her.

There was blood everywhere. He'd never seen so much blood.

Shifting her body slightly, he reached up, then twisted his cravat tighter, trying to bind the wound near her neck.

She gave a low moan.

"I'm here, sweet. Hold on, please."

He walked on.

The carriage will be around the next turn. Yes. The carriage. The horses. Something . . . something.

The horses had taken off. His coachman was dead, as was one bandit. The other had ridden away.

"Letty."

Silence.

"Letty, sweet hellion. Can you hear me?"

Nothing.

He pulled her even tighter against his chest, holding her as firmly as he could.

He began to run again.

His boots pounded down the dirt road. His heart beat in his throat. He could smell the steely odor of blood.

Her blood.

Each breath was a fight. Each stride desperation.

He kept running. His arms were numb. His legs ached. His throat burned. But he didn't know if it was from exertion or emotion.

He looked at her face. It was gray.

Her lips were lax. Chalky.

He couldn't feel her breathing. He wanted to feel her heart.

He couldn't stop. He just ran.

It hurt to breathe. It hurt to run. It hurt to talk.

But he had to. He ran harder.

Had he said it today? Had he told her today that he loved her?

"I love you," he said in a rasp of breath.

He held her tighter, leaned closer to her limp body, and almost stumbled.

"Can you hear me? I love you ... I love you ... I love you. Please, Letty. Don't ever think I don't mean those words. I mean them. I love you."

Every step he took, he said it.

"I love you."

Every breath he took, he said it.

"I love you."

He looked down at her, seeing nothing with his eyes but seeing all with his memory: an imp of a girl staring down at him from a bridge.

A young woman with her heart in her eyes as she

had danced around him during a country dance, smiling, and then going in the wrong direction.

He saw a hellion who looked at him with poignant remorse and said "I shot you." The same hellion who said "I love you."

He saw the woman who believed he had courage and knew he had a heart, no matter how hard he tried to show her otherwise.

He saw a woman who believed in fairy tales, and dreams that come true, and blind faith in someone you love.

He saw his wife. His life.

He looked up then, raw emotion turning the horizon into a misty blur of brown and green ... and dying hope.

He begged.

Just save her.

He promised penance and faith.

I'll do anything. God, don't take her too.

He offered wealth.

Take my land, my title.

He promised anything.

Take everything.

Even himself.

I'll be anything for her. I swear. Just don't take her from me.

Living without her. A thought more terrifying than anything he could ever imagine.

The only reason I've lived was to find her.

He stared up at the sky and shouted, "God dammit! You hear me! Listen. You listen." His voice tapered off. "Someone listen. Someone." He looked down at her, paused and whispered, "You have to be all right. Don't die on me now. Not now."

He began to cry then. The harder he ran, the harder he cried.

"Richard." It was barely a whisper.

But he felt it as well as heard it.

Her eyes were open.

"God . . . hellion. Can you hear me?"

Her face was wet from his tears. "Is it raining?"

He swallowed. "A little."

Her eyes drifted closed. "Thought so." She paused, then added, "You're blustering again."

"That's only because I thought you weren't listening."

Her only answer was a ragged breath.

"I love you."

Silence.

"I love you."

She licked her pale lips. "I know."

"You said I needed to see the future. I see our future, love. I see it clearly. It's really there. I see those dreams of yours coming true. I see our children, our grandchildren, playing in our meadow. Did you know that? I see myself looking down at you when I'm old and gray and saying two million."

She said nothing.

"Can you hear me?" There was panic to his tone.

She was looking at him again through eyes that carried little life, but what life was there showed her worry. But not for herself, he knew that. She was worried for him.

He took a breath and tried to speak calmly. "I see what I can be. I see it all." He leaned down so his mouth was to her ear and she wouldn't be able to see his wet eyes. "But I can't have that, hellion, if I don't have you."

He raised his head and looked at her again through a blur of emotion. Her eyes had drifted closed.

He lay his head against hers, needing to feel the warmth that said she was still alive. He ran and ran, onward, down the neverending road, not knowing how far, not knowing how long, only knowing he had to.

He heard his boots crunch on gravel. He pulled his head away from hers. He had no idea how far he had run. Time had passed without him.

He looked at her pale face, and prayed for her. For him.

Again the gravel crunched beneath his boots. A drive, he thought. A house.

He looked up.

Through raw, burning eyes he saw gates.

Estate gates.

Then he saw it.

Lockett Manor.

"Can you imagine?" said the Reverend Mrs. Poppit to the Ladies League for Moral Stewardship. "That brave man ran all those miles with little Letty Hornsby in his arms."

"She was not Letty Hornsby." Matilda Kenner glared at Mrs. Poppit. "She was and *is* the countess of Downe."

"Well, that's neither here nor there," Mrs. Poppit snipped, then raised her pointy chin a notch too high and announced, "The point is the romance of the story. Even before he became an earl, I always knew that Richard Lennox was of the stuff heroes were made of. The finest moral character."

The four other women choked on their tea.

After a moment of coughing, Nyda, one of the Pringle sisters, whispered, "I heard she lost so much blood they thought she would die."

"The earl stayed by her side every minute." Lady Harding sighed. "Such a devoted husband. They couldn't get him to move."

" 'Tis said the Duke of Belmore brought in some special Scottish doctor."

"One of the maids told our housekeeper that they came late one night, when all were in bed, none of them expecting the poor countess to last through the night. The duke had to knock the earl out with a Chinese vase to get him to leave the room so the doctor could save her. The earl didn't want to leave her for a single minute," said Nellie Pringle. "But in the end, this doctor worked a miracle."

"Did the maid say who this doctor was?" Lady Harding leaned closer to Nellie Pringle.

"No one saw him, but someone heard the name."

All of the ladies leaned closer. "What was it?"

"MacLean."

Epilogue

As long as there are dreamers,
There will be dreams that come true.

Letty sat in the meadow, hugging her knees and waiting for Richard. In the last hour she'd picked enough wildflowers to fill ten vases, thrown a stick for Gus until they were both bored, and kicked dandelions till there were none left. She looked toward the house but saw nothing.

With a sigh, she lay back in the grass and closed her eyes, losing herself in the magical moment of a daydream. Within seconds her mind's eye showed a meadow filled with children—the children they would have someday.

Clear as the Devon sky was the image of a boy of fourteen with brown hair and dark green eyes. He stood as tall as his father while he baited a fishing hook for a blond lad of about eight.

Nearby was another boy with golden hair, about twelve years old, with a rascally smile, and he was sporting a black eye from his sister's cricket ball. The cricket batter, a blond girl of ten, joined another girl

of six who played with a litter of bloodhound pups.
And a toddler rolled in the dandelions, her laughter
catching in the wind and echoing in the crowns of a
nearby elm tree. The daydream was so realistic and
so heartwarming that she almost believed she would
open her eyes and they'd be there.

A loud *clank* broke the peace of the meadow, then
the sound of a horse's hooves startled her and she
sat up.

She blinked, then shook her head and blinked again.

Riding toward her was a knight on a white horse
adorned with bright red and yellow pennants. He appeared to be having trouble staying in the saddle.

She stood up quickly, her mouth hung open in
shock, as the knight reined in his charger a few yards
away and lifted the visor on his helm.

He promptly fell from the saddle, and the crash
rang clear through to her teeth.

Muttering, Richard creaked upright, shook his head
slightly, then squeaked toward her.

Gus growled.

"Hush." She gave him a reassuring pat on his head.
"It's Richard."

Gus barked, then took off at a lumbering run. With
a flying leap he hit Richard square in the chest and
knocked him to the ground with a deafening crash.

"Bloody hell!"

Letty peeled her hands away from her eyes to see
Gus sitting on Richard's armored chest with his muzzle buried in the helm opening.

"Richard! Gus!" Letty ran over.

Gus was licking Richard's face.

"Get this beast off me!" came the muffled sound of
her husband's voice.

She pulled Gus off and made him sit.

Still lying flat on his back, Richard looked up at

her through the raised helm. "I told you this armor looked painful."

She was laughing so hard she couldn't speak.

"You are supposed to be overwhelmed by my heroic attempt to make your dreams come true, hellion. Not overcome with laughter."

She knelt beside him and tried not to giggle. "I'm so sorry. It's just so, so perfectly wonderful I feel like I'm dreaming." She smiled. "I love you."

"You'd better after this. I don't know how in the devil they fought in this contraption. I could barely mount the horse. Took four grooms to seat me. Give me a hand, will you?"

She reached out and he pulled himself into a sitting position with an ear-ringing *squeak*. He turned and reached for her, lowering his head toward her mouth. Barely a breath away from her, the visor clamped shut.

He swore, then reached up to open it. It wouldn't move.

"Letty, my hands are worthless with these gauntlets. See if you can open the visor."

She tried to push it up. It wouldn't budge. She tried again. Still nothing. She chewed her lip, then said, "Richard?"

"What?"

"I believe it's stuck."

There was a full minute of telling silence before he swore viciously. Three minutes later one gauntlet flew westward. Three minutes after that, another flew eastward.

And some two hours later, on a grassy hillside in Devon, amid a scattering of bent and buckled armor, the Earl of Downe smiled triumphantly at his countess.

"One million, two hundred and ninety-three."

JILL BARNETT

New York Times
bestselling author
of *Carried Away*
and *Imagine*

WONDERFUL

After too many years on the battlefield,
Merrick de Beaucourt is looking forward
to a simple life of peace and quiet with a
docile wife at his side. But when he finally fetches his bride-to-be from a secluded
English convent, he finds he needs more
than his knight's spurs to bring order to
his life....

Now available from Pocket Books

POCKET
B O O K S

1406